Neighborhood Secrets
Ruan Willow

Table of Contents

Dedication

This book is dedicated to people who explore their fantasies and sexuality and allow their partners to as well. Those who play in and out of the bedroom, those who never stop playing, never stop expanding and exploring their sexuality, and those who desire to please their partners and get off on getting their partner off, because that's how it should be. Mutual pleasure is mutual bliss. Sexplore it together! Sexual pleasure is your birthright!

Disclaimers: This book is an erotic romance, please read and enjoy it knowing this is the genre it is in. A Daddy Dom/submissive story of control and submission that flourishes as mutual sexual freedoms. The book contains elements of mild BDSM, multiple partners, exhibitionism, experimentation, cheating, explicit sex scenes, group, role play, kinks, and lots of pleasure, empowerment, and exploration. Daddy Dom is a consensual continuously talked about power play only giving/assigning a dominant role and a submissive role. ALL acts are consensual and characters engaging in sex are 18 and over. Enjoy a story of fantasy later-in-life exploration into open sexuality. "Daddy" refers to leadership, it's not used in a related sense.

Prologue

If I knew what my life would turn into, would I even want to live it? Would I have the motivation to wake up every day and do things? Would I even try? What would be the point? This would depend on if I liked the outcome. If I knew no matter what I did, my life would turn out the same, I'd likely lose all joy, motivation, and any excitement. I'd be a character in an already-penned story. Well, maybe I am that on some level. But in all honesty, I prefer not knowing it. I wonder if I will be happy. If I were to be asked, this would be my end goal to simply be happy.

But I guess that is all unknown. There's way more fun in that.

I glance out the window, dragging my eyes along the new lounge chair I bought to replace his. I smile. Choosing the same exact spot where he parked his lazy ass for years with beer in hand had felt like a triumph last week. As if I were claiming the spot now because his toxicity doesn't live here anymore. It felt damn fucking good.

A pair of birds fly by and I miss their chirps so I rise to immerse myself more freely in their sounds outside. I slip off my robe and saunter out the door to my deck with a smile on my face. A smile I haven't been able to fully remove even the faintest suggestion of off my soul since my divorce became final. The freedom feels that good. Like it's breathing for the first time since my younger days and without a mask on, like having thoughts all my own that don't reflect his whereabouts, thoughts that aren't shrouded by wondering what he will say this time, what old argument he will bring back up once again because it didn't end the way he wanted, so therefore it was never resolved. But it was a never-ending word salad bowl, and everything in it was his flavor, because he always needed to win. He always needed to be right.

Well, I'm done with that story.

I let the summer breeze strip those thoughts off my skin, my face to the sunshine, my soul floods the air around me, reaching her fingers to touch the world, and soars to every speck of the sky as I take it all in and let it transform me once again. Happy. This is what happy feels like. If I had known then what even happier felt like, it wouldn't have been as wonderful, surprising, full, and all out fucking as exciting as it turned out to be. I'd learned to savor the not knowing and finally accepted that it didn't have to hurt. Life that is. It's all a choice.

But damn, even in the breath of not being strapped down by a toxic person, I really had no idea what happy really meant.

Not yet, anyway.

Chapter 1

I nestled into my new soft cushion on my deck chair and drew in a breath. There was beauty everywhere I looked. The trees looked more gorgeous in their bath of sunlight, the grass greener than seemed possible, and the sky was the bluest I ever remember seeing it. I sipped my coffee with a new savoring. Today was going to be another good day. The good days were stockpiling up now and I was beginning to believe this new way of life was real.

My phone buzzed with a notification. A reminder of the neighborhood pool party popped up. Kyle and Mandy were throwing another adult-only pool party. When Mandy used the word 'adult', it had sounded like a porn movie in the making, only I knew that was wishful thinking. But wouldn't that be fucking amazing! But, regardless, it had made for great masturbation fodder last night before bed that's for damn sure. Not going to happen in this vanilla neighborhood, that's the bleak reality.

"Maybe I need to move," I whispered to my phone screen as wild dog barking from my dog announced someone was about to appear on the path behind my house.

I zoned in to see who the poor victim of my dog's barrage of barking this time would be. Two dogs I recognized and then a petite dark-haired female form came into view. Miranda. That woman took more walks than any person in the neighborhood. Her figure reflected her incessant drive to walk and work out. The woman was fucking scrumptious.

I had often thought it was all the testosterone in her house that drove her out of it on more than one walk a day. I couldn't begin to imagine her life. Mine was enough to fathom. My two boys had weathered the divorce quite well, both of them choosing to be with me but being forced to go to my ex's. But lately, they've been coming home a day early. No court could force them to stay. It wasn't jail, but more of an obligation my ex expected, which of course turned off my boys from staying with him anymore. At first, he had complained to me, blamed me, as usual, for pulling the boys back to me, as if I were their puppet master. That was his yearning. Not mine. I preferred my boys to be free spirits, and truly, I supported every little speck of such in them. I was determined they wouldn't end up trapped someday. I strove to teach them they didn't have to be.

Miranda waved to me. My eyes ran down the perfect curve of her hips to her thighs. She was round and soft without being overweight, positively and deliciously feminine without even trying. Allen was indeed a lucky man to have her. I admired her strength, her spunk, her empowered ways. If I admitted it, I took impressions of what she said and how she carried herself and tried them in my own skin. And it had made me feel amazing. That woman was feminine power on high beam. She owned it. And I'd wanted to taste her for a long while.

She waved again before she disappeared out of sight.

My phone buzzed with a text from Kyle asking if I was coming to the party. How curious. Why would he text me? Usually, it was Mandy who texted me. She must have asked him to text me, I didn't even know he had my number. I glanced at their backyard. I could see a portion of Mandy and Kyle's yard from my deck. I'd be the first to admit I'd watched Kyle swim alone on one of his many swim workouts. The man was exquisite.

I texted back.

Me: Yes I'm coming. Do you guys need anything specific?

I had already filled in with a reply of yes to the invite that I'd bring a dessert.

Kyle: Great. Mandy is having me double check with everyone. Can't wait to see you at the party!

Ah, that made sense. The text was a bit of a letdown. If only I could find a man like Kyle. But then, who needs a man? Given my impression of what a husband was, from experience, there was no free will there. What I've got is freedom now and I'm not just handing that off to any old ordinary person who wants in. That person would need to be special, perfect—like crystal perfect. Someone I couldn't imagine living without. Someone I'd give up this freedom feeling for. But would that be right? I dreamt of a relationship where I never felt trapped. Where his love was unconditional enough that I could be who I am for real, and not be someone living inside a plastic sheath that on the outside had to look like how he wanted me to look and act. Fuck that.

I guffawed with disgust.

I watched Pumpkin zoom across the yard, her tail wagging like crazy. Once again, I was so happy, he hadn't fought me for the house. Likely, he had not wanted to clean it, because he had never wanted to when we were married, so him alone in it would have meant he had to clean it because I wouldn't have been around as his slave. That was my theory anyway. Which held true when he had enough money for a house, but chose a condo instead where he not only didn't have to mow, but he also didn't even need to plow snow because the association did it. He was lazy and content to lay around getting fatter while everyone else did everything for him.

I shuddered. Why is he still occupying so many of my thoughts? I need to stop this cycle. He's gone. He shouldn't be bleeding his vile presence into my brain as his shadow. At first it was hard. I kept expecting him to walk into the living room, to barge into the bathroom while I was in it, stalking the wall, shimmying along it to wherever I was to spy on me. That feeling had waned thank goodness, but it had taken way more time than I'd expected. My therapist had told me this would be the case, I had refused to believe it until I was living it. And of course, she'd been right.

Pumpkin flew up the deck stairs, her tongue out to the right side of her mouth as she panted heavily. Her eyes were bright and full of joy. She was in her element and her soul flooded out of her eyes she was so jubilant.

I rubbed her brown head. "Aw, sweet girl. Having fun down there?"

She wagged her tail heartily in answer. She stopped panting for a split second to lick my hand.

"That's a good girl."

"Mom," Alex said through the screen door. "I'm going to Jenna's."

"Hi, Alex. Okay. Have fun. Tell Jenna 'hi' for me."

My son was a hottie. It was weird to see girls like him, knowing he was the heartthrob of his grade. All the girls pined for him. Watching him on the football field had become a fan club pastime as teen girls swooned over my baby.

I smiled at him. "Oh, don't forget to give Jenna that bag."

He nodded but the smirk on his face deepened. "When do I get to know what you are giving her?"

I let out an explosive laugh. "Not until she decides she wants to tell you."

And secretly, I hoped it wasn't that time yet, but I had a sneaking suspicion they were already beyond that. In many ways though, I wanted him to know what it was because then maybe he'd prioritize Jenna's pleasure, and not just take his own from her body and call sex 'done'. I'd tried talking about sex with both my boys, but neither could stomach the conversation with me, so I had to abandon it, fearing that with our ass poor sex ed in the schools, they were only getting their sex ed from porn. Fuck, I hope not.

"Fine. You two are mean." Despite his words, he was still smiling. "I'll be home for dinner." He waved and was off.

"Bye, honey. Have fun." Part of me hoped they'd use what was in that bag together, part of me feared it. But either way, I was happy to be able to give the toy to Jenna.

Me purchasing her the gift had been unexpected, but I'd come to realize he loved that Jenna and I got along so I went for it. Especially since her own mother was a tool, I really connected with Jenna. And hugely so recently over a cup of coffee while we waited together for Alex to get off of work. I'd broached the topic of masturbation with Jenna, only from her prompt, and because she was now eighteen. I'd never have brought up such a topic, but the desperation in her eyes as she'd told me why her mom took her phone away for the past week made my blood boil. Societal views shaming pleasure were a disgrace.

"You mean to tell me your mother took your phone away because she caught you masturbating? Are you serious?" The knowledge hurt, and I knew the pain well.

Jenna had nodded her pretty head, misery claiming her lovely face, her straight long blond locks dancing across her bare shoulders. "And it's not the first time she's shamed me about doing that," Jenna had said with deep sadness in her eyes.

I was grateful I didn't see shame in her eyes.

"Sweetheart, can't you lock your door?"

She shook her head slowly, a hint of panic growing in her gaze. "I have no door lock."

"How about a chair up against the door?"

"I tried that once, Mom freaked. Thought I was like killing myself or something. She got Dad and both of them were pounding on my door demanding I open it." She sighed and fingered the napkin she'd already twisted into a little paper log. "Then they'd had to talk with me for three hours about safety. Geez." She snorted with a roll of her green eyes. "I have no desire to kill myself, but they seem to think all teens dream about death."

She let her napkin unfurl as she dropped her eyes to the table.

I needed to help this poor girl. "Will you let me buy you something? Do you have any hiding spots they wouldn't find things in?"

Her eyes lit up in alarm first, then curiosity took over.

"Yeah, I have a few spots I can hide things in."

"Good. I'm going to buy you something now that you are eighteen. Something I wish my mom had bought me when I was your age so I could have learned about my body. See, I was shamed for masturbating just as you are. It harmed me for years. I'm talking all my life until recently. I didn't know much about my own body. I certainly didn't know much about my own clit. Our sex education is a crime against humanity and totally downplays female pleasure."

She blushed at the word. I didn't want to scar the poor girl, but I wanted to help her not live a life of shame as I had, trapped by what others thought about sexuality.

"I'm going to buy you a wand. And this is the perfect sex toy, because, if your mom or dad do find it, you can say it's a muscle massager." I grinned at her as her face blossomed into excitement.

"Oh, I've seen those on porn." She recoiled shifting her shoulders backwards after she said it. Her excitement switched to being ashamed, sending her body into a wave as she fidgeted in her seat.

"It's okay, Jenna. Porn isn't evil. I watch porn."

I immediately sympathized with her, the relief that flooded her face next soothed the shamed girl that still sometimes sat at the bottom of my gut. Sadly, that still at times claimed me.

"Will you accept this gift if I buy it for you?" I wanted to touch her hand, give her some human comfort of skin on skin, but I also didn't want to freak her out. Talking sex toys with her boyfriend's mom had to be a bit weird.

"I'll answer any questions you have. And if you don't want to ask me anything, that's okay too. But please, let me do this for you. It hurts me to see a young girl like you not know her own body and be so restricted in exploring what God gave her to enjoy. We were given a clitoris for enjoyment. It's the only human organ that is meant solely for pleasure."

Her interest was clearly piqued as she relaxed her shoulders, and her face. "I read something online about that. And my friend Missy recommended a podcast about women's sexual empowerment to me. I've been listening to it."

"Fantastic." I clapped my hands. Damn, this felt good. "I'll order it today. And then you can start playing, even if you can only use it in the middle of the night."

"Yeah, that will likely be it, or when my parents both go into work. Or when they play bunko."

"Take those moments and run with them," I assured her with a generous nod.

The light laugh she exuded was fresh as the outside air. "Thank you. It's crazy that my boyfriend's mom is the person giving me my first sex toy."

I had wanted to tell her to use it with Alex, but I knew eventually that would happen, so I didn't need to be the key to turn on that chain of events. I had just wanted to be someone who started Jenna down the right path to learning about her sexuality, because clearly, her parents weren't going to do it. I was what most would call a liberated mom, I guess. Even though my boys had never been willing to talk about sex with me, after my husband had moved out, I had laid a male sex toy on both their pillows before they had gotten home from school one day. Neither of them ever had said a peep about it. Maybe they had thrown it away grossed out by the cringe factor of their mom buying them a sex toy. But at least they knew from that, that I was not only okay with them masturbating, but I encouraged it.

"Jenna, I just don't want to watch another female wait until her forties to explore her sexuality. That's what I've done and it's a tragedy." I shake my head. "All those wasted orgasm-less days."

Jenna had laughed with delight in her eyes, which I cherished as I gave her a hug as Alex walked through the door. He had impeccable timing.

Another notification hit my phone and I glanced at it. It was an update on the party from Mandy.

It said: 'Come early for a cocktail hour to enjoy a tequila sunrise!'

I meandered back into the house. Time to make dessert for the party. I'll skip the early bird plan and have a glass of wine here first instead. At home it was much more enjoyable anyhow.

I ripped the foil off the top of the bottle as I gazed at the half-eaten loaf of banana and blueberry bread. I loved feeding my boys, now that they are older, it's one way they let me spoil them that comes only from me.

I poured myself a glass of wine with a sigh. My social life might be limited to lame neighborhood parties, but at least I wasn't sitting home alone with my sex toys and a bottle of wine every night. Well, wait, maybe that wasn't so bad. I snickered remembering my monster orgasm last night, which I'm free to have in my own bed now that he's finally gone.

The thought of mingling with a bunch of couples made my stomach turn though. Most were nice, but many also had loads of judgment in their eyes every time they looked at me. Mark was a charmer. He was a social butterfly, 'the good guy'. The whole neighborhood saw him as a great guy, which made me the bitch for leaving him. They didn't know the real Mark. Only I knew him. He'd saved his nastiness for me and me alone. His vile snake-ness lurked behind that happy guy face, and when he decided to strike, he was pure evil. No veil of smiles and jokes could shroud his true nature from me then, not once I'd been the victim of his biting insane attack spirals, which had worsened with age. My best friend had been right, good guys know they are good, they don't ever say it. Mark said it all the time, often in jest, because of course he was 'a good guy', but there was no real joke there, nor truth.

I sighed as I pulled out my mixer. Baking was an easy way to fill up my day when really what I wanted would have involved sex in every room of my house. Kinky sex. Wild sex. Passionate sex I couldn't even imagine yet. Sex I saw in porn, sex I fantasized about, that pushed my limits, sex that felt taboo, and likely was. I needed a man who loved sex. Period. Are there any other criteria? I wasn't sure yet, all I knew was I wasn't wasting another day not living as the sexual creature I was, even if it meant I'd do it all alone.

Chapter 2

Kyle was one of those men who just looked like he knew how to fuck, and fuck well. He had a sleek body that tapered to a real waist that drew my eyes to his crotch every time I saw him. I often wondered if I turned him on or if he had just been blessed with a perpetual boner.

Today was no different.

His wife Mandy loved throwing neighborhood pool parties. She was a sexy, trophy-type-looking wife with big fake tits, no belly, and caked-on makeup, which I imagined she must scrap off with a paint chipper every night.

Being more natural myself, I figured Kyle had no interest in me because he'd picked her to marry.

I was wrong as fuck.

I slipped into their perfectly manicured backyard through the perfectly painted white fence door. Their picket fence was more of a wall, being six feet and wrapping fully around their ginormous backyard. As I sauntered in, the black sheep divorcee of the neighborhood, I got a few disdainful glances, just as I expected. Mostly from the snooty women, and none from the men.

There were at least twenty-five people here already. 'No kids' the invitation had said. In the back of my mind, I had hoped that meant sex fest, but most of these prudes probably couldn't get past their fantasies of it.

I sighed and grabbed a red Solo cup of dark red liquid with bits of pineapple, strawberries, and blueberries bobbing it in. I swished down a swallow and grimaced.

Kyle's laughter made me turn my head.

"Like drinking melted jolly ranchers, huh?" The twinkle in his eyes sent a twitch through my clit. His scruffy face held a five o'clock shadow that I couldn't stop imagining tickling my thighs.

"What?" I was stupid for a moment. My jaw fell open as my eyes darted down his shirtless body to the bulge in his swim trunks. Perpetual boner man. Mandy was lucky as fuck.

He wasn't just shirtless, he was more than half-naked and I couldn't stop staring.

I forced myself to close my jaw and wiped my mouth with my fingers. It'd been way too long since I'd enjoyed a real dick.

I gave an awkward laugh. "Yeah, pretty much, but laced with a gallon of vodka."

"Yep, Mandy's specialty. I swear she works out just so she can drink this sugary slop."

I patted the small cooler hanging from my shoulder. "I have back-ups." I smiled because he was smiling at me.

My mind drifted back to the game night last night. He'd been there too. The brush of his hand along my ass cheeks as we both had been in the kitchen getting snacks had been my masturbation fodder last night. My heart raced as I once again imagined he had done it on purpose, and not just as an oops. I reasoned that a swipe could be an oops, but a grab, well that was a clear message.

"I like your bikini. Bright pink is very nice on you." He ran a hand through the gray patch at his temple as he winked at me. "It suits you perfectly."

His eyes dwelled on my D cups. My heartbeat raged.

"Thank you," I said, enjoying his eyes roaming my body.

Mandy skittered over to us. Her boobs bounced and she giggled. "Kyle, come with me. I want us to tell Molly and Steve about our last conquest."

Kyle nodded at her, but when her back was turned, he rolled his eyes and stuck his finger in his open mouth. He followed her, which I'd imagine made sense on some level.

I picked at my second plate of food and searched for a decent soul to talk to. There were only a few guys I actually liked talking to, but their wives always seemed to ruin it by hovering and gossiping about bland shit, so I just stood with my plate of fruit and nuts and watched couples play in the water. One couple was clearly fucking in the corner, so I watched them, which did nothing to quell my burning need for cock.

Maybe I'd just leave and go home and fuck myself with my new big pink dildo toy. I'd enjoy fantasizing about Kyle stripping off my suit in the pool shed and fucking me to a cummy messy pulp against the extra floaties they always kept in the corner. I imagined bouncing on them as he rammed into me from behind, my bare-skinned tits squeaking on the plastic.

I tossed my plate in the garbage and turned to leave. But something shiny caught my eye, glinting from the window of the pool shed. I squinted. The distraction helped to squelch my raging lust, at least for the moment.

I took a few steps closer. Whatever it was, it was being waved around by someone inside and it was catching the sunlight. The door opened slightly and Kyle's head peeked around the big white door.

The head of his bare, swollen cock popped into view next.

All the air left my lungs as I gasped.

His hand appeared like a claw on the edge of the door, his finger beckoning me with a come-hither motion.

"Oh my Gawd," I whispered. I quickly glanced around to see if maybe he was meaning to get Mandy's attention, but she was over on the other side of the pool, talking excitedly with her hands. Her minions nodded and cajoled along with her like good pets.

I glanced back at the pool shed, thinking I must have imagined seeing Kyle there. I'd dreamt of that more than once and with how horny I was, and being a bit buzzed, I was sure I'd been seeing things.

But no.

He peeked around it again. Thrust his dick in the air and then pulled it back behind the door.

I resisted the urge to run to him, expose him for being a mirage. I strolled along, casually walking as my heart threatened to beat right out of my chest. I was panting already, and my pussy lips felt wet as they slipped against each other with each step.

He stuck his dick out the open door again and yanked it back quickly. The teasing look in his eyes was delicious.

I stole along the bonfire pit, gingerly passing the two couples sitting in the chairs, chatting. I avoided their eyes as I moved past. They were only ten feet from the pool shed.

My heart flew to my throat as I entered the little house. I half expected to find it empty, proving my imagination had fooled me.

Kyle stood next to the pile of floaties, naked, dick fat and thick, and standing up like a rocket reaching to launch.

"Holy fuck," I muttered and left my mouth open.

"Wanna?" he asked with a flick of his head.

"How ... ?" I stammered.

He took a step towards me. Then another. And then three more. He reached around me, which made his bulging cockhead press into my belly as he shut the door.

"You could make good use of that open mouth," he said with a snicker.

He didn't even lock the door, but pressed his hands on my shoulders.

Shock froze me in place. I wanted this, but how in the actual fuck was this happening? I dropped to my knees and took his cock tip in my mouth, as if this was what I had expected.

He groaned out as I sucked his head. I lost my hesitation as I tasted his erection. It had been over a year since my divorce, and even longer since I'd had cock between my lips. It felt so good to have dick in my mouth again. Something wild and primal groaned into existence deep inside me as I savored his taut flesh.

I moaned as I jerked him off while sucking as hard as I could. It was like I was watching us from above. This was surreal. My disbelief transformed into craziness as I rode him hard with my mouth like a mad woman. I sucked his cock like I'd never sucked anyone's cock before in my life.

The groan he released told me it'd been a while since he'd gotten a blow job.

"Oh fuck," he sputtered as his hips moved.

He grabbed my arms and pulled me to stand. Our mouths collided. A hot, wet kiss sent my want for him sky-high.

He cupped my breasts in his large hands. He squeezed.

I yelped.

He kissed down my neck, making his way toward my breasts.

"What are we doing?" I asked breathlessly. "We can't do this."

He popped my right tit out and consumed it with a satisfied grunt. He sucked my hard nipple for thirty seconds, then muttered, "I just need a taste of you."

I writhed against his suckling, his cock dancing along the bare skin of my tummy. My mind drifted to Mandy and why he hadn't pulled her into the pool shed to fuck.

It was true that Kyle was at least ten years older than me, but that just turned me on more. There was a good chance he could have fathered me, at least from a breeding standpoint, if not more. Our age gap was intoxicating, but ever since I'd become single at forty, the thoughts of older men had gifted me so many orgasms, more than I'd ever try counting.

His hands migrated down my hips, then he grabbed both of my ass cheeks so hard I squealed.

His eyes were staring at me so intently, with such passion, it fueled my already frenzied mind.

"Yes," he said with force as he devoured me in a French kiss.

Our bodies tangled. I ran my hands from his shoulders to his biceps, back up to mess up his lush hair.

We kissed, writhing against each other, moaning and groaning. We sucked tongues as if our neighbors weren't just outside the walls stuffing their faces and chatting about stupid unimportant shit.

But this was important.

"Fuck, I want you," he said fervently.

I'd have laid down with my legs spread just from that sentence alone. I hadn't heard such a wonderful thing since my twenties. My mind reeled; it was at war at once both with joy and confusion. But there was no way in fuck I was stopping.

I pulled back from him, bit my lip, and smiled. "I've wanted you for years, Kyle." It was so freeing to say it out loud.

He smiled a deep smile. "I know."

I swiped my palm along the precum oozing out of his cock, deftly spreading it around his firm skin.

He moaned and slid his fingers into my bikini bottoms. I threw my head back and moaned as he tickled his fingers along my lower lips. The rapid motion of his fingers along my wet folds got me gyrating my hips. Fuck, that felt amazing.

His eyes were so hungry for me that they set my passion ablaze. A strange urge to bite him bloomed in me.

"Fuck me," I said between my pants. "Please."

He chuckled. "Beg me some more." His eyes twinkled as I'd never seen them before.

I stifled a laugh. He was clearly too horny to be serious. So I played along.

"Please, fuck me. I want you inside me."

His grin grew bigger. "More," he demanded as he began to finger fuck my sopping wet pussy.

"Please, I want your big dick slapping the inside of my walls. Fuck me."

"Fuck me what?" he asked with even more gumption in his voice.

"Fuck me hard."

He withdrew his hand from my hot, wet cunt. In one swift motion, he flipped me around and bent me over the pile of floaties.

I gasped in shock as my face smashed hard into the bouncy mattresses.

He fondled my ass and pressed his shaft against the crack of my buttocks.

"Fuck me hard, what?" he said with arrogance.

His coercive, stern tone sent a shiver down my spine. I moaned as he rubbed his palm along my labia.

The phrase was on the tip of my tongue and, as he rammed his fingers into my slit, I uttered the words I longed to say. "Daddy. Fuck me hard, Daddy."

He released a slow, satisfied chuckle. "Yes, baby girl. Yes." He left me untouched for a moment, then I heard the music outside get louder. "There. That's perfect," he declared. "If I'm going to make you scream, we need a cover."

"Oh, fuck yes," I moaned out. I couldn't contain my glee. I was going to get fucked. And by Kyle. My excitement came out as a series of whimpers.

He intended to fuck me indeed. His passionate grabs delivered the promise of his words as he pressed deep into my flesh. He continued to finger fuck me as I wiggled on the pile of floaty toys, my fingernails digging into the soft squishy plastic. He pulled his fingers out and tapped my thighs.

I obeyed and spread my legs further apart. He spanked my clit with his open palm and I screamed out.

"Good girl," he said compassionately.

His words made me shiver, they gave me pride as I let him bring me closer to orgasm. He hit my clitoris hard and fast on repeat.

He leaned over my ear and I savored his skin all along my back. He whispered, "You a clit junkie? Or do you need G-spot too?"

I nodded, then said, "Yes."

He laughed and smacked my clit into a big orgasm. I screamed again as I peaked. My body shuddered and twitched as the contractions traveled from my pelvis out to my body.

"Good girl," he said again, which threw me into another peak of the orgasm.

My body jerked through another rise to a climax. I gasped and panted as he massaged my clitoris.

"Now I'm going to fuck you hard. Be my whore?"

I nodded emphatically. I already was that.

He pressed his mushroom head inside my cum-soaked opening and we both groaned out. He wasn't gentle, but pounded me like he was desperate.

I grunted as his body smacked into my ass. His sounds drove me insane.

"More," I begged, my voice sounding like some other woman's.

He fucked me harder. My feet kept slipping on the wet concrete floor and my full body weight now pressed the pile of pool toys down. He rammed into me with so much power and stamina, I was hurled into another orgasm.

He quickly withdrew his cock from me and his cum splatted across my ass.

The door of the pool shed opened and I gave a little cry.

I didn't want to glance back for fear it was Mandy.

"You are late," Kyle said like he wasn't a bit sorry.

"I couldn't get away. Miranda kept jabbering on about the deals she got at Sam's." I knew that voice. My mouth fell open as I finally had the nerve to glance back at the speaker.

It was Allen. The neighbor from down the street who had seven kids with his wife, Miranda. His downtrodden look broke my heart. The image of his wife walking her dogs behind my house earlier flitted through my brain. I wondered what alternate universe I'd just fallen into.

He chuckled heartily as his expression went from annoyance to amusement. "Fuck. I missed it, didn't I?"

I stared at the two of them. It felt more like a dream than reality.

Kyle licked his cum off my ass, then helped me to stand up.

I slumped against him as all the feel-good hormones swam in my body, unable to stay upright alone.

"Oh, babe. You okay?" he asked like a good Daddy.

"You fucked me into a stupor, I guess." I smiled and gave a single flighty guffaw. Calling him 'Daddy' hadn't felt fake. I suppose he'd have to prove that. Maybe I just wanted it so bad that I just gave myself permission to claim it. I could back out.

"Don't look so shocked, Alexa." Allen ran his hand down the mound at his crotch.

I shook my head and didn't mask my bewildered look. "How can I not?"

"Nice tits," Allen said with a nod. "I've been hungering to see those for years."

I snickered. "Where were you guys when I wanted to open up my marriage?"

Kyle blurted, "Oh, I asked Mark once if you two were into that. He said, 'No way.' So I let it go."

My mouth fell ajar. More betrayal. I had asked Mark to open our marriage years ago and he had refused. "Are you guys open?" I asked, aghast.

Allen smiled. "My wife is vanilla, but she lets me sleep around. She knows we have different needs and wants, so she allows me to play outside our marriage, but we love each other and want to stay married."

I tried to wrap my brain around how they had so many kids and she let him fuck others. And more about how she didn't want to join him. "I have so many questions," I stammered out.

His response was to grin deeper and rub his hands together.

"Wow," I said as my eyes drifted to Kyle's satisfied face. It felt amazing to help a man come again.

"I'm not open as in open, I'm open in the dark." His expression told me all I needed to know.

I gasped. "So last night was a come-on?" My brain was still slowly catching on.

"We had the plan to pull you into the back room and ask you," Allen said with a giant lecherous grin. "But you left before we made the move."

"I told you we should have texted her," Kyle said as he squeezed my bicep.

My heart did a somersault. I glanced down at Kyle's dick, which was still erect. He held me steady, which was comforting since I was still shaking a bit. My mind scrambled, wondering who else they'd propositioned for threesome sex in the neighborhood. My brain stalled. Wait a minute. Threesome sex happened in my neighborhood? My confusion paralyzed me as I scanned Allen's body and eyes for more answers.

Allen pulled his dick out of his swim trunks and began to stroke it.

I couldn't keep my eyes off the thickened manhood in his hands, nor the desire in his eyes. It was all hypnotizing me.

Dumbfounded, I stared at his hardon, then met his gaze.

"Care to play again?" he asked, his eyes hopeful. The suggestive leer he gave me would have convinced me if I hadn't already been in.

"Yes," I said without any hesitation, and a smile.

"Very nice," he said appreciatively with a rapid stroking of himself.

What's one more married dick inside me at this point? If I was honest, I wanted Allen too. Yet I was even surprising myself as I yearned for his cock to pierce my slit as well. Dr. Seuss flitted across my brain. Not 'thing', but dick one and dick two. The ridiculousness of this 'who scene' thought that had popped in my head almost made me laugh in their faces. I shouldn't be thinking of children's books in such a moment as this.

Part of me worried Mandy would come looking for us, but most of me didn't care. Would Miranda really be fine if Allen fucked me? I was already the outcast. Now I'd be the outcast who was sexually pleasured by two of the neighborhood's married men. The me of five years ago would have never done this, but who I'd become ran headlong in.

I guffawed. "So Miranda knows this is happening?" I swirled my finger in the air in a circle to signify us.

Allen nodded with a devilish grin. "Yeah, and she also knows I will pleasure the absolute fuck out of her later because of it." His jubilant laughter filled the shed. "She's no dummy. That woman gets what she wants and then some."

"Not a bad deal at all." I raised an eyebrow, wondering if he was really telling the truth, and more importantly, if I could ever convince her to join us.

Allen pulled me to him and kissed me as Kyle pressed himself snugly to my backside. It was foreign to have these two men on me like this, but I welcomed all the yummy taboo of it. This was a fantasy come to life. Would I regret it later? Most definitely. But I was doing this. Fuck yes, I was doing it. The rush of both of their bodies pressed to mine left me breathless and weak.

Their grips roamed me and, for the first time in my life, I enjoyed two sets of masculine hands along my skin. The booze had worn off, but the euphoria had taken over. I writhed between them as they mauled and kissed my flesh. Our combined moans filled the pool shed as the music blared outside.

I glanced out the window at all the guests of the party and smiled lasciviously.

"This is fucking delicious," I said with a groan.

They both laughed and agreed.

I ran my hands through Allen's mostly gray hair and dragged my fingers to his beard. I tugged on his whiskers as he fingered my pussy. His fat fingers felt amazing inside me.

"Oh, my Gawd." I leaned my head back against Kyle as he fondled my breasts, pinched and tugged on my nipples. I reached up to caress his face as Allen knelt in front of me.

He pressed his face between my thighs as Kyle braced me from behind, still playing with my nipples. His tongue explored my pussy lips and then he locked onto my clit with a hard suck. He massaged my hips as he ate me out to a huge orgasm. His whiskers along my skin were even more enticing than I'd had imagined.

I sighed, though I wanted to scream. I sucked in a deep breath and slowly let it out. In a moan-filled voice, I asked, "Who needs to get married again with you guys as neighbors?"

They both laughed heartily, Allen's laughter sending arousing vibrations along my clit as I came hard against his mouth. He slurped at my pussy, eating my cum out of me.

As if they had planned it, Kyle raised me to my feet and Allen pressed his mouth to me. I could smell my pussy on his beard and taste me on his tongue.

We kissed as they mauled me like a rag doll between them. I'd never been so touched in my life, and it was intoxicating. Kyle swiveled me to face him, and we kissed before Allen pushed on my back.

After I was bent over, I took Kyle's cock in my mouth as Allen entered me from behind. No discussion, no rational thoughts left my mouth, though they lingered like an ignored itch on the edge of my consciousness. It was like being drunk and knowing it, but still reaching for that next swallow of beer.

They spit-roasted me into another orgasm as my body flopped like spaghetti between their thrusting hips. They'd need to carry me out of here at this rate. They could tell guests I had drank too much and had passed out. Damn, I was good at dreaming up excuses. But this was our secret, and none of their business. I closed my eyes and savored them taking their pleasure from my body as they gave it back to me as good. They both came hard as skin smacks and wet sloshing sounds filled the shed.

When I opened my eyes, Miranda was standing at the window with her phone held up. I was startled, but the appreciative look on her face immediately eased my worry. She was loving what she saw. I tried to process it as they pulled their wet cum-soaked cocks in and out of me.

They finally withdrew their dicks from me. Allen saluted his wife. She raised her eyebrows, pointed at Allen, then at herself, then left.

"Wow, just wow," I muttered. "I had zero ideas of this."

Allen sighed heavily. "Epic fuck, Alexa." He was still fully dressed in his Hawaiian shirt and khaki trunks, only his dick was out and dripping.

I immediately wondered if he came in me. What had occurred in the last few minutes was fuzzy. I'd been so overwhelmed I hadn't noticed where he spewed.

"Don't worry, I'm clean and I'm fixed." He held up seven fingers. "After boy number seven, we needed to shut this breeder down cold turkey." He shoved his deflating cock back into his suit.

I stared at him, aghast. I had my two boys. I couldn't imagine seven. And, apparently, he had women on the side. "Well, we know you are virile, so it's a good thing you're neutered."

Kyle snickered.

"Hey, I've got balls." His belly shook as he enjoyed my humor. "And I get tested regularly, so I'm healthy."

My brain flitted to what his insurance claim processor must see on a regular basis and I stifled a laugh. Though his admission of sleeping around with Miranda knowing eased my worry, there was still Kyle.

"And I haven't fucked anyone in a few years, besides Mandy. Guess I was waiting for you to seem ready." Kyle grinned deeply. "And Mark to be out of the picture."

"I'm suddenly really happy I didn't move after the divorce." To be sought after by one man was exciting, but two? "Mmm. Wow! Now I feel special."

"Oh, just you wait. Daddy has a lot in store for you, baby."

The look in Kyle's eyes gave me no doubts that was true. But Daddy statuses were earned, so I'd read, and he'd only tapped his toe in at this point. I'd play along for now, but there was too much missing to verbally agree.

That didn't change the fact that his words lit a warm fire in my gut, which I had desperately needed on those cold winter nights alone in my bed.

"Oh, we've established 'Daddy' already, huh? What's that make me? Can I be 'Daddy' too? Or two?" Allen chuckled in his usual jovial way.

Immediately my mind went to a gay couple, so I sneered, "Of course, but do my daddies fuck each other too?"

They roared with laughter.

"Not yet, baby girl, not sure we're those kinds of daddies." Allen snickered.

I didn't care. I just knew my life had just gotten infinitely better. A glimmer of hope. Plus, the possibility of reaching a sexual bucket list goal of mine swelled into potential existence ... vaginal DP. Why not dream big at this point? I didn't know whether to laugh or scream.

"You are a delight and I'm loving that look on your face." Allen clapped his hands. "I predict we are going to have lots of fun together."

Chapter 3

Everything reminded me of sex. Everywhere I looked, thoughts of fucking socked me in the gut. The pile of cantaloupes made me think of fucking Kyle and Allen, the way the cucumbers were lined up screamed their cocks, and the glances from horny men rang that memory bell too. Even if they weren't horny, I imagined that they were. I couldn't get the sex with Kyle and Allen out of my head. It wasn't just that I wanted more, it was something else I couldn't name. But it was pervasive and snaked into every aspect of my body and soul. Whatever it was called that we'd done, I was hooked.

My mind sifted through the last twelve hours of my life. Sleep had been a great distraction, which had come swiftly last night, even despite the exuberant shouts of Alex playing video games online with someone somewhere else in the world. When both he and Jasper were waging wars online, it sounded more like a party than just two boys playing separately in their rooms.

No thoughts of dreams had graced my first waking moments; only flashbacks of Kyle's skin and Allen's beard and bare dick occupied the beginning of the day. Pool shed images hit me next. They flicked across my thoughts perfectly crystalline, as if I were flipping through real pics on my phone. The memories of explosions of orgasms flooded my first consciousness of the day, and it just made me want them again. Fucking strangers was one thing, but letting men I'd known for years shove their cocks in me was another. It was so shocking to know this was my life that this crazy insanity was happening to, and that there were most definitely more hijinks on the horizon.

And Miranda. Miranda! Miranda, she knew! I still couldn't wrap my brain around that one.

I had showered and grabbed my grocery list, barely making it out the door before my sister was texting me.

I glanced at my phone.

She had sent me a photo of her, Jeff, and the kids with the ocean in the background. I gave it a heart and slipped into my car. It was inconsequential when I'd just fucked neighbors secretly in a pool shed, at a party. Who was I now that I'd done that?

During the whole drive to the store, my brain swam. I didn't think I could make sense of Allen, Kyle, and me. I wasn't sure why we fit or if that was just a one-time threesome fling. Maybe they'd even ignore me going forward, pretend it hadn't happened. I was certainly used to being gaslit.

I parked the car, and the sun blasted my skin as I rushed into the grocery store. I was brainless, but I also felt more alive than I'd had in years.

I shook my head as I selected peppers with four bumps on the bottom, which Mark had told me were the sweeter peppers. One thing he'd taught me that was helpful. I sighed as I recalled all the good meals Mark had made during our marriage. Damn, he'd been a good cook though, one of his few saving graces.

I gritted my teeth, trying to remember a recipe's ingredients, not easy with my mind full of thoughts of sex. I needed to get more organized and better with my grocery lists. All the changes of being single were still something I needed to get used to. I'd thought by a year I'd have sorted it all out. I constantly lamented the loss of Mark's cooking, but my boys ate whatever I made, even if I'm nowhere near as good as he had been.

A hand smacked my right butt cheek. I gasped. It wasn't an accidental brush, but more of an intentional slap. I spun around, ready to yell at the offender. But instead of being pissed, I smiled. Joy seized me like a blanket covering as Kyle grinned back at me.

"Oh shit," I muttered, followed by a sly biting of my lower lip. "It's you." My eyes filled with flirty lust as I met and held his intent gaze.

"I couldn't resist that butt of yours. It's way too ripe in those tight shorts," he said as he pressed his hand to my ass cheek again, pulling me closer to his pelvis. His cock was a hard log against my gut. He leaned in and whispered, "I loved pounding my pelvis against those luscious cheeks of yours. I wanna do it again. Soon."

I froze as the fullness of his words took me. The sentence sent a jolt through my clit and a spasm through my back, which forced me to arch. Fuck! I glanced around, wondering who saw my body jolt, and even the spank.

"Brave, aren't you?" But my heart filled with glee at the meaning behind his words. So, we were more of a thing than a nameless one-time fuck in a pool shed. Yippee!

"No, just horny. And I want to fuck you again." He took a step back, so our bodies separated. He glanced around, then chuckled. "Well, maybe, but I can't resist your ass." His expression turned sly and even more salacious. "I really want to drag you across the store by your hair and fuck you behind the big bins of extra toilet paper they keep at the back."

My jaw dropped open as I realized I'd really do that with him in a heartbeat. My mind started fantasizing about it before I could take another breath.

His suggestive grin told me he was serious, until he winked. "Though I'd have to be faster than a spitball from the sixth grader because Mandy is here too, somewhere in the store." His fun, flirty expression disappeared as he scanned the produce section. Frustration flooded his face.

I knew that watched feeling. I could see in his eyes. It was a horrible feeling.

My heart fell. I instantly missed not doing this risky exhibitionistic idea with him and now it was something I wanted on my bucket list. I'd started a sexual bucket list of fantasies and desires I wanted to do before I die. Actually, I'd had it mentally for a while, but now it was in black and white, legit, and in the world. Not that being in my forties is that old, but it's made me realize life is short and I'm only getting older and fatter and uglier. I chastised myself. That's a piss poor way to look at life, and something Mark enjoyed pointing out to me regularly.

"I'd do that with you in a heartbeat, Kyle," I piped up as I puffed out my chest bravely. I gave him even stronger fuck me eyes, so he'd know I wasn't just flirting.

He held my eyes in a lock and every speck of me joined him. I was getting sucked in.

He licked his lips. "Oh, I would too. Maybe we can arrange that someday, but when Mandy isn't along." Every time he said 'Mandy', his eyes changed, and I yearned for how they looked before.

I opened my mouth to speak, but nothing came out. I searched his face and wondered how I could get more of Kyle in private moments on a daily basis.

"Any regrets?" he asked as he fingered his lips. "About the pool shed?"

Fuck, I loved his lips. The way he pronounced 'pool shed' made my pussy wet. I wanted to touch his mouth, to enjoy it on my flesh again, to kiss him. Oh, how I missed kissing a man. And Kyle clearly liked kissing. My loins moved, gravitating my body towards him in a sway as if we were magnetized.

"None." I spoke firmly, but hesitated a slight bit inside my brain. Because how honest could I be with him? I sighed and decided to go for it. "In fact, I want to do it again."

His expression bloomed into a gorgeous thing. Utter glee filled his face, leaving me not questioning if he was pleased by my answer. He nodded as desire flew into flames in his eyes. "As do Allen and I."

My mind scrambled again, fixating on how Miranda willingly let Allen fuck other women and dared not participate herself. This woman seemed so smart, but now I felt her to be a fool.

"When?" I whispered breathlessly, without hiding the desperation and excitement in my voice.

He smiled deeply and it shocked me how much I adored that I had pleased him. "I'm not sure about Allen, he's tougher to get free with Miranda and the boys, but I'd be free to sneak over to your house later today. Will you be alone?"

I shook my head. "Not sure. My boys are unpredictable at best. They are flighty and I don't think either work today, but they often go out with friends or their girlfriends, so there's a chance I might be by myself, yes."

"Okay. I'll text you. I told Mandy I need to go to the hardware store later, so she already expects me to leave. I just have to figure out where to leave my car so I can sneak back to your house."

This did pose a problem. Our hooking up apparently would be per chance, and victim to the whims of others in our lives. But this was so exciting, I'd take what I could get.

I nodded. "Okay, text me. Maybe we can figure something out."

Mandy streamed into view and I bristled. Her giant breasts were encased in an obvious cleavage display of a workout bra above her perfect ass in capri leggings. Just her cleavage alone must drive boob men wild. If I was honest, it drove me a bit wild too. It was like looking at an oddity, I couldn't look away.

Her gaze zeroed in on us and her lips pursed into a firm line, but she quickly wiped the expression away with a shake of her hair, jutting her nose high in the air. "Oh, there you are, Kyle. You left me in the deli section."

"You told me you'd be right back, so I decided to come say 'hi' to our neighbor, Alexa." Kyle deflected her blaming well. It was a skill I learned as well.

She nodded at me, but there was an extra coolness in her eyes as she said, "Alexa."

"Hi, Mandy," I offered in a friendly voice, which felt very fake considering I just talked about helping her husband cheat on her with me.

I got the impression from Kyle at every turn that he felt trapped in his marriage. As had I, so I understood his dilemma very intimately, painfully so, and his desire to get away from her. I didn't know Kyle that well yet but, so far, we couldn't be more suited to each other if we had made each other up out of thin air.

Mandy stomped her foot. "Let's finish shopping. I need to get home. Tosha and I are going to work out." Mandy flung a perfectly manicured hand through her lushly curled locks and tossed me a look. "Later, Alexa." If her tone didn't fully discard me, her look did.

I almost cringed outwardly but managed to keep it internal only.

Kyle followed her, but glanced back at me with new excitement in his eyes as he pressed his index finger and middle finger together and jabbed it upward toward the ceiling.

I clapped without sound and nodded. His fingers up my cunt were exactly what I desired on a day like today, and any and every day. This new development was perfect. Mandy never did short workouts, so he'd likely be able to sneak over for a not-too-quick fuck without even having to hide his car anywhere.

The rest of the shopping trip didn't hurt as much because the anticipation of my sex date with Kyle soaked all my insides with happiness. I loaded up on apples, bananas, grapes, and strawberries, knowing my boys would eat them in two days flat. The rest of my list took me an hour and I quit when I couldn't safely add another item to the cart.

#

I looked out the window as my second son left the house. Did I feel guilty about what I was about to do? No. Guilt had totally left me. Kyle sought freedom, as I once had. I was once where he was now. And honestly, somehow the both of us getting what we really wanted squashed any pesky embers of guilt. Why should we live our lives without enjoying what we wanted? A miserable marriage was not worth staying in.

Ever since Mark had left, I had felt free. Each day I felt freer and freer from his abuse and the reality had set in. Joy had started to permanently settle in the nooks and crannies of my cells. It was that pervasive. Upon waking up each morning, the extreme bliss I felt should have been impossible, yet it shone out from me as real and as relentless as the sun's shine.

I was finally free to be me.

There were moments when I startled, expecting to see Mark appear around a corner. The old feelings of his incessant watchfulness, of walking on eggshells had claimed my sanity, but each day, more and more that black plague had lost its grip on me.

Still, I wore a stain. The haughty glances from Janna at the grocery store earlier flitted across my brain. Black sheep was a status that extended for me even from our neighborhood to the local store. Janna had once been my friend. Well, maybe, given how she treated me now, that was a stretch by a long sense of a mile. But we used to get alone time together and enjoy it. We'd talk, even go on walks, enjoy a glass of wine on each other's decks. Once my divorce was known about, she'd given me the cold shoulder and not so much as even said 'hi' or waved to me as I drove past. The dumb thing was, I knew she was miserable with her husband too. I'd concluded she hated me for having the balls to shove mine off.

I snatched my phone and texted Kyle.

"Not wasting a single second," I muttered.

Me: He's gone. You can come over anytime.

Kyle: I saw him leave. I'll be there in a minute. I want you. My cock is hard as a steel bar. Gonna fuck you into multitudes of orgasms.

Butterflies exited my heart and burst along every artery as I skipped to the stairs to make my way to the back sliding door in the basement. I was a young girl again, savoring the excitement of the impending arrival of my lover. And it felt so damn good.

The plan was simple. He'd come in back where no eyes would see him entering unless they had binoculars on the back of my house. I skittered down the stairs so fast, almost slipping several times as I lost control of my body in my exuberance. I couldn't wait!

He was somehow faster than me and inside the house already, standing to the side of the sliding door with that luscious crotch of his set in a huge bulge, a goofy adorable happy grin on his face.

"Oh, well look at you," I said seductively as I rushed to him, practically panting already. His presence was that intoxicating.

We collided as lovers who haven't seen each other in weeks do. Our bodies tangled as our hands went right into the other's hair.

"I need you. I need your pussy. I need you to come on my hard cock, baby girl," he whispered before kissing me again. "Need your cream on my cock, baby."

The fire inside my gut raged as I groped his toned body. Images of the pool shed fuck invaded my brain once again, and I savored each delicious strand of the memory. I feared Allen would be mad we left him out of this, but in truth, I missed his presence too. Kyle's passion made up for it, however, as his hands caressed me more than I'd had in all the previous years of marriage. I was still hungry, starved for the sex and intimacy that Kyle so easily offered. We were the ultimate slow burn, having secretly yearned for each other for more than a decade. All the mutual glances at neighborhood parties, the casual flirting, that unspoken click that was between us was undeniable. And it was now raging in full actuality, and I was pining for more.

"I need you, Daddy." Again, the word should have felt foreign being so new, but instead it was devilishly decadent off my tongue. "I need your cock in me. Please, make me cum."

He grabbed both my ass cheeks and lifted my body. I wrapped my legs around him as if he was a pool noodle in deep water. I was his and I'd spread my legs for him gladly. I gasped at my thoughts. Yes, I'd open my thighs for him each time he reached for me, of that much I was completely sure.

"Oh," he murmured in his sexy low voice, "I'm going to make you come multiple times. You are mine."

His claim on me should have felt unsettling. To the ordinary mind, perhaps it would. It should have been awkward at the very least. In a sense, maybe it was, in a way, but I was loving the stretch of our newly found affair into such grounds. Sometimes the doing first ushers in the reality. At this point, I had zero doubts about us stringing the hope of trust along for a bit. It felt so imminent that it was almost a thing already. I was more than willing to go out on a limb. I was hungry for it.

Maybe it was the way he held me. Or maybe it was that unnamed something in his eyes, but we had latched onto each other from a place of such desolation that our souls knew the drink we needed. Being thirsty wasn't something either of us had planned on or expected at this point in our lives, but quenching it perhaps was so undeniably amazing that instead of awkward, we'd burgeoned into a joint ball of flames. Our bodies curved together as instinctual as lust itself, and as obvious.

We savored each other as only the deprived can enjoy. There wasn't a part of me he hadn't touched already as we fell to the couch. My need for him was like for the air itself.

"I need you," I whispered against his neck.

He straddled me and slipped off his shirt. He grinned at me. "Your turn."

I had removed my bra earlier in hopes that he'd come over, so as I pulled my tight tank top off, my breasts swung out and separately.

"Oh, fuck me, yes!" he said with so much appreciation that my desire for him heightened even further. "I love the no bra. Fuck, your breasts are stunning. I am in awe." He molested my body with just his eyes in a passion I hadn't tasted in way too long.

His excitement over simply seeing my bare breasts filled me with a flood of feelings I'd not had the pleasure of stewing in since I had been young. His compliments, no, his desire for even just seeing me naked were gifts in and of themselves.

He made me feel sexy with just a look, then when he added his words, I was ensnared in his magic. I wanted him to take me more than I wanted anything in the world.

"I'm thrilled you like," I said, maintaining eye contact with him. "I'll show you them anytime you want to see them."

His grin told me how much he planned on using my offer. "I'm going to fuck you hard, Alexa. I want to pound your cunt into this couch and make you scream."

His dirty talk flared me even higher. It was so deep, this hunger I harbored for his passion, that pieces of it kept floating to the surface. We fell into a kiss that made my insides burst. I moaned and sighed as he dragged his tongue along my skin down to my right nipple. His hand cupped my breast, and it was not only comforting, but arousing as he took my hard peak into his mouth, hoovering my breast to his tonsils. I'd never been tit-sucked this long and hard by a lover before and I squirmed and squealed beneath him.

"Oh, my Gawd," I drew the word out into a moan. Sex wasn't supposed to be this good, not in the way I'd come to view the world. "You feel amazing." It felt lame and somewhat weak to say, but it was the damn truth.

He popped his mouth off my nipple. "No, you feel amazing."

Why couldn't life have been this simple? I'd been cheated out of all the sexual fire Kyle so easily gifted me my entire existence on this planet.

He dry-humped his dick along my abdomen in tune with my moans and his grunts. Foreplay being the teasing part of sex meant I got to savor every touch, knowing that maybe he'd make my pleasure a priority. That was foolish of me. I wasn't the first woman on Earth to crave being the focus, it seemed to be the plague of my gender for the most part.

I sank into being present with him and shoved those theoretical wet wishbones of lifelong lamentations to the back of my head to dry out. All I needed right now was to think about fucking him.

A surge of confidence flared in me. "I'm going to make you cum, Daddy." I reached for his cock and stroked him through his shorts. His cock felt larger today than yesterday. "You eat your oatmeal this morning or something? This cock is a prize fighter today."

He chuckled and it soothed me so deeply I almost forgot to breathe. "You do this to me, Alexa."

I believed him.

I yearned to strip off his shorts, flip him over, and ride him until we both came screaming like banshees.

"Get your pants off," he commanded.

The direct order sent a shiver down my body as easily as an oar pierced water. "Yes, sir." I already enjoyed submitting to his domination. All the words were coming too soon, but it all felt so right. According to online reading, I wasn't supposed to feel this yet with him. But who was I to argue with my feelings? I'd learned to stop being that fool a long while ago.

I wiggled out of my leggings, my phone tumbling to the floor.

Kyle picked it up and the mischief in his eyes tore right into me. "Be my pussy model."

Naughty pics as foreplay? This man was a sexual genius. No one had ever taken pictures of my pussy and I was instantly thrilled he would be the first.

He scrambled backward and I enjoyed watching his erection bob as he did. "Spread your lips, baby girl. Daddy wants a naughty photo shoot."

The thought of having our play time documented on my phone was a scrumptious layer of taboo I'd never yet broached in my life. There'd be actual proof of our time together. To be honest, I hadn't even looked at my pussy. I couldn't have even described my own body part, which seemed stupid. I could easily tell others what my hair looked like, what color eyes I had, and how my petite toes were more attractive than most people's feet. But it hit me like a ton of bricks. I didn't have a clue what my own pussy looked like.

I shoved my disbelief aside and succumbed to how sheerly naughty and wonderful it felt to let my neighbor plan to take pics of my naked womanhood.

I carefully spread my lips, and while this act wasn't unusual anymore, I had done that countless times prior to inserting one of my dildos, this time was so different. I was doing it in front of another human being, and he was grinning like the fattest Cheshire cat in the world with my phone at the ready.

I'd never been told anything about my pussy, other than the doctor telling me it looked healthy. So this jaunt into him appreciating the appearance of my pussy really turned me on.

He began taking pics. Nodding his head, widening his grin as the photo shoot of my pussy stretched into a much longer session than I'd ever expected a man to want to look at my pussy could ever be. Watching the myriad of expressions his face morphed into was arousing beyond all I could have ever imagined.

He loved what he saw. And I was sexy. I was feminine. I was a Goddess for his viewing pleasure.

"I love the different shades of pink of your skin. The curve of your lips. The deepening of color at your slit. The way your juices glisten off your skin."

Him listing all these things about my pussy flipped a switch inside me. It was tangible and already ever-lasting as much as it turned my genitals into a raging clit boner. He really thought my pussy was sexy and for the first time in my life, I accepted the sexy compliments.

"I need you to fuck me, Daddy," I murmured with such want that I barely recognized my own voice.

Him not touching me but reacting to me playing with my pussy drove me wild and I needed his cock in me, slapping my G spot and my thickened clitoris. I writhed as he took more pics, my panting was raging as I played with my swelling lips. I thrust my pelvis as if I were riding him hard reverse cowgirl.

"Please," I whispered as my need for him hit a critical level.

But he had his own agenda.

"Now for a video. Follow my commands, baby girl."

I nodded as the idea of a video of me playing with my pussy on some cloud for video storage made this feel even more naughty. Could someone access this video from deep in a hidden safe house where cloud access was perused by all-powerful internet wizards? The thought of someone watching my video and getting off to it sent my already blaring sex drive into a bursting star of want, not just an explosion, but a supernova.

"Okay, yes, baby girl, be patient. We need to savor this. Now, press your lips open. That's right." He made eye contact with me for a moment. "Now, tickle your bean. Yep. And now harder. Milk her with fast strokes. I'm going to make you cum. Listen to my words, I'm in control."

Him in control of me was suddenly what I wanted, and all I wanted. "Please," I said again in barely a whisper. I wanted this without knowing, as if deep down I'd wanted it for years.

He clearly enjoyed my begging as his facial expression showed immense enjoyment. "Not yet," he said sternly while zooming in on my pussy, then videoing my face.

My face! My face would be in this video too? The taboo showing of my whole face after my pussy excited me. Who would see this? And honestly, I couldn't wait to see my pussy. To watch myself come. The thought raged me so hard, but yet I waited, I obeyed him, not because I wasn't strong, but because I wanted him to guide me.

"Okay, that's it. Now press your index finger into your slit for me. Nice and slow."

I listened and did as he instructed.

"I can see it in your eyes, but don't do it yet. Don't you come yet, baby girl. Slowly pump those fingers into your hot wet hole. Coat your fingers in your juices."

I slipped my fingers inside myself and resisted the urge to ram my fingers against my G spot.

"Careful, not yet, baby girl. Slow and steady. Fuck yourself with your fingers." He kept grinning at me like he knew how badly I wanted his cock in place of my fingers. "Good girl." He pursed his lips. "Give me your sounds. I want to hear you enjoy."

Those words satiated and flared me hotter than any. I moaned as I slowly fucked myself. My groans hit a crescendo. I rolled into whimpering and even uttered a nonsense word.

"Imma honsa oh."

"Good girl. Good girl. Slow rise, give yourself a slow rise now. I see that loss of control raging in your eyes, and I love it. But don't you dare come yet. Hold off until I say." He stroked his hard cock and swiped his fingers along the hole at the top. He leaned forward with his finger soaked in his precum. "You're gonna taste us," he said as he held his wet finger just above my lips. "Now, bring your fingers from your pussy up to your mouth."

I obeyed.

"Now," he said with force.

He pressed his finger into my mouth as I pressed mine in as well.

"Suck us."

It was so erotic and it smacked me like a freight train that not only did I not know what my own wet pussy looked like, I didn't know what my own juices tasted like. Why had I not tried this before?

Kyle continued to blow my mind as I swirled my tongue around both our fingers as he continued to video me. The salty taste surprised me. I'd read about salty precum, but since Mark had not liked blow jobs, I was really dumb about it all. The shame of offering him a blow job once and his disdain had stunted my sexuality in ways I hadn't even realized until just this moment. He'd had a thing about mouths on genitals as being dirty, so oral sex hadn't been our thing.

Kyle fucked my mouth with his finger. "Fuck your mouth too, baby girl. Come on. That's it," he coached. He pressed his hard shaft to my body and like I had blinders on, imagining his cock pounding into me was all I could see. It was like seeing red. I was instantly obsessed. I pleaded with my eyes for him to fuck me, but still, he didn't.

He pulled his finger from my mouth, so I copied him and removed mine too.

"Now, tell Allen you wish he was here, and he'd better get his ass here or I'm fucking you alone."

I gasped as terror and excitement filled me at once. He was going to send this to Allen. The thrill of that raged my libido even higher.

I was panting so hard as I said between pants, "Allen ... come here ... to ... my house. Or ... Kyle is fucking me alone."

Kyle sat up and shuffled backward while still videoing me. He reached for my pussy and pressed in what felt like possibly three fingers. He began to finger fuck me harder than I'd ever been finger-fucked before in my life. The sloshing sounds of his wet fingers riding my wet cunt drove me so far to the edge that I had to fight hard to not come.

He rammed his fingers into me relentlessly for what was surely an eternity, but I knew in reality it was only like a few seconds. "Yeah, almost there."

I wasn't almost there, fat chance, I was there right now, practically hanging off the edge already. I writhed, trying to control myself and not come, and right when I was about to lose the battle he said, "Cum for Daddy."

My world split open in an array of pleasure that only unimpeded sunlight could rival. My body burst into one of the largest orgasms I'd had to date. My legs drew up alongside his body, bending as my torso curled. My head fell back as I made the loudest sounds I'd ever made during any sex in my life. My back was so arched I might as well have been doing the hardest yoga pose on the planet. The contractions that followed turned my face into what I assumed must have been ugly and agonizing. I squeezed the couch cushions, digging my fingernails into its softness. I was enduring so much intense pleasure that I had to let some of it out with my arching muscles too, sound wasn't enough.

"Oh, Gawd, fuck," I muttered as the pussy contractions claimed me. I cried out involuntarily, then fell silent as my body jerked. I gasped so deeply as I'd held my breath without realizing it. I needed the oxygen before I'd go blue. The contractions continued as a rise of panic filled me, my clit was way too sensitive. "Stop, it's too much."

I couldn't see his face as he said, "Suffer through it, baby girl. The next one will be even bigger. Trust me."

I didn't think I could handle that. I tried to squirm away from his jamming his fingers into me relentlessly. I wanted to scream bloody murder as the aftershocks of the first orgasm spread into the peak of another, like ice cracking towards a bigger break. I made sounds I hadn't known I could, more heretical nonsense words and shrieks that I couldn't even name. The contractions took me again and spread out their control over my body. They owned me like they never had before. This was new ground and I'd never been so vulnerable before in my life as I allowed him to force me into another wave of orgasmic shakes.

It was shocking to have that many contractions in rapid succession. I'd counted to fifteen, then couldn't fathom counting anymore, yet they kept going. My head thrashed from side to side as he slowly lessened the attack on my pussy. I'd read about this in books, but none of them had taught of this.

He sighed with a highly satisfying sigh and topped it with a low, rich voice, "Good girl. Very very very good girl."

The affirmation primed me for what I assumed would come next. "Fuck me, Kyle," I said in barely a whisper.

"Fuck me, who?" he demanded.

I managed a small smile in my euphoric state. "Daddy," I said through my grin.

"That's right." He stared at his phone. "Allen is at a soccer game. Poor bastard." He typed something but didn't share what as he handed me my phone. "Watch yourself come, baby. Then I'll fuck you."

I took my phone like it might break and tapped the video. My pussy was pink and wet, the squish sounds were almost as loud as my moans. Watching the video made me slightly dizzy as the video jerked up and down as he had held the phone while aggressively fingering me. Glimpses of my face made me gasp. Oh, how I looked! I didn't think I'd ever made such expressions before in my life. I was flickering between shock, expressions of pain, which were most certainly not pain, but pleasure, and episodes of eye-rolling which were punctuated by my almost eerie mouth movements. At times my mouth was wide open and at others my lips almost met. I looked more like a zombie having a seizure than anything remotely sexy.

I couldn't take my eyes off my pussy in action though. Watching Kyle's fingers barraging me was one of the most erotic things I'd ever seen. Likely because I paired it with how I had just felt. Shut up and don't analyze, Alexa. Watching my body curl and shudder taught me that even though I'd never come that hard before, my body sure as fuck knew what to do instinctually with that much pleasure. And that by itself was jarring.

"Wow, that was amazing. But I look like a freak." I met his gaze and was startled by the raging lust in his eyes.

"Oh, it was beautiful. I've never watched anyone come that hard in person, to be honest. It was a masterpiece." Doubt filled his eyes for a split second. "It was your biggest, right?"

I nodded. "Epically so. I've never in my life ... " I didn't get to even finish my thought before he laid on me and kissed me deeply once more.

"I want to give you more pleasure. Make you come again. Getting you off gets me off."

Confused, I furrowed my brow as we kissed more. When he lifted off of me, he cocked his head.

"Ah, what's up, baby girl?"

"You need to come." His concern for me climaxing again perplexed me. He should be ramming himself into me by this point to get his. "Don't you want me?"

He stroked my cheek. "I've already had you. I made you come under my control."

"But, you haven't come yet."

He chuckled until he frowned. "You are serious?"

"Well of course I am. You need to come."

"No, I don't. I would be satisfied just making you come." He pulled himself off of me and it was a slap in the face. "I get pleasure from giving you pleasure. Sex isn't about just me coming."

"No, I know that, but it's not done until you come too."

His phone buzzed. "Shit," he muttered as he lunged for it. "Hello?"

He sat on the end of the couch, and I watched his dick deflate.

"Yeah, I can do that." He was silent for a few more minutes. "Okay. I'll go and take care of it."

He hung up and it was a sign, our fun was done. "I've got to go. Mandy's biggest client has an emergency and she's on her way home, so she can't do it. I have to go do it."

"Wait," I said as I sat up. "I can make you come quick. Please. I want to."

He shook his head. "Baby girl, I don't have time. And Mandy will be home soon. I can't."

I'd never felt so good and so bad in such a short space of time.

"You know, I think it's good this happened. I don't need to come to enjoy you. My coming is not what makes what we do sex." He slipped his shorts back up over his softening cock, which had stiffened up after he got off the phone with Mandy. "I'm actually happy this happened. It's not like I won't come at some point today. That's easy."

It wasn't just that it was a letdown, it was that it wasn't finished. He'd blue-balled my idea of what my idea of sex was. The man was supposed to come. That was the finale. That's what it was and he'd stripped it out. Confused, I sat up and watched him prepare to go.

"Alexa, let me ask you this. Are you any less satisfied if I don't come?" His eyes showed he was chuckling inside while I was just more perplexed. He was so damn sexy even being this obstinate.

I widened my eyes as the full realization of this hit me like a chokehold. Refusing to let this feeling paralyze me, I said with absolution, "Yes." I crossed my arms under my breasts as I let my anger show all over my face.

"Then this is a good lesson. Sex is about your pleasure. It's not about mine. I can come in a heartbeat. Sex is what I can gift you." He slid on his shoes but then walked across my carpet.

I watched, pretending to be offended, though the word 'lesson' rubbed me the wrong way. But I refused to let that color this moment. "I'm making you come. And that's final. Come back after."

"I will if I can." And he left.

I stared at the space his body had just filled. I sat frozen with my mouth ajar. Dumbfounded didn't even fit what I felt. Flabbergasted did but that still wasn't enough. There were men like this in the world?

My phone buzzed.

Kyle: That was delicious. Send me the video please. And then play with your gorgeous pussy and make yourself cum again for me.

Me: Yes, Daddy.

My brain mulled it all over as I prepared to follow his instructions.

Calling him 'Daddy' even over text sent surges of excitement and arousal through my body. I had never thought it would.

I selected the video and hit send.

He sent me devil and fire emojis.

Kyle: It's not the same as hearing and living it live, but damn it's good to have—Good Girl.

I sent him a smiling emoji with hearts and a fire emoji.

I flipped my camera on and pointed it at myself. I gazed at my pussy on the screen, still in shock over what I looked like down there. I was hot! I spied some cream parting my lips, so I squeezed them. Cum oozed out of me, more than I'd ever dreamt I could make.

"Oh, my Gawd," I uttered as I tapped record to catch this for him. "He's got to see this." I pressed my lips together and watched as my cum oozed out of my pink moist lips. They felt puffy between my fingers as I pressed them.

"Look what you did to me," I whispered. I swiped my finger along my slit to scoop it up and brought it to my lips. I videoed myself sucking my own cum off my fingers. Salty and indescribable, a flavor I'd never tasted so couldn't quite name the taste, floated about my taste buds. "Yours is next," I said into the camera before I tapped the recording mode off. I sent it to both Kyle and Allen and sat up.

Fluid oozed out of me as I pulled my leggings up. I shimmied into my pants hoping the fabric would just effortlessly soak up my juices.

"Well, that was certainly a first." I stared out the sliding glass door, utterly amazed by my own body.

I headed to the kitchen because I was hungry. I started a sandwich before I realized I hadn't obeyed Kyle and made myself come again.

My stomach growled and I smiled. "Sustenance first, then I'll come again."

With all my new toys, and newfound understanding of my own body and triggers to climax, I was becoming so skilled at making myself come. And now I knew what that looked like. I had never believed when I had read that women had to oftentimes learn to come, it's natural, it should be instinctual, but it's not. Whereas for men, it really was so easy. It just happened, and often with such little effort. It was unfair that women could have sex without being aroused, but men couldn't. It pissed me off and explained why women were so easily targets of abuse. It seemed like a cruel joke nature had played on us. But, then there was the female ability to orgasm multiple times in a row. I smiled. I'd forgive nature for giving us that perk of being a female.

"I guess that's nature's way of evening the playing field between the sexes." I chuckled to myself all alone in the kitchen. "I'll take being female!" I said with triumph. The power of that statement was so good and so real. I hoped the boys were still gone, they'd wonder what the fuck their mom was doing shouting all by herself in the kitchen.

Chapter 4

Having had Kyle already today, and now with Allen sneaking over, I was beyond excited. I loved the triad of us, wanted way more of that. But now getting Allen in my own home without the boys here was a rare bonus I'd likely not get very often. I had to grab it by the balls and use it.

With how happy Miranda always looked, Allen was surely an amazing, caring lover. She always looked so satisfied. He was a big, burly man, and next to petite Miranda it seemed he could break her even when he tapered back his strength. I'd fantasized all kinds of sexual scenarios between the two of them, including him holding her body up from beneath her thighs and bouncing her on his cock. The mere thought of it wetted my pussy.

A knock at the door proved to be Allen.

"Come in," I said hurriedly as I glanced around. Who would be starting the rumor of a neighbor entering my house alone? It was if people around the 'hood acted like he was entering my pussy, not just entering my door frame. I don't give a fuck. Let them talk. I now knew Kate and Devon were swingers, and Max and Emma, and even the most boring neighbors, Melinda and Bosch, were too. I couldn't fathom all of them doing each other like orgy partners in a million years, but according to Allen and Kyle, they'd been at the carefully curated free-use lifestyle longer than they had.

Gazing upon Allen's face was like a hug and a clit kiss at once. If I were to sum him up, he was a mama bear and a brute in one, well, but add in the horny stallion too.

He pulled me into a hug so fast, I was lost in his warmth and manliness instantly.

"Oh, how I missed meeting up with you and Kyle earlier. I was so excited when you texted you were free now. I need me some Alexa now too."

My first thought was of Miranda, and if she knew he was here, so I wiped that out of my head like a pesky bug. This was our time. Nothing should be clouding it. "I missed you too."

"Kyle told me everything. That ok with you?"

I nodded. It felt a bit strange having them discuss me without my input, and without me even there, but I was willing to go with it thus far. I'd been leaping in fully to all this since we first started. Letting the doing of the things be first was a daring, but exciting, fun, and sexy way to live, I'd decided. Risky, but at this point in my life, I was ready to take big chances. "It was amazing! I came harder than I ever have!"

"And you saw your pussy." He nodded as he spoke. His expression showed me how thrilled he really was. "For the first time."

My face flushed as it hit me how they both intimately saw my pussy on that video on the same day I had. And though it felt wrong, I only had myself to blame for accepting that I shouldn't look at my own pussy. "It was quite liberating and very surprising."

"I personally think all you women should have pulled out hand mirrors and laid them on the floor at sleepovers when you are teenagers." He chuckled like Santa Claus or a jolly giant. "Oh damn, just imagined my boys being flies on the walls of that scene. They'd go nuts."

I cracked up with him. I stepped back and pulled him inside. We had held each other with the door open, but somehow, he hadn't even seemed to care that we might be seen.

"That would be quite the sleepover. But having never looked at my own until now, I agree. I think it's a must-do for all teen girls."

He caressed my bottom as I walked, then cupped my right cheek and gave it a hearty squeeze.

I yelped. I pointed to the couch. I had two beers set out for us with a bowl of pretzels.

"Snacks," I said with a sheepish grin.

"The only snack I need is your pussy." He pulled me to straddle his lap.

"No beer?" I asked in a skeptical tone.

"Oh, I'll take the beer, yeah." His eyes were always so happy, and his slow way of speaking always helped me relax. There just was no rushing with Allen, he made sure of it with his demeanor. "So, tell me about the big O."

He rubbed my back, then my ass cheeks. Sitting on his lap should have felt odd, but instead he made me feel as if I belonged there with his soft inquisitive eyes, his firm touch, and the way he kept touching me in non-sexual places as well.

"Oh, my gosh. It was better than any orgasm I've ever had in my life! Kyle wouldn't let up, and then he pushed me to go further, and the next one was even bigger," I said with excitement and great animation. It was special to be able to tell him about it.

"We need to talk about this. We will push you. But you know your safe word. Use it whenever you feel unsafe. You can feel out of control, we will be here for you, but if you cross that line that puts you in a place where you no longer have good feelings and it's intolerable, say it."

He knew things I didn't, and I couldn't even imagine them pushing me to this point of using the safe word. They just weren't like that.

"But, I ... "

He put a finger on my lips. "I know you don't understand how that could happen. We have your utmost safety and enjoyment as our preset, but you don't always know how you will feel, baby girl, until you are in a scene doing it. You might be turned on by the thought of being inspected by horny men, or being used, for example, but the reality is not always what you envision."

I froze, wondering if I'd spilled some fantasies while drunk one night. How did he even know I had these kinks?

"I'm just saying all this and preparing you for life as a sexplorer."

Images of dungeons and sex clubs flitted into my brain. I'd wanted to visit such places in my youth, but the closest I had come was once when I attended a drag queen show at a bar, that had given me a taste of alternatives, and I'd never forgotten how scrumptious it had been.

"Wish you and Kyle could take me to some places like ones I've never been to. Like a sex club." My face must have looked wistful because he caressed it with a sweetness in his eyes that quickly transformed into excitement.

"I likely could take you, it's Kyle who won't be able to join us. Would you like to go somewhere? A strip club? To Canada, to a sex club?" He grinned hugely. "Road trip!"

I busted a gut laughing. "You couldn't take me to Canada! Not with all those boys and Miranda."

"Well, I do go on fishing trips from time to time. Maybe you could meet me up there. I'm talking with my buds and my brothers, and we are actually considering a trip next year."

Butterflies swirled inside me. The desire to do just that swelled in me. "Really? Oh, fuck, that would be absolutely incredible!" My hopes sank like sand through my fingers as I realized it wouldn't work. "But how would you get away? It's not like you could say, 'I'm taking my girlfriend to a sex club. Bye.' Could you?"

He laughed so hard I was almost jostled off his lap. "Maybe not, but I'd come up with something, darling." His eyes twinkled and he raised an eyebrow. "Kiss me?"

How could I not? He was irresistible. I nodded and our lips met. Our kiss deepened immediately as I pressed my abdomen to his thick erection.

"Been dreaming of you all day, Alexa."

Before I could stop myself, I asked, "Does she know?"

He planted kisses along my neck as he fondled my left breast.

"Who, Miranda?" He filled his mouth with my flesh in a series of kisses that brought him to the hem of my shirt above my cleavage.

"Yeah, she knows. I don't hide anything from her as a practice. I'm not perfect, but I believe in open communication. And that will go with you too. I expect it." His tone got very stern in that last sentence, and it made my clit twitch.

"Or else what?" I taunted with a flirty grin.

"I might just spank you to teach you to obey this rule."

I laughed until I realized he was serious.

"No, are you serious?" My heart beat quite a bit harder as the real domination threaded throughout his sentence smacked me in the head with a hefty dose of reality.

"Yup." The mad dad face left him and he smiled a lecherous grin. "Now kiss me again as I finger your pussy. Watching you ooze cream in that video has got me prepped to taste you. Let's get that pussy of yours cooking up another dose of that for my mouth."

I shuddered as he grabbed my pussy with force. I squeaked and he chuckled. "Tell me which pressure you like best, baby girl." He proceeded through a series of soft to strong pressures on my clit.

I pursed my lips and shifted my eyes once he was done. "I don't know." I guffawed. "Can I say all?"

He roared with laughter and pressed his large hand to my pussy lips. "Yes, you can. And noted."

We kissed some more until he was removing my shirt and suckling my nipples. I grasped his head and threaded my fingers through his hair and beard. He took his fill of sucking my teats as his mouth triggered stirrings in my loins.

"Please, Daddy, I need your cock."

He shook his head. "Not yet, baby girl."

My mind flipped to the morning and how Kyle had been. "But soon, right?" I'd need cock inside me today and my pussy wasn't taking no for an answer.

He slid his hand up my skirt and pressed his fingers to my pussy. "Commando. Good girl."

Those words struck a chord in me that shook me to my core, gripped my libido, and shook it wild. I was all ready to come, and there was no way of derailing my denial. Being called a 'good girl' was a big trigger for me. I'd need to tell my Daddies this and often.

"Good girl," he said again. The salacious gleam in his eye told me he already knew this. "You are so wet."

He pressed his fingers along my slit, fondling my lips as he migrated towards my clit. "Make no mistake, I'm making my girl come. And hard. And several times." His voice came as warmth against my breasts as he lapped at my erect right nipple.

He stood up while holding my thighs and swiveled me to the couch. He let out a big sigh and laughed like I'd expect a lumberjack would, hearty and full, capable and strong, unapologetic was the charm he gave off.

"Beer to set the mood, then I'm covering your pussy in beer as I guzzle you."

I giggled in delight. "That sounds kind of messy, Daddy." Calling him 'Daddy' did a similar thing to my clit and raging desire for him as his calling me 'his girl' or 'good girl' did. It wasn't like I thought of him as really my Daddy, that would be gross. It was different. It was a reverence, a respect, an acceptance of caregiving, an acknowledgment of his leadership and direction, and a submission to him being in charge. Not in a brute way, but in a way that I'd feel safe and protected, and that my boundaries would never be crossed.

Having known Allen for years and trusting him somehow made this really easy to fall into, as if it were meant to be, nothing forced, but right with my world, and his. I felt the same thing with Kyle, but there was a difference though, although it was too murky and nebulous to spell out yet. Both of them were natural doms, that much was obvious. Only I couldn't figure out if I was a real sub. Something I thought I should know, but had always kind of felt it was lower somehow. Reading on, though, told me the sub was the elevated one, and the Dom only did what the sub gave 'the okay' for. The whole thing was opposite from what I had originally thought. I'd spent so many hours reading up on D/s relationships since we had joined together. And that was at Allen's urging, she was always sending me links to articles and podcasts. I couldn't help but wonder if he and Miranda were this way too.

He handed me my beer and tilted his bottle my way. "Cheers to our newfound union."

I blushed. It felt weird to blush, but I quickly swallowed a big gulp of my beer before he swiped it.

He chugged another generous pull from his beer and then pushed me to lean back on the couch. "Pussy munching time, my girl. That pussy definitely looks like it needs to be munched." His breath on my inner left thigh sent my excitement and anticipation for him higher.

All I wanted was his mouth on me, his cock in me, and his dirty words filling my ears.

"I've never been 'munched', but I'm pretty sure I want it more than anything," I said breathlessly.

He belly laughed as he moved his mouth closer to my hot, waiting pussy. "How many times have you come today, baby girl?"

I shivered as he hovered over my lower lips, his breath bathing my flesh.

"I think like four." My voice was shaky, my heart was pounding, and I wanted to scream already.

"That's at least six too few." He inched closer to my womanhood until his lips all but pressed my skin. "I'm going to make you come harder than you did this morning, and I'm going to eat your cum right out of your pussy, suck it out of our hole."

I got stuck on the word 'our' but lost my brain as he attacked my clit with a hard suction for what seemed like many minutes. I knew I wasn't going to last. I was going to climax and soon. He held my hips down with his big man hands and pulled all my loose bits into his mouth. His beard tickled me as he commanded full control of my cunt with his mouth. I screamed loud enough for someone to hear outside as his mouth molested my clit and pussy lips. As he shoved his fingers inside me, and finger fucked me as hard, well, even harder than Kyle had. I had no choice, and I couldn't move because he had me pinned. I climbed my orgasm hill and soared, knowing the fall into my body shaking would be so intense I'd likely get close to my safe word off my tongue if he pushed me as Kyle had earlier. I seared the air with my screams as I soared to the brink of a motherload of an avalanche of an orgasm.

The intensity was far greater than any pleasure I'd ever had. Maybe it was the beard, maybe it was him holding me down, maybe it was the force with which he sucked me, but the loss of control curled my body around his head. My legs bent, my back arched, and my head flipped back like I was living an exorcism. I dug my fingers into the couch and the vaginal contractions started. They boomed out and squeezed his fingers inside me, but he didn't stop. He kept shoving them in me. With one hip loosened from his control, I writhed, but his head kept me from going far.

I yelled out and I lost control of my face. Suddenly I didn't care if he saw my wacky face, I couldn't care about anything, all I could do was endure the pleasure wave he'd set me on. The contractions were strong and stole almost all my consciousness as I rode them. They melded into one long, strong contraction with peaks as I whimpered.

I became aware of his grunts as my contractions slowed. I was panting so hard, but the vague recollection of the sounds I'd just made blasted my brain. He had been right. I had come even harder than I had this morning. Either he planted the seed, and my brain took it, or he was just that good at stimulating my pussy.

"Wow," I whispered in a hoarse voice.

He chuckled with his mouth still covering my sensitive clit.

I whimpered and tried to pull away from his suction, but he pressed me into the couch harder. There was no way I could get away from his stimulation.

I screamed. "Too ... much."

He didn't stop.

I considered my safe word, but reigned in my panic and gave myself a pep talk. I can do this. I can do this. Just feel it, Alexa.

The second orgasm came at me like an out of control freight train and sent my resolve spread-eagle to wallow on the ground. I was his prisoner, his cunt-slave, his munch meat, and I was going nowhere but up the biggest orgasm climb of my life.

I twitched, I yelled out, I created words that mean nothing yet expressed everything as I let the next big O tell me it was the boss.

I curled up around his head again as I yanked fistfuls of his hair, and still he never let up his mouth or his rapid finger fucking of me.

I spasmed, curled against his head in the most intense climax I'd ever experienced. The cries that left my mouth made me sound as if I was in true pain.

As I floated down, Allen let off the pressure and then fully left my pussy. The aftershocks were almost as big as some orgasms I'd had. I laid there with my mouth open, staring off into nowhere as if I were frozen in a seizure. It was too hard to speak, too much to move, and only the panting and throbbing of my pussy and body grounded me, otherwise I was floating up above. The tingling set in next, and I waited for the ability to speak to return.

"Wow wow wow," was all I could push out of my lungs.

I opened my eyes, and he was kneeling between my legs with the biggest grin I'd ever seen.

"I love wow. And I got three wow's."

I formed my mouth into a slow, savoring smile and sighed. "Wow."

"Four." He caressed my thighs. "I love four."

"That was ... epic." I was living it, but it was like I couldn't fathom what had just happened to me. How had I never had such orgasms like this in the past? I haven't really been living. My mind fixated on it. I ruminated on what all this meant and what my future with Allen would be. Would my orgasms get even better? Or was this the max?

"You look a little shocked, babe." He couldn't stop grinning. "I'm proud of you. That looked pretty amazing. You let me guide you through two biggies. Maybe next time we try for three." He sat next to me and pulled me towards him, so my head was on his lap. His hard-on was pressed to the back of my head as he stroked my hair. Despite the big O's, I wanted it in me too.

"That was beautiful. You are beautiful. Your pussy is so sexy and really quite beautiful. Are you tired of that word yet? I'll be using it a lot with you. You tasted amazing by the way. You give good cum, babe."

He caressed my arm and back with his other hand. "My girl," he said softly in an encouraging voice.

If I had never understood what it was to be mute, I did know now. I was still so overwhelmed that thinking of speaking was a true challenge. Finally, I said, "Wow."

He laughed softly with great happiness.

"I never ... "

"Just rest, Alexa. Let me love on you."

My brain got stuck on the word 'love'. Was this just Daddy Dom routine? Or did he have feelings? I wasn't sure I cared because my heart and soul soaked up all his tenderness. Then he began to sing a song and I started to cry.

He didn't stop singing, but kept combing my hair with his fingers and rubbing my bare skin softly. He wrapped his arm around my front and placed his hand between my breasts. I hugged his arm to me as my tears finally slowed down.

He leaned down and kissed me on the side of my forehead. "That's a good girl," he said in a soft voice, softer than I thought he could get his voice to be. "You can take a nap if you want. I love to pleasure you to sleep."

Sleep. My body seemed to want it, but I fought it. I wanted to savor more of his 'love'. This cuddling was foreign to me. I was used to sex and roll over, go to sleep. As I lay naked on my couch, cradled by Allen, I pictured the three of us having a threesome again. My brain roamed the fantasy as I felt sleepier by the second.

I woke with my head still on Allen's lap.

Panicked, I asked, "What time is it? The boys might come home!"

I sat up quickly and Allen caressed me. "Okay," he said calmly. "I should go too. I have a lacrosse game to get to for Logan." He touched my cheek and held it. "How did you sleep?"

"Really really good. Too good." I blinked as I looked around for my clothes. "Wait! You can't go! You didn't come."

He rubbed his beard as joy and relief filled his expression. "Oh, I came, baby girl. I came as you did."

I relaxed. "Oh, good." Then I eyed him skeptically, "Are you some kind of octopus? You had one hand on me and the other was in me. That seems impossible."

He burst out in raucous laughter. "I wouldn't try to fool you. I did come, without touching myself."

I dropped my jaw. "What? Unheard of! Are you serious?"

"Yes, and I used the couch a little to stroke me." He tilted his head as he ran his index finger over my lips, pressing the tip of his finger between.

I licked at his finger as he poked it in.

"How do you taste?" He pressed his finger into my mouth, and I sucked myself off him.

I popped off. "I taste like me." And I was excited by the fact that I knew that.

He pulled me into a hug. "We are going to have so much delicious fun together, babe. I'm really excited for where we are going to go."

"I am too, honestly. Entering into a relationship like this was the last thing I thought would happen to me, but it's the best."

"Good. Before I go, I have a few questions."

I nodded and settled into the crook of his offered arm.

"I will share your answers with Kyle. We came up with these questions together, and normally we will talk together, but we wanted to address this sooner rather than later. How do you feel about anal?"

"Not really into that. It hurts. I know some love it, but I'm scared of it." I drew up all my courage. "Hard no."

"Good. Thank you for your honesty. How about name-calling? Any words or names off limits?"

"No. In fact, all the dirty words turn me on. I love them. Use them freely." I smiled. It felt yummy and dirty to say them. "Cunt. Whore. Cumslut. Bitch. Even degrading words on occasion, use me."

"Mmmmm. We will have some fun."

"Yeah, I'm very into auditory stuff, I guess. I'm learning."

"That's what we are doing, learning and exploring. I won't speak for Kyle, but I love dirty talk, but I am going to spoil you, baby you. In fact, do you have oil? I'd love to give you a massage."

"I don't have any."

"What? Oh, come on. Time to go shopping," he chastised. "Well, lay on your tummy anyway, and I'll do it without." He stood up and motioned for me to get flat. "I might play with your bottom a bit," he confided. "Never in. You can trust that."

I trusted him because, so far, he'd never given me a reason not to. He rubbed and kneaded my shoulders and on down my back, then back up and over my biceps. He planted kisses here and there as he massaged my muscles. I thought back over my marriage and only recalled about two five-minute massages from Mark, yet I'd given him several hundred.

"I love your feet. Would you let me suck your toes next time?" The breath of question hit my skin before he planted another kiss.

"Yes," I said dreamily as he worked the muscles in my lower back and upper buttocks with his strong hands.

"Good. You have gorgeous, sexy feet. Now for the butt. My favorite part to massage." He aggressively grabbed my bubble butt as I sighed. I was on the verge of pain at times but not safe word worthy. "Fucking amazing ass you have, baby girl."

I didn't feel a bit guilty about accepting his love and his gestures. I'd come a long wait and it felt so good, I almost started to cry again, but I choked it off.

Like a genie, he knew. "Don't ever be afraid to show me your true emotions, baby girl. It brings us closer, and I want to know everything you want to share, okay?" He stood up. "I'd better go. I'll text you later. How do you feel?"

"Oh, I don't know that I've ever felt this good, to be honest, Daddy."

He grinned deeply when I said 'Daddy'.

"Perfect. Exactly as I want it. And I love how you say 'Daddy' by the way. Makes my cock harder." He pulled up his pants over his raging boner. "Yeah, I'm hard again. Impossible not to get hard massaging you like that. You are so fucking sexy. And don't worry, I didn't come on your couch earlier. I shifted so it went on my shirt."

I laughed as he grabbed my hand and started pulling me toward the front door.

"I hadn't even wondered, and I wouldn't have cared if you did. A mess means a good time."

"God bless you. Give me a kiss, babe."

We kissed and held each other close.

He turned to leave and opened the door. The blast of the summer heat warmed my naked body.

"And Alexa, I won't ever do anything that's a hard no for you." He smirked. "And that includes spanking you." His joy in teasing me was obvious, and he clearly surmised that I was a bit turned on by it.

"I have a zero for my poker face game score, don't I?" My heart fluttered like flapping bird wings again. I wasn't quite sure how I felt about being spanked for real, but it set my heart racing a little more than I'd expected.

"We will have lots of discussions, you, Kyle, and I, but also, Kyle and I will always talk about you on the side too. As your Daddies, we want the best for you and everything we do, you are first and foremost the center of it all. We are just incidental and lucky to be a part of your Goddess nature. I want to watch your sexuality bloom, without any pressure or restrictions from me and Kyle, and absolutely none from society. You be you, Alexa. And we will be at your side protecting you from the nastiness of the world. I sense great exploration and potential in your sexuality, Alexa. I predict you will take all three of us places we never even dreamt of. I want you to taste everything your heart even remotely desires."

And with that, he turned and left.

I stood there, naked, where anyone in the neighborhood could have seen me. I stayed still and watched him walk away. Part of me wanted to rush out and haul him back in, but I knew that couldn't happen. He had a family, and a wife he loved. I would just get tastes of him, as he would of me. And that's how it always would be. He waved from the end of the driveway, and I shut the door.

I leaned against the closed door and shivered. I recoiled with a faint glimmer of shame. Not my own, but my ex's—which still colored my life at times, and I hated it. Most certainly he would have freaked out and shoved me inside. The levels of freedom I was now enjoying never ceased to amaze me. I just needed to figure out how to eliminate the stain of his shame that still apparently plagued me.

I smiled as I thought back to what Allen and I just did. I couldn't help but wonder why me. Of all the women in this neighborhood, all the women in the world, why and how had I gotten so lucky?

Chapter 5

With a full belly, I spread out naked on my bed. My giddiness made me relish the anticipation of the moment. I might be a glutton for sexual pleasure, but I knew I was just making up for all of those lost chances, so it was all good whatever I did. The fresh scent of just-washed sheets reached my nose as I writhed. I sighed, savoring all the scents and feels of my soft, plush bed. This was me time. Time I had never taken for myself for like literally years and years. Well, I couldn't, he'd have thrown a fit and burst in. But back then I hadn't even understood that my body and mind needed this kind of thing. I had never been taught the healing nature orgasms had on the body. I most definitely was a total dunce. I had not been connected to my sex center for most of my adult life. The mourning of lost time had been hard to get over, but the fresh blast of new freedoms in my life and in my sexuality had been gifts. This reverberated around my soul and mind every day and I wondered if it would ever stop. It felt softer, though, in some moments, like the whisper of a ghost at times. That gave me hope.

Not that I needed the affirmation of knowing orgasms meant so much more, but it felt so amazing. It wasn't just a feel-good act, it was everything. This was exactly what I needed. Kyle was so right. Allen was so right.

I scanned the six sex toys lined up next to my belly, the ylang ylang scented gel lube, and my earbuds, just in case I wanted to watch porn as I played. I'd always been afraid of porn all my life, almost angry at it until I realized it was a tool, entertainment, and not happening to me personally. Porn was not a personal attack. Nor was it an attack on the characters. Being indignant and fearful hadn't been fun at all. Before, it had seemed like a legit assault on my person, on women, but that foolish notion had died in me, and I now realized how judgmental and stupid I'd been. Most of these actors were simply acting, and getting paid a lot of money to do it. They wanted to do it, and they were just playing off of people's fantasies, secret and otherwise. Of course, there would always be scammers and abusers who posted sex with their partners without them knowing, but I didn't have to let all porn get cast into that well. I refused to be so short-sighted as to fall into such generalizations anymore.

It was liberating too because I no longer thought of porn as an insult to humanity, but let it dwell in the same space movies and books occupied. It wasn't a damn documentary or account of reality (most of the time, unless it was amateur and they did it intentionally, which was fine and their choice). But, really, and largely, it was just a damn show! One that happened to be about sex, love, fucking, messing around, and delving into all the rich levels of human sexuality and power exchange, but it wasn't inherently evil as society and culture set out to make us all believe. And the best part was, I could enjoy it as I desired. I began to view porn as a gift rather than a plague on society. And it was mine to use when I desired.

It had been freeing and it had ushered me into not only sinking into my existing kinks, but it had helped me unveil new ones, which was even more freeing.

I reached for the rose clit sucker and rubbed some of the gel lube on it, dipping my finger in the hole to coat it so my swollen clit could slide nicely in it for the pulsing. Reading about my own anatomy had also been so eye-opening, and finding out the clit was analogous to the penis had been mind-blowing. I'd paid attention too, and it was true! I got morning clit wood!

Without anyone home, and without any time constraints or audience, I could pleasure myself as much and for as long as I wanted. And as loudly. I'd found the making of sound to be not only heightening on the rise to climax, but also in the release of it. It was surely bliss on so many levels that just the mere thought of doing it started the process of owning it, of being relieved from stress, of it providing comfort to me. I could take this time because I wanted to. I didn't have to perform, I didn't have to try, I could just enjoy and let all of it flow naturally, even the very taboo and almost disturbing ideas.

I pressed the toy to my clit and yelled out at the first touchdown.

"Fuck," I muttered appreciatively.

This toy always got me there quick. I plucked it off and put it back on over and over again, slowly edging myself towards climax rather than letting it take me there in less than a minute, as it had proved it could. All those articles stating 'it takes women twenty minutes to climax' had obviously never tried this fucking toy. I'd surmised the twenty minutes meant that she just wasn't getting the right touch, in the right spot, for the right length of time enough to come, so it needed to build with longer exposure, because I'd made myself come in thirty seconds with this toy when I had been really horny. Just like a man! I could climax fast! Who knew? Honestly, the realization had been a true confidence booster in my own ability to orgasm.

I reached for my black vibrating wand with the big head. I smeared the lube all over the large bulb and pressed it to my pussy lips. I was aroused, so I knew my vagina had likely already lengthened enough for this large dildo toy to slide in me easily and I'd comfortably have the room inside to maneuver it. It didn't take a genius to understand women, yet we were called a mystery. It only took paying attention and trying different things. And to think I'd been a mystery to my own self for years. That was the most unsettling part of all.

At first, when I found out all this, I'd been mad. I felt cheated by the sex ed I'd received, shielded from my true feminine nature by a society, and a husband, who devalued women's pleasure. I found I didn't mind being a sex object, in fact, I got off on turning others on, but my pleasure had to be the center of it, not just my body, or I wouldn't enjoy it.

I pushed the phallic toy in and as it popped past my G spot I groaned out, "Oh, Gawd."

It was an overwhelmingly exquisite pleasure that'd only come from such a fat-headed toy thus far in my life. But I was totally prepared to have Allen and Kyle change my mind on this. In fact, I expected it.

And pulling it past the sweetest spot inside me and pushing it back in made my eyes roll. I moaned out. It was not possible for me to remain silent while receiving this much fine-tuned and directed pleasure. G spot stimulation was good, but clit was better, and both? Both made me roll into giant waves of climax like I'd never enjoyed before this combo occurred to me. It was fucking magic!

Nothing else mattered. Nothing hovered over me. The fullness of the freedom to do what I wanted when I wanted had been jarring after my separation had started, but then it wasn't even nearly as full as it was now. I was truly my own self, master of myself, and I could take my time, or I could rush. It was like I'd been living under a roof and every speck of the air had touched me, not cradling, but suffocating me. And now my personal space had an open ceiling to the sky, no walls watched me or told me where to walk, what to do. I wasn't in that cyclic maze of hidden abuse anymore. The invisible walls my ex had put up to contain me were now truly invisible, and all but gone. I was free, freer than I ever imagined possible, and the joy was jarring. And each day it had only gotten wider, this open roof. This feeling of myself without prying judgmental eyes, confining me by his opinions of how I was to be in the world. In the lengthening of his absence, his control of me was blessedly ever-waning.

Looking back, I'd lost myself. I had become no longer me, I'd become everyone else's version of me, and especially my ex-husband's. As I came out of this fog I'd suffered in for years, I realized I was still inside me, and when I let her breathe for the first time, the exhilaration had flooded me. After the crippling realization of all this, I began to walk, then run, and now I was embracing it, soaring. It was like how the freedom of running outside as a child was sweet, but not nearly as sweet as it was after being stonewalled in the jail of homework, school, or being grounded ... all of which had cruelly kept me from the pure joy of it. To be denied simple joys and freedoms had been the most damning jail of it all.

The memories were justification for how it had been, and for how I wasn't ever going to be again. Whereas this new life of mine was pure healthy air, brilliant sunshine, mysterious curious moonshine, and fields of frilly, fragrant vegetation. It was breaths of fresh sky and loads of nourishing comfy sleep. I could sleep again! I could sleep without any fear. I was who I was meant to be, doing what I was supposed to be doing, and I had zero guilt or obligation to people who didn't have my best interests at heart. I wasn't a tool for manipulation, I was me ... glorified, intensified, and celebrated. Rebirth meant reclaiming myself, and owning my own sexuality.

I pressed the clit sucker to my clitoral head and yelped out. The goodness was succulent, moist, and ripe. The sensation was a closed rosebud, and a full fragrant bloom at once. It was lying on the sand on the beach while the ocean licked its sandy shore like a generous, giving lover treated his woman's pussy lips. The depth of the ocean, the world's vagina, pleasure was as endless as the sands and as fleeting, but ever stretching, always available, landing on shores in different colors and textures of rock and shell. It was flying, skating, skiing, and like being wrapped in a blanket near the fire. Sexual pleasure was it all, and the world of it was just opening up for me. There were so many places to travel, to visit, to explore that I'd never be done. And that was the best part.

I imagined Kyle touching me, caressing me, talking dirty to me, just like he had earlier. I envisioned his sexy face, his kind, giving eyes, and his delicious, hard erection. His gentle persistence had been such a surprise. His firmness about my pleasure coming first had totally confused me. I wasn't used to such a generous mindset in my lover. And Allen took the same approach, but even to a new different level than Kyle. How had I gotten this fortunate to find these unbelievable men, and right in my own neighborhood? And in men I already knew and partially trusted, even at the get-go because of this? That had been the key to ushering us into this threesome Daddy triad. Shocked didn't even come close to how I felt about all that.

I smiled as I relished that this all was true. We were a thing now. Something that started as a fling was becoming … something.

My arousal climbed with yummy waves of pre-orgasm thrills as I let the toys pleasure me. I began to pant harder and undulate my hips as the vibrations flooded delicious feelings all across my body, gifting me glimpses of the impending euphoria. The rise kept going, building stronger with each second. Time didn't exist as I floated about in the hormones that bathed my body. Foreplay didn't even make sense as a stage anymore, it was all just play on different levels and a natural progression so that it didn't need to be thought of as just a pre-stage anymore.

Next, I imagined Allen jerking off to my video and I almost fell off the cliff. I yanked the toy off my clit and the avalanche of the peak backed off.

"Not yet, Alexa," I muttered.

If Kyle and Allen had taught me anything, it was that edging brought stronger orgasms, or at least had the potential to. And the journey to the rise should be enjoyed and savored, not rushed into like checkbox sex.

Sex wasn't a set math formula as much as it was a holiday all-day buffet with naps. Obligation sex had become a thing in my marriage, which took out all the pleasure, all the spontaneous passion, all the teasing dance of flirtation. Sex had become a nail that held my shaky marriage together longer than it deserved, rather than a journey of enjoyment and making love. But I was certain Mark wasn't even capable of all that anyway.

I shoved him out of my brain and focused my mind on Allen and Kyle. Caught up in the lush, pleasing thoughts of them, I pressed the clit sucker hard to my clit.

After all, Daddy had given me this homework.

My body lurched as the intense wave spread from my clit. With nerve endings locked and loaded, the rolling sensation blossomed. It seized me and pulled me over its scrumptious edge as my torso began to curl, bringing my shoulders into a hunched position. My head fell back, but I was too curled for my head to touch the pillow. My legs drew up towards my body, my toes scrunching too, and the vaginal muscle spasms took control of my body. The clenching vibrations repeated as I counted twelve of them. I stopped counting because it was clinicalizing my orgasm. It kept going as I yelled out. It was too intense, I couldn't handle any more pressure on my clit as I reached the count of eighteen squeezes. I couldn't resist knowing the number. I wanted to tell my Daddies what peak I reached.

"Aw fuck," I squelched out. I made a painful ugly face as I ripped the toy off my clit. I panted as I whispered, "Fuck, too much."

If Kyle and Allen had been here, they'd have guided me to keep the toy on and push through so the next orgasm would be even bigger. I loved being their sexual plaything as much as they loved it. And I adored that they wanted the sexual journey for me to be the best it could possibly be.

I pulled the wand vibe out of my pussy and examined how I'd coated it. I licked it with a lecherous grin, already excited about telling my Daddies about this play session. I lapped my tongue all around the head of the toy to scoop up all of my fluids. This too was a new adventure for me. I didn't suffer shame or disgust, no washcloth needed to touch this toy. I cherished that I enjoyed the natural acceptance that I wasn't gross. I wasn't abnormal. I wasn't my Daddies' toy but a toy I could declare as theirs, if I so chose to. I owned myself. I owned my body. I owned my sexuality and no one else could ever own it. It was mine to share when and if I wanted to, mine to give, and mine to take back. And mine alone.

Chapter 6

"Mandy," I hollered as I waved across the yard. She was weeding her flower garden in a bright yellow bikini, much to the delight of the teen boys that currently occupied my back deck. They had a perfect view of her bent over, hanging cleavage that went on forever, and makeup that was model worthy, even from a distance. She was gorgeous. I couldn't deny that. But I still didn't want to fuck her the way I did Miranda. The two were like night and day.

"Mandy," I said quieter as I approached her.

She still didn't acknowledge me. Rather than be offended by her rebuff again, I strode on towards her.

She finally caught sight of me and pulled the air pods from her ears.

"Hi Alexa," she said coolly, but at least I wasn't a ghost.

She didn't know about me and Kyle, at least I didn't think so, but maybe her intuition could smell the stain of his cum leaking down my thighs. Either way, her eyes spit daggers at me every time we were near. He'd snuck over at midnight thirty and fucked me to within an inch of my life last night. I'd fallen asleep juicy and well-fucked before he even left the room. I'd woken this morning to the memory of one of the best sexual experiences of my life. In truth, all the epic sexual experiences were stacking up and I could write a book.

Her eyes narrowed and toxicity seemed to bleed out her pores into the air between us. Even if she didn't know I'd been fucking Kyle, maybe somehow she smelt my pheromones that were claimed by her husband. I couldn't explain her new coolness to me in any way other than something chemical, instinctual perhaps. She'd always been fake with me, but she'd always been one of the few neighbors who hadn't treated me like yesterday's garbage, or the town harlot with a big read 'A' on my forehead. 'A' being for a useless 'asshole' who left her husband. Well, he had left me years before in mind and partnership. There was no marriage in that marriage.

"I was wondering if I could get my crockpot back from you. I'd like to use it for the barn dance coming up." I didn't need it back quite yet, but it was an excuse to talk to her and see if she still hated me.

"Yup." She nodded, which also made her tits jiggle.

She glared at me as if I were the sun. "I'll have Kyle bring it over later. I'm cunt deep in weeding this shithole of a flower garden." Maybe her pissy mood was just Mandy being Mandy. Trophy wife traded for sailor mouth. I bobbed my head in agreement.

"It's a never-ending battle." One I had given up on. If flowers bloomed at all, I called my gardens a success and that was that. But I certainly loved having them in my yard, weeds or not.

I waited for a few seconds to see if I'd get any nice chit-chat from her. Nope. Guess not. Then I turned on my heels and walked off.

Rather than watch the boys ogle Mandy from my kitchen, I grabbed my sweet baby girl dog and slipped her leash on. It had been way too long since I had taken Pumpkin on a walk. Well, two days was an eternity to a dog, and I'd let three pass by without bringing her out on one. I felt guilty not giving her this simple pleasure. She jumped and yelped her excitement as I ushered her out the front door. I swore she loved telling me about her excitement about the walk as much as she enjoyed the walk itself.

I smiled at her as we strode out into the summer sunshine. It was glorious today, a nice eighty-degree day. Minnesota had its ridiculous weather, fluctuations that brought thirty degrees one day and eighty the next, or summer in March for a week, but today felt like a perfect summer day. Blue skies and a light breeze, I knew I'd be sweating from the walk halfway down the 'hood.

Allen's texts flitted through my brain as we strolled along. He'd guided me through a play session this morning. My Daddies never left me alone for long. And I loved it! They were as hungry for my sexual pleasure as I was. It made us a very well-matched throuple.

I approached Allen and Miranda's house. A batch of their boys and their friends were playing a game of basketball in the court on the side of the house. A bunch of high school boys with a few neighbor teen girls watching filled my vision. I remembered those days well. I smiled, thinking back how I'd done such things with my girlfriends, watching our boyfriends fight out their macho hierarchy on the ball court. Watching them strut and hoot brought back all those intense memories. It'd been a fun teen life, until it wasn't. But I wasn't about to dwell on that.

I strode along the neighborhood that had once accepted me. Regardless, I held my chin high. It was easier to dismiss being hated though, because I was so happy. Truly happy for the first time ever. Not happy in just moments or birthdays or my kids' milestones, but happy in every moment of every day, mostly, and even happier yet in others. I had never dreamt life could be this good. The only thing better would be living married to my Daddies. Well, if I'm honest, both of them.

I hushed that thought immediately. Plus, it was impossible. They were both married, though I often wondered if Kyle would snap and leave Mandy with how miserable she was to him. I secretly hoped he'd recoil like a too-stretched rubber band and land on me. We'd have to move, of course, but I was okay with that. No way Allen could, or would, leave Miranda, plus I sensed he really loved and enjoyed her. I wasn't a man stealer on any level.

I heard footsteps behind me, someone running. I glanced back and it was Miranda and her dogs. She had on a form-fitted fuchsia tank top and matching legging workout shorts with aqua tennis shoes. Her thick hair was in an upstyle, and she had two braids embedded with her other locks in the hair binder. She looked beyond stunning, but she was most certainly eye candy for any libido, and mine. I longed to test the waters of my bisexual self even more in her presence.

"Can I join you? It would be nice to walk with someone for once." Her eyes were bright and friendly. Her cheeks were flushed, and even though she'd been running, her panting waned immediately as she slowed to a walk. Damn, this woman was fit.

"I'd love to have you." Unlike Mandy, Miranda had been more cordial to me since I'd hooked up with her husband. Which, honestly made no sense to me, but who was I to shun a friend? Even one who knew I fucked her husband on the regular. Maybe she liked that I scratched an itch for her husband that she couldn't. Either way, Miranda was a mystery to me.

"I've got to get a breather. My house is overrun with young hordes of testosterone." She snorted.

"I know the feeling. I have a gaggle at my house right now too. I'm afraid to go back, they probably already killed my last grocery store run."

She bent over with laughter. "Oh, you have no idea. I go to the store every other day, full cart." Her gaze was lit with passion, a passion that was obvious to all. She loved being a mom. She made motherhood look easy, though.

"Oh, I'm sure. I can't even imagine! I have two who have friends over all the time raiding the kitchen, but seven? Plus, friends?" I laughed with her. "That must be insane."

"One hundred percent, yes. We are lucky Allen does so well financially. I'll tell you that." She guffawed, and even that craziness looked lovely on her. "I seriously can't keep up with them. And I will think I made enough dinner, but someone always ends up asking for more of something that goes gone in a flash."

"You are super mom, you know that, right?"

Our dogs walked in parallel, which was dog body language for 'I'm okay with you right now'. I smiled at their camaraderie because it felt similar to how I sensed Miranda and I were.

"Well, I wouldn't say that. But I try my ass off every day." A wistfulness flickered across her face, and I immediately wished it gone.

"You do amazing, Miranda. I see you, girl. You do work your ass off." It felt so wonderful to have a woman to chat with, and to build up. I knew her struggles, at least on a more minimal level.

"It's also the laundry, the activities, the driving, the sports equipment, the homework. Even summer school. That's why I go on so many walks, it's the only time I don't get accosted, and that's just because I'm not there! I get texts and phone calls when I walk, so I've started turning my phone off!" She laughs heartily. "I can't even take a bath alone without someone knocking on the door unless I do it in the middle of the night. Now with one in college, though, I don't even get a weekday alone." She sighs. "I wish he'd have chosen the dorms, but this way is cheaper, I must say."

"Oh, that's a whole new level for me to think about. College. I kind of wish my boys would arrest at this age, yet I want them to succeed and become happy, healthy, functional adults. It's the bittersweetness of being a mom." I sighed. "You don't want to stunt their growth, but you want them to stay at the same time."

"Yep. And Allen, he helps out a lot, but it mostly lands on me." She grins big. "But it's my job too, and he has his, so we end up flowing pretty decently. He's not a slacker."

I nodded. "True, and that's good, but you also deserve a break."

"And I'm getting better at taking one. Like right now. So, thanks for being my walking buddy."

"Oh, anytime, Miranda. Just text me and I'll hop and scoot out the door to meet you."

"Honestly, I'd love to go for a glass of wine sometime if you are up for that too."

"Totally, I'd love that." It felt somewhat odd to be planning social time with her, given that her husband's dick had been in me recently, and his mouth had brought me such pleasure that I'd screamed my head off. If only she'd join us. Maybe it was my mission to get her to make us a foursome. Wanting to ask her why she wouldn't consider it, I chose a different route. "Want to grab one in a bit after our walk? I'm open."

She sighed heavily. "Maybe. But I do have a lacrosse game to get to. And then a soccer game. And then it will be dinnertime and they will all be looking to me for food."

A weariness flickered across her eyes, and I immediately wanted to hug her. I smiled. "What if it's pizza night and mom goes out to dinner instead?"

Her eyes perked up. "I rather like that idea." Her stride relaxed a bit, and she slowed her walking, but didn't stop. "You know, you are right. Let's do it."

"Awesome. I'm free whenever, so just text me and we can go."

The rest of the walk was all mom talk and the challenges of raising teen kids. I wanted to bring up her lobbing into our little sex club, but the timing wasn't right. Maybe at dinner would be the right time. We said goodbye and I sauntered down the street feeling like I'd made a friend. It had been a while since I'd hung out with just a woman and I was honestly looking forward to our friend date.

I strode into my house with the fresh breath of the walk still savoring my skin. It felt invigorating, as it usually does after a long walk, and my body was thanking me. I undid Pumpkin's leash and she zoomed to the water bowl to lap up gobs of water. I filled my water bottle too until I heard his voice.

What the fuck? Mark is here? I threw my head back and froze as I listened. Oh. My. Fuck. What the fuck is he doing here? My skin crawled and that familiar dread filled my body.

I slammed my water bottle on the counter and charged outside to the deck, where he was joking with the boys. He was always the charmer to everyone, but me, except when in public he faked it with me to look good to his audience.

"Mark, what are you doing here? We've talked about this. You aren't allowed at the house unless I invite you, and I'm a million percent sure I didn't extend an invite to you," I said coolly.

My boys sent me a look of apology and their friends smirked uncomfortably. I knew I was making a spectacle of myself, but the audacity of Mark to just show up enraged me. And in my absence, he had the gall to hang out as if he still lived here.

Mark smiled that fake mask of his and said, "Aw, Alexa, I was nearby and just wanted to stop in and see my boys to say 'hi.'" He sounds like a good dad when he says such things.

Mark didn't do anything that didn't have manipulation and forethought behind it. He was about as spontaneous as a fucking school textbook. This was just another attempt at controlling me and making me feel watched. His whole existence revolved around him, and his use of and attempts to control me, even after our marriage ended. He was a leech and as ugly as one.

"Please leave now. You've said your hello. And please refrain from just stopping in. You can't just come to the house. You don't live here anymore, Mark."

He laughed lightheartedly. "Oh, baby, I didn't go in the house." There it was. The workaround to get what he wanted.

One of the kids laughed.

True. He hadn't gone in, as far as I knew. "Please leave, Mark." I didn't want to have to get a restraining order because we still needed to talk about the kids and face-to-face was better for that, but this was getting bad.

He sent me a defiant look that flashed for only a second, so just I'd see it and not the boys. Then his expression turned kind again. His vile snake self was always lurking beneath his friendly façade. And almost no one got to see the true nature of his nastiness but me. The boys had seen some, but no one got the full depths of his cruelty but me. And I had to come to terms with this because he only showed that part of himself to me. Which made others think I was insane for leaving him. From what they saw, he was a 'good, nice, friendly, All-American guy who loved his family'. I knew better. Painfully so.

"Okay, I've got some shopping to do, boys." He paused and looked right at me with mocking in his eyes. He continued, "For a date. So, I should shove off. Enjoy the sunshine." He motioned to where Mandy was still weeding her flower beds. "And the views." He snickered and left off the deck stairs.

I was fuming. And did he really think I cared if he dated? Is he really still in that space? That was actually laughable. I felt sorry for his date. If only I could somehow warn her to run far and fast, but Mark hid his red flags quite well. She didn't need to stick around to suffer the monster he'd surely unleash on her at some point, Mark didn't deserve anyone. He'd just ruin her if she let him.

After I made sure Mark's car left, I headed out to my garden. The sun was warm and felt amazing, but I also expected to sweat more. I'd garden for a bit, then shower so I'd be ready for when Miranda texted. I glanced at the boys on the deck, and they were sipping sodas and laughing. The sounds of them joking were nice. Soon I wouldn't get this because they'd be off to college.

I rounded the corner of my shed and stopped cold. My new clay flowerpots both had been caved in, shattered to obliteration. Shards of clay lay amidst the spillage of dirt. The flowers were all skewed sideways, and a few had fallen to the ground. Nothing could have done this but a hammer or a mallet. I had one in the shed.

"Mark," I said vehemently. "Oh, my gawd, that fucking asshole!" His vileness was reaching a new level. Anger boiled in me faster than I took a breath. He'd always taken joy in ruining or devaluing all I liked or did. And now this was extending to times in divorced life too? I would not accept this. He no longer had control over me to torture and manipulate me. If I tried a new venture and he didn't approve, he'd tried to get me to stop. He'd never admit to trying to control me, yet he tried every narcissistic tactic in the book. And that included gas lighting. No. Mark was the life of the party, and a 'nice guy', which he affirmed to me all the time. He wouldn't ever do those kinds of things to the woman he loved. And then he'd gone off and acted like he never said the things he said. But I'd had the texts to prove his nastiness, even so.

I pulled my phone out as my eyes flared. I was pissed. No, I was beyond pissed. I was livid. I took a deep breath. This is what he wants. He wants a reaction out of me so he can call me irrational again, tell me I'm crazy. I'm not playing into his hands. I'm not going to be a player in his sick game this time.

I slipped my phone back in my pocket calmly and walked over to the boys.

I steadied my emotions so I wouldn't sound like a freak. "Jasper, can you come here for a minute?"

He lumbered down the stairs, looking every bit the sexy teen model he could be if he wanted. That had been hard to stomach as a mom, to know that he was truly sexy and all the world could see it. I smiled as he approached. What a wonderful young man he was becoming, though, and thankfully he was nothing like Mark.

"What's up, Mom?" he asked good-naturedly.

"Did you see Dad lurking down by the garden?" I motioned towards the broken pots.

"Oh, shit!" he exclaimed. "Wow! What the hell? I'm sorry, Mom. Clearly, someone did that." There was no skepticism on his face.

I shook my head. "I know. Looks like a hammer or mallet." I ran my hands through my hair. I hadn't wanted to sully their dad in my boys' eyes, but I'd shared some things with them that Mark had done. I'd had to with the divorce. And they had both admitted they'd seen some of it in their dad, even as hard as he worked at hiding it, it was obvious.

"Do you think it was Dad?" He looked sorry and he'd done nothing wrong.

"I don't know. But it's very possible. Did you notice him down here?" I asked it meekly as if Mark were listening in. His stain still hovered over me at times even in his absence.

"No, I didn't, Mom." He ran a hand through his hair as his expression turned painful. "If he did this ... " His anger seethed in his words. I had seen my boys rage over their dad ever since we'd had our talks. It was in hindsight and both of them felt guilty for not seeing their dad fully for who he really was.

"Jasper," I started.

He shook his head. "Bet it was him." His voice dripped with venom.

It was sad to me that Jasper didn't doubt that it was.

"I'll help you clean them up after my friends leave, Mom."

"Thank you, but it's okay, honey. I'm going to do it now. Guess I'm not weeding the garden." I sighed as I attempted a weak smile at my son. "Thanks for caring. I want to try to save the flowers so I'm going to replant them."

"Okay. I'm going with the guys to get a sub in a bit."

"Alright. I'm going out to dinner with Miranda, so I'm glad you've got dinner covered. Is Alex going too?"

Jasper nodded. "Yep."

"Okay, have fun, honey."

"Yep. You too." He turned to leave. "Mom, I'm sorry Dad did this."

I reigned in my tears and chalked this up to another casualty of my life with Mark. I was further saddened to know that not only was I still being hurt by Mark, but my boys were too, through his actions against me. The worst part was no one knew the full truth of how vile Mark could be, but at least my boys now saw past his veil. Mark had saved that camouflaged part of himself for me alone for years. When he'd spiral, he'd become a true monster. When others were present, he was a loving, caring dad and husband. It had been sickening to watch him shift so easily from one to the other, like it was a simple light switch between the two modes.

I gingerly scooped up the undamaged flowers and, through tears, set them on the grass. I didn't want to bare root them for too long, so I poured dirt over them to protect them. I found old pots in the garage and replanted my flowers with tears not only staining my cheeks but choking my heart, re-staining my scars there with fresh pain.

Chapter 7

I was fearful Miranda was standing me up as I swirled the last swallow at the bottom of my wineglass. Several men had eyes on me and I returned them lustily. It was fun to nonverbally acknowledge such flirtations as intentional eye contact. It was something I'd missed from before the start of my relationship with Mark. His jealousy would have flared, and I'd have been paying the price had we still been married. I'd ignored way too many red flags on this front with Mark when we were dating. I should have run. But then I wouldn't have Alex and Jasper, so I couldn't wish my marriage hadn't happened. But damn was I a young fool back then.

I smiled to myself because I could smile back at these men, and it felt so good. I could acknowledge attention and compliments without being made to feel guilty or how somehow it was my fault that men had eyes. In Mark's eyes, it was my fault they found me attractive. I'd been duped for years and hadn't even realized it until one day a friend pointed things out to me she noticed as we talked about my marriage. Things I'd seen as normal because it was my norm. Once I had started to investigate this type of abuse, I had been floored. It was rampant in my marriage, and even in the young life of our dating. I'd been taken in so completely, and not even realized it, for literally years. No wonder I was so unhappy. I'd been being abused. I shuddered because I'd always thought of myself as a strong independent woman, with fiery passions and zest for life, not any sort of victim by any means. But it had been covert, insidious, but not blatant to me.

I checked my phone again, but no message from Miranda.

"Damn," I muttered. Typically, things go this way it seems for me. I contemplated heading over to the bar for one more drink, so I didn't look like a loser being a single person in a booth. Or maybe I should just give up and go home and see if Kyle is around. It had been nice at least to get out of the house and be near people having a good time for a bit.

I flagged the waitress and said, "Can I settle up?"

I swallowed my sadness. I hadn't needed this rejection on top of the flowerpot incident. A day that had started out so good was now choking in the filthy gutter. Well, that was taking it too far. I need to stay positive. I made eye contact with the man who had nodded at me earlier. He was alone at the bar and for a split second; I thought of going to join him. I knew it was hard, but I needed to get myself out there. At times, I wanted to keep our triad going indefinitely, and stay single. At others, I thought maybe it'd be better for me to date single men. By being with Kyle and Allen, was I limiting myself? But I wasn't sure I wanted that kind of life again, though, the one woman, one man kind of life. I valued my freedom and mostly I was enjoying the fuck out of being a single swinging female. But at the same time, my Daddies and I were starting to feel like a relationship. I was so confused and them being so amazing, it just entrenched me further into not knowing what to do next. I was resigned, though, to just live this out for as long as it lasted because they were so supportive in helping me explore my sexuality. I was healing. And if that's all that ever came out of this, I'd be forever grateful for their assistance and for helping me fully realize and explore my sexual self.

As I stood up, Miranda bounded in the front door. Her appearance was impeccable, but her eyes were harried. She rushed over towards me.

"Oh, you are leaving?" She was panting. "Am I really that late?"

"Oh, no. Not anymore now that you are here." She looked gorgeous, but by the look in her eyes, she was a mess.

"I'm so sorry," she said with exasperation, her 'so' all drawn out. "Disaster happened because the boys dropped the whole stack of pizza boxes. I had to try and salvage the pizza. But then Allen got home and told me to go, and that he'd order new pizzas."

"Aw, shit, that really sucks. But nice of him to swoop in like Superman."

She let out a huge sigh with wide eyes. "They were hangry, so I was washing fruit and plopping it out as I tried to save the pizzas." She plopped down in the booth. "It was my usual chaos." She let out another huge breath. "Damn, I'm exhausted."

"Let me order you a drink." I gave her a very pleasant smile. I understood her pain, but hers was intensified by being a mama to so many boys. "What would you like?"

She hopped up. "I gotta pee." She turned to go, but flipped back to face me. "I'll have whatever you are having. And two."

I giggled. "You got it." Poor woman.

She hurried off to the bathroom and I headed to the bar to tell the waitress to cancel closing my tab. After I ordered three more glasses of wine, I settled into the booth and savored my budding friendship with Miranda. I still wanted to get inside those tight workout clothes of hers, though, and make her scream.

The waitress was quick and brought our wine before Miranda returned.

"Is it weird that I sat on the toilet for a few extra minutes?" She looked sheepish, but I loved her humility.

"Not a single bit. Been there. Done that. Especially when my boys were young."

"A breather is a breather, right? Even if it's on the shitter."

I laughed. "Yup. Agreed." My mind flew back in time. "I remember this one time I was so stressed, and I knew both my boys were outside the bathroom door, and I just sat there until I calmed down. They calmed down too. They just started to play with each other. Eventually, when I was smiling, and they were having fun, I opened the door. It was like a reset for all three of us. It was kind of eye-opening for me. From then on, I'd take bathroom breathers." I smirked as a twinge of bittersweetness for times long gone settled upon me. "I miss those days when they were young, but it's easier in some ways now. Yet harder in others."

She pursed her lips. "Yup, exactly. Parenting teenagers and young adults has its own set of crazy to wrangle."

"But Allen seems great."

"Oh, yeah. He's a wonderful dad. He's always been one in the trenches with me. He probably changed more diapers than I did!" She laughed with her nose wrinkled.

"Oh, I definitely can't say that!" I wanted to touch her hand but resisted. "And he's even always worked full time? That's quite amazing."

"Yeah, I can't ever complain about him shirking anything. He's been a gem." Her face went forlorn, and I regretted bringing Allen up.

I wasn't about to dare bring up my interactions with Allen. I was thankful for the wine because I didn't want to make her feel uncomfortable. I held up my glass. "Cheers to kids growing up and more alone time."

She clinked my glass and we both took a generous pull.

"Fuck, I needed that," she said as she sat back. Her round breasts heaved as she raised an eyebrow. "How about that bartender?" Her eyes filled with lust. "I'd let him take me around the bar, bent over every section. Like all night!"

I guffawed. "I know, right? Damn, he is hot as fuck."

"I've seen him before when I've been in here. He's a nice guy too." She was visibly more relaxed, already slouching back in the booth seat.

"Is he? I haven't talked much to him."

"Yeah, I was in here with Georgia last week and we sat at the bar. He talked our ears off. And flirted with us like a fiend. I loved it!"

Immediately, I wondered why she wouldn't swing. I mean, obviously, she likes attention from other men. Dying to know, but not brave enough yet to ask, I focused on our kids instead. "So, any games tomorrow, or are you free?"

She rolled her eyes. "Five. Don't get me wrong. I love watching my boys, but the number of games from all of them combined is very overwhelming."

"Not much time left for you alone, is there?"

"Nope. Not really. I'm used to it, but there are some days where I wish I could go to a hotel all by myself and just veg out. Enjoy a bit of just existing. I wouldn't be bored at all."

I cocked my head at her. "Why don't you do it? I bet Allen would be okay with it."

"Yeah, he would be. I did it once. Like five years ago. It was wonderful. He didn't even contact me other than to say they were all good and he loved me."

"He's a really amazing man." I needed to stop talking about him.

Every thread of my being was begging to confirm with Miranda that she was okay with her husband fucking me. Maybe she got her alone time walking, and maybe she gave Allen his reprieve by fucking others. I wasn't sure, but I really wanted to know. My mind spun. How had Allen brought this up with her? Had she been hurt when he first asked to swing? Was she still hurt on some level, or was she happy about it? Did she even like sex? Maybe that's why she was okay with it, because she didn't want sex herself, but didn't want to deprive Allen of a sex life. All the questions burrowed around in my insides, leaving hollows where I needed answers.

Instead, I asked about her garden. "Do you still plant your garden?" Thoughts of my unweeded garden plagued me. Fucking Mark and his destruction.

"Yeah. But I do all easy things like zucchini, tomatoes, strawberries, potatoes. I pay my youngest to weed it and pick stuff. He loves it. And I just can't seem to keep up worth shit." She blew out a guffaw. "On anything!"

One thing was clear, Miranda needed more stress release. "We should do this once a week. Or we could do lunch, or a coffee. You need some more time to yourself." I shirked a little at suggesting this because she might not like my company that much. Or was this feeling colored by my fear that she hates Allen fucking me?

"I need to eat. Are you getting food? We could get an app at the very least. I'm famished." She looked around and waved at our waitress.

I tapped my wine with my freshly painted fingernail. "Yup. I'm pretty hungry too. And I'd better eat something. This wine is taking advantage of me."

"I need to be where you are. I need me another glass so I can join you. But I'm very hungry. I was ready to eat the mangled pizza back at home." She raised her hand to grab the attention of the waitress again and I admired her shapely arms.

Her impatience was a bit cute. "How do you find time to exercise so much? I need to be better about that."

"That's my alone time. The one time that hardly anyone bothers me about anything, so I take it. But I'm really thinking I need more alone time like this where I'm getting to talk to another woman rather than be by myself. You are so right on that."

"Yeah, I can understand. I've gotten so I can finally relax alone without feeling like I'm being watched or timed. I'm loving not being interrogated about my every moment these days."

Her expression turned serious. "I'm totally okay with it, you know. You and Allen and Kyle." She bit her lip. "I get it. I just don't want the stress of all that."

Stress? It was a huge stress reliever for me. I wasn't sure what to say, so I said nothing.

"Don't ask." Her pouty lips went slim as she pressed them together. "I'm thinking something cheesy."

I tried not to worry, but her admission only stoked my wonderment fire. How was sexual pleasure stress? It was the opposite, being a stress reliever.

We enjoyed cheesy nachos, chicken wings, and a pizza amongst several more glasses of wine, then called Allen to come pick our drunk asses up.

Chapter 8

My Hole of Glory Over Allen's Desk

If I had known then what I know now, I'd have never wasted time disliking Miranda. Because of her, my day of long-awaited glory happened. I had always thought she was a snooty prude, but her allowing Allen to fuck other women, which she apparently used as a tool to get Allen to please her, shed new light on her past bitchiness. In fact, she was rather brilliant. Our girl date had relaxed some of my fears about her but also created new ones. I didn't want to hurt the woman. We were becoming friends.

I smiled as I entered Allen and Miranda's house. Miranda's words from the other evening at the restaurant floated about my brain and helped ease my worries that she hated me. It really helped that she knew Allen and I would be messing around on a regular basis.

Allen had told me to just come in the back sliding door. Miranda was working out in the exercise room off their master bedroom, and she'd be in there for the next hour. Allen had assured me it was safe. Not that she'd care that Allen was fucking me, but I was still getting used to her being within earshot of us while Allen's dick was inside me.

There weren't many other pleasures as monumentally naughty as getting fucked by a man whose wife was in the same house. Add to that, none of it was as taboo as I had imagined it would be, but it was still utterly delicious, nonetheless.

I smirked as I walked past the blueberry muffins cooling on the counter. How domestic. The fact that they were all still there meant Miranda must have made them after her seven boys had headed out for the day. In my house, my two boys would have eaten them in twenty-four hours. In this house, I bet they were gone in thirty minutes flat.

I strolled past the laundry room, heading toward Allen's office. The washing machine and the dryer were going, and Miranda's bras were lined up, hanging from the cord that was strung corner to corner. There were jock straps, thong panties, football pads, long sports socks, and pantyhose hung along the line as well.

As I neared Allen's office, I heard him on the phone. I snuck in and closed the door as he nodded and smiled at me. He was naked, and his cock was pointed at the ceiling. Kyle was supposed to join us, but that depended on Mandy's mood.

My mind wandered as I gazed upon all the pictures of his boys on the walls. Boys in hockey gear, baseball gear, football gear, lacrosse gear, soccer uniforms, and two holding saxophones.

In the corner was a sex chair with a large hole in the seat. Delectable images of Miranda's tight, perfect bubble ass stuffed in the hole above Allen's waiting mouth flashed across my brain. How did they get away with a sex chair in his office with a house full of kids? The boys must wonder, or maybe they just avoided the office because lawyers' offices are boring as fuck anyway. But the chair piqued my interest. Miranda must like sex, at the very least, she used to.

Allen jabbered on for a few more minutes as my pussy began to throb. We hadn't had sex for two days and I was wanton as fuck.

I dropped to my knees, unable to wait any longer, and crawled toward Allen. A wicked grin spread across my face as I slinked along, my ass up. My pussy slit flared as I felt my breasts swing like pendulums in my sheer shirt. I had sprinted down the street braless, like a bold whore rushing to her lover. At least in this neighborhood of secret porn watchers and decadent hidden swingers, I realized I actually fit in more than I was the outcast.

Allen held up a finger as if to chastise me, but smiled instead. His grin was naughty and appreciative. I sat and pulled my shirt off and shook my body to make my tits swing.

His grin deepened and he stroked his cock. His erection looked mad today, like it might burst. It was almost purple it was so red and angry looking.

It was perfect.

He pulled open a drawer and pulled out a small bottle of oil. I had been planning to suck his dick while he told his client his options for divorce, but oil meant titty fuck.

Once I reached him, I sat on bent knees and massaged my breasts while keeping a seductive look on my face. It wasn't an effort at all, but a pleasure.

I grabbed the oil and drizzled it all over my tits. The oil was warm, as if he had heated it. I smeared it all over my boobs and cleavage and then began to molest my nipples.

His grin grew evermore salacious as he watched me, which was the best fucking fuel for just about everything.

I desired to be desired. And he had that fucking scenario down pat with his expressions and his eyes alone. When he mixed in his words, I was pure and malleable as warmed putty in his hands.

I wrapped my generous tits around his fat cock and began to bounce my cleavage along his dick. I maintained eye contact as he gently stroked my hair and cheeks. His eyes were blissfully full of desire.

My nipples were hard and wrinkled as he fingered them, pinching and pulling on them as I rode his cock.

He hung up his call and let out a giant groan.

"Oh fuck, that was so fucking hard to hold in." He grunted and thrust up into my cleavage for a few pumps. "Fuck, you are good at that. You are sexy as fuck, you know that?"

The little girl inside me glowed. "Thank you, Daddy," I said in my sweet voice.

His eyes flooded with dominance, which made my insides quiver and quake.

"But now I'm bending you over this desk and railing you until you scream."

We weren't waiting for Kyle, clearly.

He grabbed my hips and spun me to face his massive wooden desk. He bent me over the only bare spot and my torso smacked the surface with a loud bonk.

He reached between my legs and played with my clit as I squirmed and moaned on his desk. Images of Miranda running on the treadmill upstairs as her husband's dick spread precum across my ass cheeks raged my lust further.

Even though she knew he was now fucking me all the time, I still loved that we snuck around, and most times I couldn't help but wish she'd walk in during a ram session and join us.

Allen rubbed my clit and pressed my buttons like a master. I slid right into the peak of an orgasm. He spanked my clit hard. The skin smacks were loud, but my moans grew louder. I held off as long as I could, but when he shoved a dildo up my pussy at the same time as he ran his finger in circles around my clit, I lost it and screamed.

My body jerked as I climaxed. I arched my back and my head fell.

The door of Allen's office opened as my vagina squeezed the dildo in a massive deluge of constrictions.

It was Kyle, and he'd brought his boner.

As my body slowly slid down from my orgasm, Kyle stripped with a smile.

Fuck, it was so good to see him.

"Nice," he said as he nodded. "First one?"

"Yup," Allen said as he kissed along my spine while still pumping the dildo inside me gently.

He pressed my clit and I yelped.

He chuckled. "Still sensitive."

All I could do was nod.

Kyle strutted in front of me, his erection bouncing.

"You ready for this?" Allen asked.

I felt a slight humiliation when I realized he'd asked Kyle and not me. But I'd learned this was also a turn-on for me. I loved how they always had a plan. I fantasized at night with a clit sucker pressed to my bits, imagining their conversations about me, when they came up with what they'd do to me next. It was particularly delicious to think that they perhaps talked about me during their chats in the streets of the neighborhood or while in line for coffee at church.

"As ready as I'll ever be," Kyle chuckled with a hint of hesitation in his voice.

I had given them my sexual bucket list two days ago, so I had high hopes they had plans to satisfy one of my list items. The anticipation of wondering which one they'd chosen was arousing indeed.

My heart raced as Allen fondled my ass cheeks, then reached for a double titty squeeze. He pinched my nipples and pulled them away from my body harshly as I groaned out.

As they both lined up behind me, my heart skipped at least ten beats. My breath caught and I forgot to restart breathing again as both of them danced their cock tips along my ass cheeks. I was amazed they were letting their cocks touch.

Allen whispered, "Baby, breathe. You are holding your breath."

I sucked in a deep breath. I released it. It was as relaxing as a warm spray of water along my skin. My body loosened further as he rubbed my back.

"It's going to be both of us. You be sure to tell us to stop if you are hurting or feel like you might tear." Allen's voice was low and fatherly. There was no mistaking that these two men were developing strong feelings for me, perhaps even stronger feelings than I had for them.

My heart raced even harder as Allen pushed his dick into me.

A drizzle of lube dripped down my ass crack and made its way toward my slit.

I held my breath again with high hopes.

Kyle rubbed my back this time. "Breathe, Alexa." His whispering voice conveyed such excitement and tenderness at once. It was intoxicating.

Allen pumped his cock into me and my pussy wetted further.

Kyle pressed his cock into my pussy hole too, and I gasped. I frantically gripped the papers and files on the desk, fully realizing I might be destroying legal documents that Allen would have to reprint. But the two of them stretching my vaginal opening to this extremity was way more shocking than I had anticipated.

I gulped, then gasped again. The phrase 'holy fuck' resounded inside my head like an echo.

At first, they thrust into me opposite of each other, then they did it in tandem. My walls accepted their fat load. My lips took their cocks. They were riding me harder and harder with each second.

I wished I could see their cocks sliding along each other as they fucked me, but enduring their dual penetration stretching me open was bigger than any vision of it could be. I writhed and moaned, knocking files off Allen's desk, frantically smacking over pen jars as I clawed my hands endlessly around the top of his desk. I needed to express my anguish, that sweet bliss of being almost too full up my pussy that I wanted to not only scream in pleasure but in shock. It was devastating, and I loved it.

They rode me like Daddies should, their cocks dancing along the wet creamy home of my last climax, mixing their own precum with my orgasmic juices.

They each had a hold of my hips, four hands pinning me to the desk, two cocks inside me, two bodies slapping against my ass cheeks.

I couldn't stop the scream that belted out of my mouth as I raged up the ramp of my orgasm.

Someone began to rub my clit hard and it blasted me into one of the strongest orgasms of my entire life. I saw red, then black, as my body curled and twitched on Allen's desk. I wasn't sure my vaginal walls could squeeze with how full my pussy felt, but the twitches flared. The contractions kept going and I lost count after eleven. It was like my hole was being choked.

They both grunted as they pounded into me. Each of them groaned so deliciously that it brought on another peak of the orgasms for me. I was dizzy and gasping, a mess of a rag doll.

Allen pulled out first and his hot cum spurted across my ass cheeks and back. Kyle whipped his boner out of me next. His spunk flew higher and hit my hair and upper back.

My body jerked as I panted, then my satisfied sighs took over.

Kyle rubbed the cum all across my back and ass cheeks and tried to wipe it from my hair. He chuckled and said, "Oops, I got your lovely locks, babe. Sorry about that."

I giggled. "It's hair gel."

He laughed, as did Allen.

"That felt better than I thought it was going to," Allen said in his sing-song Eeyore voice.

"Gotta admit, I agree." Kyle let out a big sigh of relief.

"It felt so tight to me," I whispered, still unable to move. Their cum began to dry on my skin as Allen pet my hair.

"First time double v for me and it was fucking amazing," Allen said. "Never thought I'd be okay with my cock sliding against yours, Kyle."

"Maybe we are those kinds of Daddies," Kyle said with a laugh. "But that's about my max for cock. Did you enjoy it, baby girl?"

I beamed at being called 'baby girl'. I nodded as they pulled up to a standing position. They each took one of my hands and led me to the couch.

They sat down next to each other and pulled me onto their laps. They hugged me to them and snuggled me. I couldn't stop smiling.

They kissed me and caressed me. They went beyond my bucket list and gifted me more love than I'd felt in all the years of my marriage.

"That was just number one on your list," Allen whispered in my ear. "And that will be repeated, darling."

I was sure my face shone with my excitement and satisfaction. There was nothing better in the world than having two Daddies, but not being their wife.

Chapter 9

I stirred the chili in the crockpot. Summer in Minnesota is a weird time to eat chili, but when Jasper requested it, I loved the idea. Chili is usually a fall thing or winter, or a Superbowl party, when it's so cold out your nostrils go into shock breathing outside and just being outdoors hurts your skin. But the idea of summer chili hit me as a good idea. Plus, I knew I didn't have that much time left with my boys home every day. College was coming, step by step, day by day, and I could see the under-eighteen finish line looming.

I grabbed the corn chips and placed them on the counter. Out the window I caught a glimpse of my tiger lilies. I loved my tiger lilies. They had beautiful orange blossoms that bloomed in the summer. I'd grown up with tiger lilies in my garden and I enjoyed keeping the tradition going at my own home as an adult. I peered closer and stopped cold. The blooms were on the ground. Which made zero sense. They should be up in the air like two to three feet. Were they bent over? Had someone trampled them? My thoughts went to my sweet doggie. She'd never done that before.

I slipped on my flip-flops and raced out the door. My heart was sinking with each step. Something was wrong.

My heart hit the grass blades at my feet. Someone had cut all the blooms off and laid them beside the flowers. I dropped to my knees and held one blossom in both my palms as tears threatened to stream from my eyes. All fifteen flower heads lay severed on the lawn beside the bed.

"Oh my Gawd," I gasped as tears fully filled my eyes. Not only had someone come into my yard, they had stolen this joy from me. "Who would do this? Why?" I couldn't stop the tears and I flat-out ugly cried in my backyard, trying not to crumple in a heap.

After a few minutes of crying, I heard a sound behind me. As I turned, I saw Kyle rushing towards me.

"Alexa, what's happened? Are you okay?" He gasped as he approached. "Oh, my God."

His voice and presence soothed me instantly, though I couldn't speak.

"I saw you from my living room. I don't have much time. Mandy is showering. But I had to check on you."

He knelt beside me and held me.

This was very risky. If Mandy or my boys looked out the window, this simple hug would raise suspicions.

"Someone cut them," I said through sobs. "Cut them right off. Who would do this? This is just plain mean."

Mark. He was on a manipulation scheme again, and I had no idea why he was back at this. We'd been divorced for months and months. Why was he coming back at me now?

He hugged me close, and I turned so we could hug along our fronts.

"It was Mark. I know it."

"What? Mark came here?" There was alarm in his voice.

"Yes, and the other day he smashed my flowerpots."

I motioned over to where the bottom half of the pots still stood. I'd left them because I had the idea that I could still use them, and they'd just look rustic, but now they just looked broken and sad. "I found Mark on the deck talking to the boys. He was being his charming self, until I appeared. Then the things he said, no one would construe as bad, but they were digs. That's how he works, he comes off as charming, and all the things he says to me are like inside cuts that only he and I know are cruel stabs."

I sobbed again and Kyle held me.

"Oh, fuck, baby. Maybe you need a restraining order?" His voice was soft, comforting, but with some resentment, which showed me he was pissed too. "I knew he was a snake from all the things you've told me about what he said, but this is low. Coming into your yard and damaging your things."

I attempted to control my sobbing so I could talk. "No one but me got to see his abusive side." I gasped to calm myself down, then continued. "It was insidious. Vile. He'd get mad at me about something, sometimes it was over a really minor thing, and he made these incorrect leaps, then he'd rage and spiral. I couldn't even keep up half the time with the crazy leaps his brain would take. He'd berate me. He was, at times, not even making any sense at all. And it was like a rush of crazy talk. At times, like a word salad, he'd bring up anything and everything. It was like an attack, I couldn't follow his reasoning or even respond properly. If I'd tried to talk, he'd twist it and use it against me. And if he'd been drinking, it was worse. Then the next morning, he would act like nothing happened at all. And if I brought it up, he'd deny it or say I was overreacting." I gasped as my heart raced with anger. "I used to get so confused."

"Gaslighting," he muttered with a surge of anger.

I was acutely aware that every second that Kyle stayed here with me posed a greater danger.

"Yes. Finally, once I realized what he was doing, then I understood, and I could protect myself better. He often did it when he'd been drinking, like I said. It was like he lost control and would just blurt things out, cruel things. Lash out. Like his empathy was just gone."

"Let's go inside." He took the blossom from my hands and laid it gently on the ground.

I followed him inside to the basement, which was a safer place to be with the boys up in their rooms.

We sat on the couch, and he cradled me to him as we sat side by side. He rubbed his fingers on my bicep.

"He's a cruel person."

I met his gaze. "Oh, he's vile. He's a snake. But he puts on this face for everyone else and everyone thinks he's a really good guy." I sniffed. "But I know better. I've seen his nastiness many times, which always made the nice guy act sting even more." I let out an exasperated sigh. "Like, I never knew which Mark I was going to get from day to day.

"Of all the things he did, the gaslighting was the worst. I started to question if I had remembered events wrong. I wondered if I was crazy. And if I brought something up, he'd flip it on me and play the victim. I learned to not bring things up anymore. He'd never apologize, hell, he'd never even admit the things he did, the things he said, or he'd flat-out deny doing or saying them." I let out another defeated sigh. "He even tried making me think I was the crazy one."

"It's like he was Jekyll and Hyde."

"Yes. Very much so. And no one knew but me." It felt really good to talk about this and have someone believe me. I'd often avoided talking about it much with others because everyone believed Mark was a good guy. No one would ever believe me, and Mark told me that many times too.

"I'm sorry to hear you suffered this largely alone."

"I'm just so happy I learned about this type of abuse so I could protect myself. Shit. I didn't want to have to get a restraining order. We are almost at the age of 18 for both the boys. Once they both turn, we won't need to co-parent so much anymore, and we will have less things to talk about. I was hoping to make it to then without a restraining order. And honestly, I didn't want the boys to have to know that their mom had to get a restraining order against their dad."

"Do they know about Mark?"

"Some. I had to share some with them at the start of the divorce. The crazy thing, well the eye-opening thing, was that they understood what I meant. I didn't have to explain it too much. It was like they instantly knew what I was talking about. They've both been so supportive of me. And I'm really glad the boys know how Mark is, so they don't get sucked into his manipulations too."

Kyle's phone buzzed. "Shit. It's Mandy."

My eyes rounded to saucers. "What will you say?"

"I'll sneak out and head to Allen's. I know he's home."

"But what if she sees you leave my house?"

"She won't. She said she's making banana bread."

"Okay, you'd better go then."

"Are you sure you're okay? You could come down to Allen's too after I leave, and we could talk more?"

"No, thanks though. But the chili is almost done, and the boys have to work, so we need to eat."

He grinned at me, and it was like sunshine. "It smells amazing in here." His eyes lit up with lust. "I wish I could fuck you quick. Make you feel better."

I smiled at him. He understood me so well. "Me too."

He stood up and pulled me into a hug.

I nuzzled into the safe comfort I'd come to feel in his arms. I gasped and placed my hand over my mouth. "Shit, my eyes will be all red."

"They will see the flowers, Alexa. And I think you should tell them that Mark did this. They need to know so they can be on a watch out for him lurking around." He grabbed my chin and stared into my eyes. "You need to get a restraining order, babe. He's unstable. Be a good girl and protect yourself, okay?"

The cloak of his protective nature cradled me. He really cared about me, and our connection was growing stronger and stronger. I no longer felt separate from him and my need to have him in my life now felt like my need to breathe. "Yes, Daddy. I will."

"Good. That's my good girl."

It wasn't wasted on me that the 'good girl' now always extended beyond our sexual relationship, and it was glorious. I'd never expected to feel this way. In the past, I'd have thought this would feel restrictive, limiting to have a man take care of me like Kyle does. I'd had thought of it as me being coddled, weak, but it was more that I had greater strength in our relationship. As time went on, it was not only sexual freedom I was gleaning, but in other areas of my life too. His support made me stronger, made me more of who I was and less and less of the guilt and self-doubt Mark had fostered in me could exist.

He peeled himself away from me. "I'd better go."

I nodded, but every shred of me didn't want him to leave. I wanted him to stay. Forever.

I watched him disappear out the door and off to the left, away from his house, and in the direction of Allen's.

I pulled myself together and headed upstairs. Neither of the boys had come down yet, so I texted them it was time for dinner. I dreaded telling them about the flowers, but I knew I needed to. As painful as it would be to tell them, they needed to know what a secret monster their dad really was. And mostly, I prayed his influence didn't turn them into him someday.

#

I woke from a nap with the urge to suck cock. This was something I'd not experienced much until all the interactions with my Daddies. In the past, I hadn't seen much pleasure it in for me. But with how my Daddies reacted as I blew them, and how much they focused on my pleasure, I was freed up to enjoy giving them head. I had found my inner slut for sucking meat, and now I actually craved it. Perhaps it was because my Daddies put me first, or because they always made me want to come, that I could then find joy in doing this with them. It was no longer a one-sided event, nor was it a chore. Reciprocation wasn't a duty with my Daddies. They never demanded anything from me but obedience to their guidance, which I dictated the boundaries of in the first place. I knew—no, I trusted—they'd never breach my boundaries. It turned me into a sexual Goddess and freed me to explore what I wanted, under their leadership.

Freedom can only come from the setup of control like we had. Freedom in expressing my sexuality was what was birthed from our relationship. And theirs too. It was unconventional, likely, to most minds, but to us, it was ideal. It was another rich layer of our triad, dominance through freedom, and it made us all climax hard, really hard. I couldn't be this way without them, and they couldn't without me. It was us, and I'm not sure we could ever be this way with anyone else. I knew I couldn't. We had freedoms from each other that we'd never had with others, so we were satiated as we'd never been with others. We enjoyed the carefreeness of not being judged by each other. No topic was off-limits for discussion, and we discussed everything. We debriefed after sex, and it was actually quite fun to do so. We looked forward to it almost as a layer of aftercare.

I didn't think less of them for having the desire to dominate me, and they never saw me as lesser for enjoying being controlled. And since they never took advantage of that, we were smooth as wind on air. Dirty talk was allowed, name-calling was allowed, degradation and using was allowed. But only in the context of us would it work. Being called a 'whore' or 'cumslut' was delicious role play and it enhanced our interactions. I'd been itching to do that on a larger scale with a group of men, like the gangbang idea on my sexual bucket list. The idea terrified and excited me and I was on pins and needles, wondering if my Daddies would go there. I had dropped a hint via text to Allen the other day, hoping I'd get the chance to experience it. Maybe I'd hate it and it would be a one-time thing. But I wanted to experience it so that I'd know for sure.

I texted both my Daddies to see if I could give them head, but neither responded so I grabbed a toy and imagined it. I started the movie in my head of both Allen and Kyle standing in front of me, cocks hard and pointed up. I took turns sucking one cock while stroking the other. The rise to climax was swift because I was quite horny. I even imagined gagging on them. In reality,

I hated it, and wanted to kill whoever forced me to do that, but in my fantasy, in my head, it was hot, sexy, and turned me the fuck on. So, I gagged in my head and my clit exploded into a wealthy plethora of contractions. I came hard. Like a whore. I liked the word. But I had a being used kink. I loved the passion, the desire of those using me. It turned me on to be wanted so desperately. Another thing I'd learned, I didn't need to be afraid or ashamed of my secret kinks, instead, I got to use them. I felt comfort in knowing I never had to do them in real life, but in my head, they were painless and only filled with lush pleasure, arousal, and climax.

Chapter 10

The smell of lasagna cooking reached my nostrils as I was finishing up work. I'd taken an afternoon break to prep it and I was so pleased with myself. I had been able to work up until actual dinner this time, and not felt interrupted by the need to meal prep. It was glorious to do it ahead of time, and being a single parent, this was becoming very apparent that doing things ahead was a necessity. It was a blessing to be able to work at home, but it also kept my brain fragmented because I was pulled in so many directions of need at once. The laundry was a big pile of stink, the carpet needed vacuuming, the dishwasher needed emptying, and mealtime always raced at me like it wanted to eat me. But I'd take single life over being married to a controlling two-faced jerk who didn't think twice about unfurling his inner demons on me at a moment's notice. It was like his guilt would throw up and he'd have to spew it on me because I wasn't doing things his way. My biggest regret was my boys witnessing his behavior. Even though he tried to sugarcoat it, we all knew the snake that lived inside him. I had once seen a piece of advice on social media from a therapist, 'When he shows you who he really is, believe it'. It couldn't be any truer than it had been with Mark. His nastiness was always there, lurking. When he'd drink too much, it raged, and he flung it all on me in torrents of various types of attacks. And he saved them all for me. No one else got to see his monster in this full and devastating form.

The aroma of the Italian dish wafting from the oven felt like a hug. I was super hungry and strode toward the kitchen, intending to pour a glass of wine to enjoy with dinner. As I rounded the corner, I smiled as I watched a little bird on the base of the pillar of my front porch. It was cocking its head and chirping. I couldn't hear it through the window, but it was so cute I carefully crept closer to see the details of its feathers. Smiling, I squinted to see if I could take in all the intricacies of the lines of its feathers better.

Something looked odd in my front yard. There was a pile of something in the center of the front lawn.

I gasped.

I shook my head. It looked like a pile of hostas, which was very odd. I had just planted them all a few weeks ago and they'd been flourishing. Bare roots stuck up in the air like the spokes off a giant's head. Despite the bird, I yanked the front door open and stepped outside. The poor bird flew, terrified of me.

All of the hostas I had planted were in a pile beside my newly added flower bed near the street. I had added it after Mark left. He always complained about mowing around things and never let me put one in.

"Oh, my! What? No!"

My hand flew over my mouth as I took in the stacked plants. Many of the leaves had cuts in them, as if someone had taken scissors to them. I glanced around, wondering who'd want to hurt me like this. First the lilies, and now the plants. Fear struck me. And was this horrible person still around? Was it Mark again? I didn't want to lay eyes on my ex right now.

This was recent, the plants weren't even wilted yet. I had mailed something earlier and this was not a crime scene then. The offender might be hiding nearby, wanting to watch my reaction.

Could it be Mandy? She'd been very cool towards me lately. Maybe she'd found out about Kyle fucking me. My best thought was it was Mark. He'd not wanted this in his yard, and he still tried to stake claim and control things, even though he no longer lived here. The cruelty of that man, though mostly hidden from the world, never ceased to amaze me.

I shook my head slowly.

I knelt down and fingered the tender leaves. The July sun had made some of them wilt upon closer inspection, but not many. I was sure they were ruined. I'd have to buy new ones and start all over. Planting them now, half-dead from the strongest heat of summer, seemed like a long shot for their survival, kind of like trying to salvage a half-rotten apple. Plus, dinner was about to be done and we had planned to eat dinner together, for once. Both boys were going to be home and I had been looking forward to eating with them.

I dashed to the hose on the side of the house and turned it on full blast. Maybe water would save them, and I could re-plant them after dinner. I dragged the hose to the front and began to spray the dying plants. I bit back the tears of frustration. It hurt to have someone destroy something I'd spent tears and sweat over. It wasn't fair, and this was very clearly intentional. Malicious.

A black car came down the street. As it came closer, I saw it was Mark's car.

My anger boiled inside to a peak, which was made hotter by the blast of sunshine beating down on my skin. He parked and slowly sauntered towards me, a nasty smirk on his face.

I kept my eyes mostly on the damaged hostas, but glanced up at him every so often. His walk to me seemed to take forever.

"You are supposed to plant those before you water them," he said sarcastically, then he laughed heartily, mocking me as he had often done, disguising it as a joke. I was always wrong and never as smart as him. His level of condescension was always there, though he'd never admit to it.

"Shut up."

"Seriously, Alexa, these look mangled. What did you do? Buy the leftovers? You were always cheap." His face held the nasty sneer long after he shut his mouth.

He had to attack me on all sides. One of his usual tactics. He'd surround me on multiple sides with cutting remarks like raptors surrounding prey. He'd keep going, stabbing me with verbal jabs, until I snapped, then he'd called me the 'crazy one' or accuse me of 'overreacting'. He was just kidding, after all, and I 'should lighten up'.

My fuse blasted inside like wildfire in summer. "What are you doing here?" I said, still trying to not lose it. I knew all he wanted was to get a reaction out of me, an emotional outburst, so he could use it against me.

"I'm watching you water dead plants." He held an ugly, mocking grimace. His handsome face shone with arrogance and disdain.

I couldn't hold it in. "You did this. Get out of here before I call the police."

He jumped back, his hands raised, a look of astonishment on his face. "You crazy bitch. I just got here. I didn't do this. You are insane, as usual."

"Rather convenient you are here just after this happens, Mark. I know you smashed my pots, cut my lily heads off. Why do you keep tormenting me? Just move on!" I screamed.

He had one thing right. I was a crazed bitch. But I'd had it with this shit show, and this had to stop. "I'll get a restraining order."

He shook his head, a disgusted look on his face as he crossed his arms across his chest.

I glanced at his eyes. There it was. That vile look that translated to pure evil, just like many of his verbal assaults from our marriage.

"You really are nuts, just like always, Alexa. Rabid and stark crazed mad as a sick dog."

The rage in me made me dizzy. I turned the curve fast into an irate ex as I took one step towards him and pointed at his car. "Leave. Get out of here. You aren't welcome."

He did me one better and took four steps towards me. He glared with daggers in his eyes and I watched him once again spiral into a rage-filled ogre, a rare occurrence in the front yard. He cowered over me, looking like he wanted to beat me. That's one way he never hurt me, but his loss of control in other ways had made me fear physical abuse at times.

I tried desperately to calm down. But I knew I was easily triggered by him, and I had no way of stopping myself from losing it.

"How dare you! I didn't do this!" He spit on me as he spoke. He was breathing heavier by the second. "You don't get to accuse me of this too! I wouldn't ever do such a thing. You accuse me of all these things I've never done. You blame me, make me out to be this ... evil monster. When I did none of it!"

I stood tall and glared back at him. As usual, he denied doing anything. He believed he was a 'good guy', but skimming the top two percent off himself and dismissing the rest, then rewriting history where he was a rosy angel was his usual way. The rest of the stuff he just flat-out denied doing, saying, spewing at me. I'd been so confused by his denial, for like years, wondering if I had remembered things wrong, until I'd been educated about what gaslighting really was and my heart had plummeted. But then it had soared. I wasn't 'crazy'. And I finally understood him. He literally believed his own false stories, which explained how he was so genuine. I'd been taken in by his performances because he even believed them himself.

"Dad," Alex said sternly from the porch. "Leave her alone." The voice I heard was the voice of a man, not my son. It shocked me, but I was proud of his tone. "Don't treat her like that."

Mark's expression transformed into a look of utter surprise. He backpedaled so fast that I almost laughed. "Oh, Alex. I didn't see you there. How are you, bud? You ready to go fishing?"

"I know you didn't, Dad. And you are way too early. I said 7:30."

"Oh." Mark took a step back from me. That was another trick he'd often do, come early and try to mess up my plans with the boys.

His eyes were now kind and jovial, transformation complete. "Well, I can come back, bud."

"I don't want to go fishing anymore, Dad. See you another time. Bye."

My heart swelled. I had feared my boys wouldn't believe me about how severe Mark had been at times. And I'd waited to tell them so many details until after the divorce was over, and in truth, I had wanted to wait until they were both a little older. I didn't want to lie, but back then, I hadn't wanted to bash their dad in their eyes. They'd seen and heard more of Mark's raging than I'd expected, and it had been a blessing, because they really got what I was saying. Not that I needed validation, but it helped me realize I wasn't the crazy one. I knew I was right, but Mark had me so beat down that I sometimes didn't recognize reality.

Mark shuffled the grass with his foot. "Oh, bummer, bud. Okay." He sounded so dejected. If he hadn't been so beastly to me just now, I'd have felt sorry for him. He pressed his lips together, clearly fighting the urge to attack me, to accuse me of turning his son against him, no doubt. "You sure?"

"Rain check, Dad."

My heart rate had slowed a little since Alex had shunned Mark, but it still beat way too fast. A sick feeling choked me inside and threatened to cave in the mountain of my healing. Mark triggered me quicker than anyone, it was all those episodes during our marriage. The path from calm to hysterical had been shortened by way too many occurrences. All the times I'd had physical reactions from a look from Mark, a seemingly harmless comment, a coy manipulation descended on me like a dump truck of mud. Instantly, it was like we were still married, and I was still trapped. This was proof I hadn't healed as much as I had thought. Maybe I did need a therapist. I bit back the urge to burst into tears and held my chin high. It took every bit of strength I had.

I tried to slow my breathing even more as I watched Mark hesitantly leave. Alex came down the stairs, took the hose from me, and dropped it to the ground. The water was still flowing out full blast, but Alex pulled me by my hand back into the house. Once inside, he smiled at me.

"It's okay, Mom. He's gone. I'll go turn the hose off. Why don't you go sit on the couch? I'll be right back."

I glanced at Jasper in the kitchen. He was cutting the lasagna and he smiled at me too. I needed their smiles like I needed oxygen. "I got this, Mom. Just go rest for a minute and then we'll eat."

I fought tears as I made my way to the couch. The relief I felt was stronger than I ever remember feeling, ever in my life. I wasn't alone. My boys had me. And they were angels in the storm I'd lived in for years, with them present, but shielded, but yet, they still came to my rescue. I wasn't crazy. I wasn't overly emotional. I wasn't insane, nor imagining things. I wasn't remembering things wrong. It was all clear. Trauma isn't always apparent until the scar is ripped open again. I'd made my first step towards healing by leaving Mark. And my boys were holding my hands to the next level.

I gasped as a few tears fell. I swiped them away as Jasper handed me a glass of wine. Astonished, I realized I had left the bottle on the counter, and he had opened it, poured me a glass, and was serving me it with a kind smile.

"Thank you, honey." My voice was shakier than I had intended it to come out. I didn't even know my son knew how to open a bottle of wine.

"You don't have to talk to him, Mom. We can talk to him ourselves."

"Well, he just showed up."

"I know. I saw him start his tirade. I'm sorry."

I shook my head. "Not your fault, honey."

He sat next to me and held my hand. "I know. But I'm still sorry."

I let a few tears fall as his words wrapped me in comfort.

Alex came into the house. "I threw away all the hostas. We will buy more and help you re-plant this weekend, right Jasper?"

"Yep. Definitely."

They set the table and we all sat down to eat. After a lovely dinner where we talked about everything but Mark, they went out with friends, and I settled on the couch with another glass of wine. With a full tummy and a fuller heart, I pet Kyla, savored the silence, and took the time to just marinate in all the wonderful gestures of my boys. I was loved. Dead plants meant nothing compared to the joy of knowing I was understood, supported, and admired by my own children. I was the lucky one.

Chapter 11

After my boys had helped me plant hostas again, they had gone fishing with their dad. He was still their dad, there was nothing I could do about that. But I was very glad they were equipped with understanding him better, and having been warned by watching how he had treated me. They would be more able to protect themselves from Mark's ways, being that they already knew. They could safely, and smartly, put up boundaries to protect themselves. I could only hope they wouldn't get hurt as much as I had. But I also knew I had to let them go. Be their own men, their own adults. Their actions had shown they were definitely becoming, or already were, thinking, discerning adults. That gave them power, strength, emotional intelligence, and it gave me some peace.

With my sons gone, Allen and Kyle were coming over. I really needed them to fuck me, but they said 'no sex'. But I still planned on pleading, begging for it, because then maybe I could change their minds. After they heard about Mark's treatment of me, they planned a cuddle session. They said I needed comfort more than I needed to come. I disagreed. But being that they were the dominants, and wanted to take care of me, I had to defer to their leadership. And honestly, I wanted to. They loved guiding me and creating our play, and more and more, it was a catering to, a tending to, of our deepening relationship.

We weren't separate, even though at times we were grouped separately, like me alone with Kyle, or me and Allen, but we were a throuple. I delighted in them telling me what to do in the bedroom, whether it was the three of us, or two, but no one else could do what they do. And they played this out beautifully. We were starting to work together like a well-oiled machine.

Allen arrived first. His hair was disheveled and his shirt sweaty. His eyes were wild, but his whole demeanor was his usual jovial self.

"Hi baby, how are you feeling?" He scuttled into the house quickly.

"Kyle is not going to be happy with you being stinky with a cuddle session looming." I gave him a warning look that was mostly a joke.

"I brought fresh clothes. I'll take a five-minute shower first, if that's okay."

I nodded. "Of course."

"Been playing ball with my boys. I couldn't say no. They don't always ask me anymore, plus they're so busy with school, sports, friends, girlfriends. I'm an afterthought, so I can't not take advantage when they think of me." He smiled big as he said 'girlfriends'. He pulled me into a hug and deeply French kissed me.

I pulled out of it and darkened my eyes. "So, you are going to kiss me like that when you guys said 'no sex'? How is that fair?" I pouted with exaggeration.

He chuckled heartily as he kissed my forehead. "You need comfort, not cum."

"Not true at all." I stomped like a brat, my fists balled. "I need both."

"True. If I wasn't here to cuddle you, I'd likely spank you." He smirked and dashed up the stairs.

My clit twitched as I fumed. "A kiss and talk of spanking?" I released a disgusted guffaw.

"It's for your own good, Alexa," Allen called down the stairs.

Dang. He'd heard.

Kyle appeared next with chocolate and a bottle of wine. "Hi, baby girl, how are you?"

He pulled me into a hug and immediately I lost my brain. I gave him fuck me eyes out of habit.

"Oh, damn. Now don't you go making this a tough day." He looked like I might be able to get him to cave in and fuck me.

I wiped my face clean of any desire to fuck and took a step back from him. "You two are now not fun, Daddies."

"Oh, we are really fun Daddies. We also have a surprise to talk about."

My curiosity bloomed. "Oh?" I asked inquisitively. "Do tell."

"Only with Allen. But we have a dual reason we aren't going to fuck you today."

"Oh, it's not just for my emotional well-being and adjustment," I complained dryly.

He smiled and let out a short laugh. "You make it sound so boring."

"Well, it's not boring. But I really want your cocks."

He pulled me into a hug and kissed the top of my head as he rocked us back and forth. "And I always want to give my cock to you. Fuck my girl."

He paused and leaned back from me so he could look into my eyes. "But not today, babe."

I was confused. They always wanted to come, to fuck me like horny stallions and make me come, to beat my butt and mouth with their bodies, doggystyle or otherwise. My brain almost couldn't process this new development.

"But we could have sex after I'm all loved up. We can do both." I wasn't giving up. Not yet.

"Nope."

I let out a fast sigh of disgust.

"Let's go upstairs. I heard Allen in the shower."

He pulled me along up the stairs. The dog followed, wagging her tail. She loved both Allen and Kyle and had to be around when they would come over. I loved that she got extra attention when they were here.

Allen was naked when we walked into my bedroom.

"Really?" I asked aghast, my lust raging. "You guys are just teasing me, aren't you?"

"No, I just hadn't gotten dressed yet. Sorry, honey." Allen's eyes told me he was being genuine.

"First you kiss me, now you stand with a boner in my bedroom and tell me you aren't going to fuck me? Is this torture Alexa day?" I stewed in frustration as I sat on the bed and curled into a ball.

They immediately curled around me, Allen still naked.

They said nothing but unfurled my tightly bound body. They sandwiched me between them and my arousal skyrocketed. I reached for Allen's cock, and he gently slapped my hand away.

"Baby girl, you need to just let us do this." His voice was tender, no-nonsense, but very fatherly.

He softly caressed my arm as Kyle pet my hair.

"Just close your eyes and let us love you." Kyle's voice was like butter on my hot skin.

"Aftercare with no sex before is severely lacking," I said as I made a sour face.

They both chuckled lightly.

"You need this more than you know," Kyle said as he curled himself around my head.

They both held me tight to them and, as I quit fighting my impatience, I began to relax. I was still turned on, but it transformed into a calmness I couldn't explain.

After about twenty minutes of silence and them holding, caressing, and cupping my body in non-sexual places, the fullness of the meditative state began to manifest. I could not only sense their love for me, but it permeated through to my soul.

"Alexa, I love you," Kyle said as he caressed my cheek.

"Alexa, I love you, baby girl," Allen drawled out.

I was glowing from their declarations as I let my love for them fill me. "And I love you both." I thought back on how accepting this affection would have been hard for me in the past. Well, it still was a little. I kept expecting them to cash their check with me, get theirs since I got mine. But this wasn't even about orgasm. It was about being unconditional, a foreign concept in my marriage. There had been no free giving of anything. It was given with the expectation of return, or the act was taken without reciprocity to me at all. He had thought nothing of me giving to him without him returning the favor. But vice versa was nonexistent. Or it was about him needing his validation, his credit.

I couldn't stop the tears. I let go of my embarrassment and I let them stream freely. The sobs started and I was lost to the emotions. They both melted into me stronger and just held me tight in the cocoon of them as I balled.

All this wasn't just talk and moves to get me into bed and fuck me so they could climax. They had real feelings for me, and I'd never really allowed myself to fully grasp that until now. I was so used to Mark needing something reciprocated, everything was owed or paid as if a debt. It had always been about him. That way of life had molded me, and I hadn't even realized it. There was nothing sexy about tit for tat. There was nothing lovingly unconditional about it either. Nor was there any emotion in it, or spontaneity. And zero passion. But Mark had molded my idea of intimacy without me knowing it. I hadn't really ever had intimacy until now. The atmosphere of unconditional love was not only a foreign concept to me, it was something I hadn't ever even fathomed. My Daddies had taught me even more than I had realized.

It was hard to view myself as a survivor and yet damaged at the same time.

They held onto me, even through both their erections, they just held me. Caressed me.

"Right now it's all about you, baby girl. You cry. We love you. You are beautiful. You have an amazing heart. You are a wonderful, powerful, and sexual woman." Allen whispered it softly in my ear.

Kyle kissed my forehead. "That's right. Loving on you right now, and that's it. Nothing else. Just loving you. And you absorbing it." His murmur was more than a statement, it was a means for me to truly accept that they'd show me love and I could just accept it. I could marinate in it and let it make me stronger.

I nodded.

I could be happy.

And that it was okay for me to be happy.

Chapter 12

In my past life, I'd have never guessed I'd wake up on a random Saturday morning and wonder how many guys I'd fuck that day. But there I was, wondering. It was a gift. And it was real.

I sipped my coffee with a smile on my face, sitting on my deck with the summer breeze lifting my hair and urging me to close my eyes and live in the moment. Today would prove to be more epic than my wildest dreams, and I'd had some fucking wild ass dreams.

And I had wondered if any women would partake in me. Because that was on the list too.

I wiggled my toes in the July sunshine, freshly painted in case someone wanted a foot job. I'd be ready. That was Allen's idea. He was the one with a thing for feet. I hadn't been at all surprised he suggested I paint them a deep maroon to match the dress I'd picked out for my first gangbang event. It seemed a fitting setup to pop my gangbang cherry.

Allen's attention to my feet had been quite a surprise, and one I hadn't expected to enjoy. In fact, I had thought I'd cringe but, instead, it made my pussy wet as he suckled my toes and then thrust his erection between my curled feet. The spurt up of his cum had shocked me. I had never understood the whole foot fetish thing, but Allen's expression as he came as his spunk landed across the bridges of my feet and the tops of my toes explained it all.

I'd never been fucked on a farm before, so I was excited. When Allen and Kyle suggested we tick another event off my bucket list at the barn dance, my mind raged into all sorts of scenarios.

I tapped my phone to respond to Kyle.

Kyle: Can I come fuck you now? Are the boys busy?

Me: they are asleep so yes, sneak over

Kyle: be right there

My heart skipped a beat. I loved being a booty call for two men. I was horny all the time, and now I had dick to satiate my lust day and night. I smiled up at the sun. My life had transformed into a thing of beauty.

Kyle texted again.

Kyle: I'll be your appetizer for tonight's events

I sent him a smiling devil emoji and a yummy face before I fingered my pussy. Miranda was walking on the path behind my house. She was expertly handling two big labs, yet managed to salute and wave to me. I secretly relished that my fingers were on my clit as I waved back.

I watched her curvy ass tick-tock and strut by. If only she'd join us someday. I dreamt frequently of being the one to make her body twitch so I could eat her cum. I sighed. Allen was a lucky man.

"Maybe someday," I muttered as she disappeared from view.

My phone buzzed again.

Kyle: I can't come. Mandy wants me to go shopping with her. Sorry. But tonight, I'll fuck you hard after all the men are done with you.

Instead of being aghast, I adored that comment 'after all the men are done with you', it made shivers skitter all across my body and clit. My torso jerked from some force inside.

Me: dammit. Ok. I was looking forward to your dick. But I'll wait.

Well, that answered my question if any women would be fucking me tonight.

#

The barn was lit with Christmas lights and twinkling stars hung from the ceiling. The bar was loaded with drunks already. I had drawn in a deep breath as I caught gazes from several men. There was something in their eyes that told me they had been contacted by Allen and Kyle. I'd always been able to tell when a man wanted to fuck me, and their gazes held no mistakes.

I sauntered over to the bar as a single woman with more dates lined up than the high school slut. Living out slut-dom was also on the bucket list. I had big plans for the next bucket list once this one was done. But one cock at a time, I'd get there sooner rather than later, thanks to my Daddies.

My belly to the bar was met with an ass grab from Aaron, the older hottie who had the paper-thin excuse for a wife. She looked like she'd faint at the sight of an erection, let alone the penetration of one.

"Nice to have some ass to grab onto," he whispered in my ear as he pressed his cock into my ass crack.

Yup. And he will get to be round one. "I know, right?" I said as I looked him directly in his lust-filled eyes.

"Your Daddies speak very highly of you, Alexa." His voice was gruff and manly. The kind of voice I wanted telling me to bend over.

"Tell me to bend over and I'm yours," I said flirtatiously as my clit gifted me with a sweet twitch.

"I plan to turn that twinkle in your eyes into a bonfire later." He winked at me and gave my left ass cheek a little slap.

"Make me a wildfire and you'll never forget me."

He laughed and grabbed two beers off the bar.

"You sure that beer is going to fit inside Lori?"

He snickered.

Through a smirk he said, "Bad mouth my wife and I'll spank you for insulting her."

I love that the men had been prepped by my Daddies. "Oh, that's a promise." The thought of being spanked in front of all the men wetted my pussy further. I made a mental note of that to tell my Daddies about that idea too. But I do recall saying it once to Kyle in a hazy after fuck glow so maybe …

I searched the crowd for them, but neither Allen nor Kyle seemed to be there yet. My heart sank. I was impatient to become the neighborhood free-use cunt. My lust shoved me into brat mode and I pulled out my phone to let her roar, but a text from Kyle stopped me cold.

Kyle: Get your whore bitch cunt out to the hay bales behind the tool shed and make sure it's wet and ready for seven cocks

My heart hit my toes as I stood motionless. The horror of being passed around flickered across my mind's eye and my desire swelled. I was about to get more dick than I could swallow. My breath caught, then raged. For how hard my heart was now beating, I should have just been running for my life.

After a quick piss break, I ran out of the barn. My pussy throbbed as I wiped my index finger across my clit in the shield of the darkness. I'd purposely not masturbated to a full climax this afternoon so my first orgasm would cream my first customer like he had stuck his dick in a can of frosting.

The night air was warm. The stars were brilliant bright beads on black. The men stood in a semi-circle, cloaked by hay bales taller than all of us. Their cocks were all out and thick. Three of them were stroking and all smiled at me. I had taken a deep breath and let out a slow sigh as my salacious smile greeted them all. I couldn't wait to feel the harsh brush of stacked hay scratching my skin as one of them rocked my tits into the wall of it.

I couldn't imagine a better location to lose my gangbang virginity than behind a barn with all their wives inside, likely gossiping and bitching about their men. They had no idea how to appreciate real lust.

"Wow," I said. "You all look like a bunch of dicks." I snickered and grabbed the hem of my dress and swung it about like I was innocent.

I was nothing but.

They laughed and I feasted on the passion in their eyes. They were locked and loaded, and I was thrilled to be their communal target.

Kyle pressed his erection against my ass and placed his hand around my throat. I leaned back into him and gazed up at him lovingly. Lately, I'd feared Mandy could see my feelings for Kyle in my eyes when we chatted at the grass borders of our lawns. But mostly I didn't give a fuck. She's a vanilla. She could use a good whack to the sexuality to wake her up to living.

"Yes, Daddy?" I asked, my pussy melting from his rough touch, his tender eyes.

He yanked my dress off over my head so fast I gasped.

"Suck Mike's dick." Kyle pointed to the older gentleman with the biggest cock.

I froze, though I loved being made naked in front of all these men in such a grand way. Did he have to start with the largest monster cock in the field? I drew in a deep breath. Smiled. Nodded. I froze too long, so Kyle swatted my ass.

"Go," he commanded. The new love never left his eyes for a second.

I desperately desired to please my Daddies. It was becoming my kink. And since their kink was to please me and get me off as strongly as possible, we were meshing like a crocheted blanket, no seam between where I ended and they started, other than off the edge. But the edge was the beginning of others, so that was separate.

Allen put a hand on my shoulder and squeezed. "Wait, I want this in you while you suck." He held up the pendulous toy and it swung from his fingers.

I obediently lifted my right leg, exposing my thigh and vulva lips to all the men. They cheered and I almost crumpled with delight, but Allen helped steady me. Quick hand this one. Must have been all the training, having all his little sons to keep safe over the years. Allen pressed the pink toy inside my pussy and tapped it on low, using his phone.

His eyes shone with mischief and affection before they shifted to great amusement. He chuckled deeply before he raged the toy to the highest mode, then dropped it back down to low. This big-cocked man before me had already seen my pussy, tits, and asshole from the naughty, slutty, show-all account Allen had set up for me on Only Fans last week. I'd met Mike a few times but hadn't talked with him much. His wife looked like someone who never would give a blow job. I could be wrong, but usually my intuition was spot on.

I smiled wide at him as Allen played with my pussy using the many modes of the toy. I twitched as he brought it to the max level, which was about every other third second. Some of the men cackled when I'd react. I smiled at them. I loved that they enjoyed my reaction. It fucking raged my excitement to new heights. So much better than my husband had ever been. Being in front of this many men on display set my lust on steroids. I'd always secretly yearned to be a stripper on stage.

As I approached Mike, I fell to my knees while keeping eye contact.

He sighed. "If only I could bottle that look in your eyes." His deep grin flipped a switch in me. I wanted to make him come, and hard.

I drew in a breath as my face neared his skin. He smelled of timber and vanilla, likely a nice solid man soap. I touched both of his thighs and he flinched, but then relaxed.

He twitched his cock in front of my face. "Been a while," he said with deep forlorn.

There were heckles behind me, words of encouragement and enjoyment that I only half heard. My focus was on his beautiful erection right in front of my lips, and the goings on in my pussy from the toy. I pressed it firmly to my clit and groaned.

"Good girl," Allen said. He was right behind me. "Now, take his cock in your mouth, baby, and ride him to cream."

I wondered why he wanted me to make him come so quickly. What about fucking?

I took his mushroom head into my mouth. It filled me even more than I had expected. This wasn't going to be much of a shaft suck. I ran my tongue all along the ridge and the groan he released made my clit spasm. His sounds were so deep and appreciative that they sent my enthusiasm to the sky.

I bobbed my head while I rode his rod with the sheath I'd made with both my palms. I constricted my fingers around his shaft and bounced. My tits swung up and down as I rode him. The men shouted out as if it were a rodeo. I chuckled, slightly choked, wondering if I was more the bull or the rider.

Allen blasted my pussy with the toy and I moaned with my mouth full of his cock. My Daddies had told me how delicious sound vibrations were on their erect dicks. I tried not to smile when Mike jerked and twitched with extreme pleasure when I did it for him.

"Fuck," he said with a deep gasp.

He held my head steady, pressing his palms to the sides of my head.

Allen set the toy on high mode and left it. I pressed the thin tail of the toy to my clit and the sensation took over. I came first, my body curled against him as I struggled to suck while I moaned out my climax. He lost it and spurted in my mouth. It was a big, juicy load. Allen pressed himself against my back and caught me as I fell off Mike's dick. Allen rubbed my clit vigorously and made me come again in the circle of men. Their expressions were all full of lust and want and happiness.

I was in the bliss of heaven.

I came so hard my whole body scrunched, my face went ugly, and my vagina shoved me into a twelve-contraction, or something near, orgasm. I involuntarily yelled out sounds I didn't think were pretty, but they all hooted and hollered. It was damn yummy.

As the orgasm slowed down, Allen pulled me onto his lap and held me, stroking my hair. I became aware of Mike's cum leaking out the corner of my mouth and I swiped it up quickly and pulled my tongue into my mouth to finish tasting him.

"Messy," I said with a giggle. I gazed up at Allen, whose eyes were so proud.

"Good girl, you made Mike come hard. He hasn't had a blow job in fifteen years."

My jaw fell open. "Fifteen?" I asked with a gasp.

Mike looked like someone had socked him in the face, awestricken but wonderfully floaty, deep relief flooding across his face. "That was unbelievable." His cock hung as a semi, still out and glistening.

I smiled. "You make a good intro to a gangbang." I wasn't sure how I'd be able to stand. Flaccid rag doll post giant orgasm was truly a thing. "I might need a few hands to keep me upright after that monster O."

Shouts of volunteering rang out and I knew I was in for the biggest, raunchiest fuck session of my entire life. They were all very eager and I couldn't wait.

Allen held me and rocked slightly. The affection he dished out filled me with joy and satisfaction. A sheepish feeling flooded me. I was finding I needed this aftercare more than I'd like to admit. Pleasing him made my heart swell and my lust balloon. I loved being their sex tool. Being used was something I'd experienced in my marriage, but not in the right way. Allen and Kyle had it down pat. It was like liquid lightning orgasm fuel when done right.

As I met his eyes, his beard looked like something I wanted to grab as I watched him. He'd told me to use it as a handle to direct his mouth many times and it never got old.

I smiled. "Who is next?"

He nodded and raised his head to the men. "She's ready." He connected to my gaze once more. We were getting to the point where we didn't even need words because we communicated through our eyes.

He whispered in my ear, "Sweetheart, I want to add a layer of safety to this gangbang. If you are too overwhelmed to speak but want a sex act to stop, clap your fingers down to the base of your palm. I will be watching you very closely and will see this. I promise you. I don't want you to develop any trauma from this."

I was no fool, I knew how likely such damage could happen. Allen had been sending me articles to read and they taught me how to avoid such emotional damage in sexual situations. He was a very smart man, and he'd been studying this stuff long before I even knew what some of it was. I gave him a single nod. I understood what he was saying. I needed to protect myself in this vulnerable state or I'd wind up with negative emotional triggers, and possibly even scars that'd never heal.

He pointed to his eyes, then directed his spread fingers at mine with an extended linger. I smirked because the men likely saw this as a dominant move to get me to behave. As if warning me to do things right or risk punishment from Allen. Well, that was a thing but, in truth, I wasn't opposed to them thinking this at all. It made this impending gang bang even hotter.

Allen helped me to stand, and Kyle caught my line of vision. He gave a tick of his head, and I knew he was on board with what Allen had told me. They discussed everything together before they approached me. I felt safe with them here. This was only about my pleasure, and honestly, more about mine than all these men. But the men didn't know that. They thought I was here for their pleasure, but I knew the truth.

Allen pointed to a younger man, who was about fifteen years younger than me. He and his new wife were new to the neighborhood. She was pregnant and they had a one-year-old little girl. The lust in his eyes felt dangerous. It stabbed pings of delicious terror down my spine. He was going to rock my world like I couldn't even fathom. All that energy and power that he held in those eyes were surely translatable to how well he fucked. Our mutual gaze said it all, we both knew sex could just be sex, and nothing more.

He stepped forward to the center of the circle of men and stopped. I sashayed toward him like a good slut. He was strong looking, as if he lifted weights, and his flannel shirt clung to his chest as if it were sprayed on. He had it half unbuttoned, showing me the firm bulges of his pecs. His cock protruded out of his open jeans like a proper farm boy ready to fuck, fully clothed, beastly, and with the zest of youth.

I closed in on him and dragged my finger across his chest, then I circled, pulling my finger along his toned back before returning to face him.

"What do you like?" I asked in a seductive voice.

"Doggy," he said with an absolution that swelled my clitoris further. "I'd like to chase you and tackle fuck you."

His words hit me like a straight-line wind. I physically recoiled and my clit sang. This was a fantasy on my bucket list as well. I glanced at my Daddies, wondering if they had shared my bucket list items with these men to please me, to hit my buttons, to rage my desire to maximum expansiveness. I didn't care one bit. They were in charge and they led me, and I enthusiastically followed their lead with my swollen clit in hand.

"Okay," I said in a shaky voice, though I smiled to tell him I approved. I laughed. "Why do I have this strange feeling that I'm not going to get very far before your dick will be up my cunt?"

He raised an eyebrow over chocolate brown eyes that seared me deep. His aggressiveness was not shrouded by anything. It was flat all over his face and delicious as fuck. I'd never wanted a man to ride me more.

"Go," he commanded.

I stalled. Stupid. Wait, we were starting now?

If he hadn't paused, he'd have caught me right where I stood, and I'd have been his, a tight MILF hole to have his way with before the chase had even begun. But he waited, a teasing look in his eyes.

I ran, realizing I was naked and running in a field. The fleeing sent chills of excitement through my body. I wasn't a mom, I wasn't a neighbor, I wasn't even the Alexa anyone knew. I was a free goddess of sex as the breeze liberated me, stripped me of all the labels I didn't claim at that moment. I frantically looked around and veered left, away from the barn. The rough vegetation hurt much worse than I expected as I padded along, and I couldn't run nearly as fast as I had expected. But I was free. Free to be caught and made to orgasm, to give orgasm, to be vibrantly and brilliantly truly alive as never before.

My heart pounded and I squealed. My body filled with glee as he grabbed me roughly from behind. He didn't even bother spinning me around, but forcefully bent me over.

"Grab your knees," he commanded, his voice full of anger that struck an odd but arousing chord in me.

I obeyed, like a good girl.

I gasped, anticipating his rough touch. I fingered my knees as my heart raged in my chest, and my panting crippled me. In truth, I'd never be able to outrun a man, and that humbling acknowledgment alone excited me to the point of almost groaning. There was something irresistible about being taken as the weaker sex.

He gave me three hard slaps on the ass and I screamed out, my sounds mixing with the song emanating from the barn, even though I'd brought us further away from it.

"Good girl," he said. How he said those words was exactly what I needed to get me ready to go.

My pre-fuck arousal thickened as I waited for him to push his fat cock inside me.

I heard snickers and shouts egging him on from the men. It turned me on so damn much that they'd followed us, these licentious men, that they'd see this youngster rage fuck me in an open field under the camouflaging blackness of night. They'd witness his absolute domination of me. My fantasies were released into the dark air like a jar of hungry fireflies. I couldn't wait to watch them soar, feast on the scene of us, then return satiated to my fully satisfied cum-soaked body. The promise of it all was astronomically thrilling.

He hit my ass cheeks with his cock before he leaned over my back. He whispered, "Going to fuck you like a whore for them all to see and use your wet hole to make me come."

I shuddered. It was the perfect thing for him to say.

He pressed his fingers into my wet lips while he fondled my right nipple. He pulled my tit hard and I squelched out a scream. He finger-fucked my pussy with stamina, not stopping until I was about to come. Then he left my body abruptly and I waited.

Nothing happened and it felt like an eternity until he hit my butt again. Being spanked in front of this many men sent me right to the edge of my climax, and I almost tipped over it as I moaned out and whimpered.

He pressed his erection against my ass crack and whispered into my ear. "Run again, Alexa. Run like the wind. I'm the wolf. You are the deer. And you are mine."

I froze, like I hadn't learned my lesson the first time. I had expected him to press his cock into me and ram himself like a piston until we both came. But this. This was completely unexpected. My heart scrambled as I finally pulled myself from the stupor of mind-numbing arousal and dashed ahead, just like the deer he told me I was.

I ran hard across a fallow field littered with dried vegetation. My panting grew out of control because my heart wouldn't stop increasing the speed with which it was pounding.

I was terrified. Each step I took scratched my bare feet. But I pushed on, gathering strength and speed from unknown places as all prey do, feeling the adrenaline blast me into a faster run than I'd ever accomplished before.

His footsteps pounded behind me as he hunted me. My entire body was on fire, so much so that I thought I'd explode across the entire field in a spray of fireworks.

He caught me around the waist in a tackle and we both bolted to the ground in a heavy heap.

"Oh, dear Gawd," I gasped out in utter horror.

The brutal slam down sent waves of searing pain through my hyper-alert body, and I was sure tomorrow I'd find scratches, or worse, all across my skin.

I was panting heavily, but involuntary sounds spewed from my lips as he arranged my body head down, ass up. He pressed my head to the coarse, lumpy dirt and strands of hay cut into my forehead.

He jerked his cock into me so fast before I could even take another breath. He rammed his hardened shaft into me with so much power and force that it pushed me into what I figured might be subspace, but surely ecstasy. I floated around, absorbing every thrash of him against my backside, but it was as if I could also look down upon myself and see him wildly fucking me in a field with many men cheering around us like beasts. For a split second, they all had horns protruding from their heads.

It was like an ancient ritual that I'd seen in a movie made about times before things were civilized. Nothing mattered but him fucking me like a monster.

The sensations he brought me through made me want to scream banshee-style, yet I was unable to make anything other than primal guttural sounds.

By the time I slipped back into my body, I was coming with such force that I couldn't remain upright. He gripped my hips as my body went slack and held me up, my knees rose off the ground, with him pounding himself into me like I was meat and his cock was a knife.

He let out a deep man growl that almost sent me into another orgasm alone because of the sheer and complete dominance contained in it. I imagined him howling at the moon, telling her he was the boss of my cunt and he'd use me how he saw fit.

I shuddered again as he continued to slaughter my pussy. I was so sloshy inside that the slick sounds of our wet union reached even my orgasm-fogged ears.

He grunted like an angry boar. His sounds as he climaxed were of a caged man who desperately needed an animalistic fuck. He pulled out of my pussy and shot his cum all across my ass and back. The air around my body felt thick as billows of cotton, but my bare skin still sensed his release as loads of multiple streaks of cum splats. It was a succulence to savor.

He panted hard as I crumpled to the ground.

"Holy fucking shit," I heard him say. He gasped and sputtered like he was drained. "I don't think I've ever come that hard in my entire life."

The relief in his voice was so beautiful.

I smiled, cheek to the dirt, and hoped the next man could devour me as well as he had. But I had serious doubts about that.

Kyle rubbed my thigh and leaned over me. He kissed my forehead and rubbed my back. In a soft, caring voice, he asked, "Are you ready for the train? It's gonna come hard and fast."

I nodded, even though I wasn't sure I was ready. But I had zero doubts about wanting it. Still, on the major high of orgasming so explosively, I managed to get to my hands and knees.

Kyle patted my back like a good doggie owner and said, "Good girl." He cleared his throat. "First cock coming in like two seconds."

The stab into me sent my back into a severe arch. My head was forced upward and all the stars above me were visible at once, dark blinding me with the power of his thrust. The slamming of this man's cock into me was sharper than falling into flames. He rode me tenaciously, with the force of a cannon. My body twitched and danced along the hurdles of pre-climaxing as someone's hand, clearly not his because had me by the hips, molested my clit.

I burst into another mogul of an orgasm. I shrieked out to the night sky that was soon filled by the presence of a body that proceeded to shove a cock into my mouth.

They spit-roasted for a few minutes until they both unloaded cum across my body and two more cocks slipped into me.

The endorphins made me drunk, and it was almost too difficult to keep my vision focused, but then he came into clarity. It was my overweight neighbor, Manny, gripping my head and face-fucking me. He did it almost gently, his belly bumping my forehead. I couldn't breathe, so I jerked back, which enticed the man fucking me from behind to fuck me harder.

I wanted to say, 'Fuck me harder', but I couldn't get a word out, only grunts, sighs, moans, and stuffed mouth gasps.

The men took turns fucking me. I couldn't have counted the number of orgasms if I had tried. I was shoved into a dream-like state as my body was taken over by hormones to the point that I wasn't even sure I could manage coherent talk if I tried.

Then someone was picking me up and carrying me.

The voice was familiar before the words. It was Allen, and his body was warm and instantly recognizable, strong and loving, as he cradled me. "Good girl. Good girl. Good girl," he repeated in a soft, comforting way.

It's all he said, but his tone said more. He was proud of me. He loved watching me come and service so many cocks with my goddess pussy. He couldn't wait to fuck me. Well, more make love to me in the post-coital warfare my womanhood had just endured, enjoyed, savored. His words carried the truth that I was an empowered woman who was gifted more orgasms in a single night than I had thought possible.

He transferred me to Kyle's waiting arms, where he sat against a hay bale. Allen talked with the men as Kyle cuddled me.

I didn't have to ask, I knew they'd celebrate me next and push my orgasm boundaries to max mind-blowing heights. Happiness flooded my endorphin-fed body and I let my eyes close as I relaxed against Kyle's body.

Chapter 13

My eyelids fluttered. Hay bales under the sheen of moonlight slowly came into focus. Parts of me were tender and throbbing, but I was also completely exhilarated. The scent of Kyle's skin and the protection of his palms on my back prevented the shiver that almost took over me. I wasn't cold. More, I was shocked.

The whole evening flooded my brain, crowding out the present. Images of dressed men with bare, hard cocks out like fleshy rods, ghost remnants of hard barraging against my pussy lips, all somehow still lingered. Like an eerily too real dream, as if it was in part happening now, but yet a memory at the same time. These apparitions took turns ramming me relentlessly, my butt cheeks gyrating from backside thrusts. All our wicked sounds echoed in my head. The euphoria of having orgasmed more times than ever before in my life, combined with the bliss of sleep, brought a gentle smile to my lips, and a sense of comfort and elation to my being. Yet my heart was raging with excitement.

I'd done it. I'd fucked them all, been fucked by all of them, short of Allen and Kyle. Which I relished would come next.

"Baby girl," Kyle said as he stroked my back with his warm hands. "How do you feel?"

I loved that his first words to me were about my emotions and feelings. This hadn't been about him. This had been all about me. His jealousy never snuck in. I often thought it was because he already knew he had my heart, so he realized that it was more that others were jealous of him.

"I feel unbelievable, incredible, amazing, wonderful ...out of this world happy," I said slowly, dreamily, savoring each syllable.

Allen swiped the hair off my face. "Do you have any idea how amazing you are? How beautiful that was? Watching you pleasure that many men while getting all those orgasms for yourself was one of the most incredible experiences of my life." His tone was so full of awe and pride, it washed over me like a bath.

These two men were my Daddy Doms. I'd read about it, even envied such caretaking lustiness in relationships, such gifting lovers, but never imagined myself as a good girl to two. Even though I cherished it, my mind constantly roamed it, looking for places to grasp onto it where it felt tangible. Then, at times, like now, it was all touchable, and it consumed me. This was real. And they were mine.

"I never thought I'd actually be able to handle that many dicks. At one point, my body felt ready to explode into a spray and join the sky like fireworks. It was like I was on fire and flying at the same time."

"I was transfixed watching the pleasure exude from your face. It was gorgeous. Then your sounds, oh wow, it was better than the best symphony to listen to them push you to all of those sounds." Kyle kissed the top of my head. "A few times, though, I admit, when I saw something flicker across your face I didn't like, I tensed, my fists balled for a second. I was ready to rip him out of you, but you always switched so quickly to pleasure again that I let it play out."

"Yeah, I saw that too," Allen said, coming from behind a bale. "I even took a step once."

"Mmmm," I murmured. "I don't even recall any moments of pain or distaste. They were likely too fleeting to register in all that pleasure. All I remember is how fucking unbelievably delicious every second was." I squirmed in Kyle's lap. "You feel so good."

Allen sat on the ground and pulled my feet into his lap. He began to play with my toes and massage my feet and calves, making me sigh.

"Would you do it again, angel?" Allen asked sweetly. I didn't need to see his face. I knew the inquisitive, pleasant smile he wore from his voice alone.

"I don't know." That was too much to think about.

Kyle let out a light-hearted laugh. "It's a lot to process for me. I can't imagine for you."

I nodded, my cheek brushing his bare chest. He was indeed shirtless, but his pants were still on. Likely he had taken off his shirt because he knows how I cherish skin-on-skin, how his and Allen's bodies comfort me when I'm wrapped up in their flesh, and when coming down off a sexual high.

"At one point, I had one of the biggest orgasms of my life. It rippled through my pussy and I focused really hard. I counted eighteen strong contractions. I think." I guffawed and gasped as the memory took over me.

I swung my hand in the air as if I were dismissing it, but it was nothing like that. "It was totally indescribable."

"Whew, that sounds epic," Allen said as he caressed up my legs, cupping my knees in his large hands. "The whole scene was beyond anything I've ever been a part of."

Kyle continued to rub my back as he said, reflecting, "I think I know right when that was. At one point, you fell and crumpled. If you hadn't had an expression of sheer pleasure, I'd have rushed in to rescue you."

I sighed as I snuggled against his skin. "I think I know that moment too and, yup, that was when it was."

Kyle's cock was hardening against my belly.

"I'm getting aroused just thinking about your expression."

On the next stroke up, Allen's finger grazed my lower thigh, arousing me more.

"Higher," I said seductively.

You'd think I'd have had enough sex for the month from tonight's gangbang, but I was raging up the desire for them to fuck me next. I imagined it wouldn't be violent so much but passionate, loving, affirming as they claimed me back as theirs with an aggressive, but tender, fucking session. Being dominated by men was a massive turn-on to me, but being dominated by my Daddies was so full, lush, comforting. There was nothing like it. And it could only be with them. No one else. It often took me like a storm, or how yearning to eat a delicious meal overcomes me, or how waking up after the best night's sleep ever refreshes me. Most likely it was all that. Actually, it was more.

I reached for Kyle's groin and massaged his erection through his pants.

"I want to reclaim you something fierce. I want to fuck you back into my folds, but when you are ready." Kyle's voice was strong, but compassionate. There was no arguing if, only when.

I glanced up into his warm eyes. They were so flooded with love and desire at once, I was overwhelmed. I too deeply yearned for them both to claim me back.

My pussy had just taken a brutal beating, albeit one I had asked for—and loved. Unsure if I'd feel sore with another cock pounding me or not, I caressed his dick and pressed my toes to Allen's crotch to assess his level of excitement.

He groaned out as I curled my toes against his thickened shaft.

"Aw, fuck, baby girl, you know my weakness." He pressed my foot to his boner as I curved my feet harder to cradle him.

I unzipped Kyle's pants while I held his gaze. "It feels like midnight," I whispered.

"It's later than that. The barn dance is over. Has been for a while. Allen helped clean up while I held you as you slept. Everyone went home."

I sank into that image, imagining Kyle staying here against this hay bale, holding me as I lay out cold under a sky filled with brilliant stars and a perfect moon.

I snuck my hand into Kyle's pants. His cock felt very hard and full. Instantly, I wanted it in my mouth. I popped the waistband of his underwear off him and pushed it down his shaft.

"Mmmm," I murmured as I maneuvered down so I could take his cockhead in my mouth.

He stopped my descent with his hands. He held my skull firm between his palms. "No." He shook his head at my confused expression. "No cock sucking."

I jerked my head to the side, releasing his grip on me as confusion spread across my face. He'd never told me this before.

He moved his hands to my cheeks and pulled me into a kiss that was hungrier than I'd ever felt from him, which said a lot, because Kyle was a hungry kisser to begin with.

I moaned as we kissed, our tongues bodies of their own, writhing and caressing each other. Allen slipped out from under my feet. He took my right big toe into his mouth and began to suck as I shuddered. My run through the field flickered across my brain. I had hardcore mad dashed through the dirty fields, my skin raw and scratched up from all the pounding of my feet against the vegetation. I cringed and tried to pull my feet from his mouth, fearing what germs and diseases he was picking up off my feet from the dirt-covered field.

Like he was reading my mind, Allen said, "I washed your feet. You seemed asleep, honey, but I washed them in hot soapy water, so all is good."

I pulled myself from the kiss with Kyle. "Seriously? And I didn't even wake?" I tried to picture him carrying a bowl of soapy water across a field and I almost laughed. It seemed impossible, and it must have been an odd sight.

Kyle chuckled like he had all the secrets. "No. Well, you stirred a little, but I was holding you, so you nestled back into me." Kyle's face told me how he cherished cradling me as Allen bathed me. Both my Daddies knew how to make a good girl feel extra special.

I sighed with deep satisfaction. "Wow. Well, good. I was afraid you were eating worm guts and manure remnants off my feet." My laughter seemed too loud, but I knew no one was around to hear but the three of us.

Allen sputtered a cough before saying, "All this disgusting talk doesn't deter me from the fact that I want to fuck your guts out and make love to you like no one ever has before in your life."

The yin and the yang of aggressive passion and the wrap-up of love were exactly what I would have hoped for after being a fuck toy for so many. It was the aftercare I needed. It was the aftercare my Daddies needed.

"I've never wanted either of you more," I declared as Kyle pulled me back into a kiss.

"Your wish is my command, and my gift." Kyle devoured my mouth with his.

My nipples hardened as Allen reached up to play with my pussy lips. I spread my legs for him, his groan of appreciation wetting my pussy further.

The warm summer air enveloped me as a slight gust of wind blew past us. The smell of earthy hay and damp dirt brought me back to a primal state of want once more tonight. I at once wanted them to rage fuck me, use me like all the holes I am, but I also craved their sweetness, their flooding caretaking, their mutually pleasuring goal their leadership in sex always brought about.

What was once a slow, sensual playing of their mouths on me became a hurried, horny grabbing as both of them began to lose control. I ardently wished for them to destroy me to a million orgasms. It was like I could touch the transition in mood. It was all-consuming.

Things began to blur as my Daddies moved about, raging in their passion. Kyle was standing, hoisting me over his shoulder, and carrying me and my throbbing cunt somewhere. It wasn't far, and he laid me down on a plush comforter in the middle of the half circle of hay bales.

Not more than a second after I was laid down, Allen spooned me from behind as Kyle caressed my breasts and tummy from my front. His hands cupped my exposed hip before pressing swiftly into my mound. He quickly slid his fingers between my cleft and fingered my clit. He dipped his forefinger into my wet hot hole, then brought my juices to slather my clit.

Dipping my head back in a moan as they handled me while I was viewing the full bright moon above was electrifying. Allen fondling my ass cheeks brought twinges of pain as he pressed his big digits against my red spanked flesh. It hurt, but was comforting at once. I welcomed his press in the chasm between my thighs like a beacon of his desire to please me, fuck me, take his own orgasm as he gifted me mine.

Kyle took my mouth in a kiss as his hands groped all along my body like he hadn't seen me in months. His movements oscillated between rash and demanding to slow loving caresses, his shifting mood obvious from each of them. I imagined in his head he was wrestling with the desire to fuck me like a whore, yet make love to me like the love of his life, and I loved him all the more for both.

He rushed my pussy in a brash loss of control and pressed his fingers into my vagina, finger-fucking me in a barraging onslaught. Both of their fingers found the inside of me as they both finger fucked me hardcore. Their fingers slid past each other, their flesh tasting the wet of my insides, bringing out my juices more to my lips with each push in and pull out.

I writhed between them as their mouths explored me. I held Kyle's head, my fingers in his hair as he suckled my boobs from mound to tit and back again, all the while reaching up to touch Allen behind me. I dropped my head to the plush blanket as Allen's mouth savored my neck, his hard-on caressing my buns.

"Oh, fuck me," I muttered with a musical sigh. They always said they loved my sighs, as if they were soothing sounds of the sea, a siren's call mixed with an angel and a lioness who liked to fuck like a whore. I released all my pleasure verbally into the night air for them. My eyes opened and closed as their desire for me lit up my lust like an explosion. "Please fuck me, Daddies. I need your thick cocks in me. Make me cum. I want to take yours."

They both pulled their fingers from my pussy as I lifted my leg for Kyle's entry into my hungry sweet spot. Allen rode my buns ravenously with his wet dick as Kyle pressed his erection further into me with a giant groan. Our three voices filled the air with passionate exclamations and insatiable grunts.

We fucked like animals. We fucked like saints. We fucked like whores for sex and love, like thirsty vampires, like only lovers who truly fit can.

It was glorious. It was monumental. It was sure to be unforgettable.

A wanton clit can take a beating better than any flesh. It amazed me how something so delicate and vulnerable, yet so capable of such intense pleasure, could also take a beastly beat-down thrashing. It seemed impossible, yet each day I proved it possible as I took both my Daddies inside and out of my pussy, them both riding my clit like rabid fiends.

Allen entered my pussy next. The press in of him was shocking at first, then the euphoria set in. The crowding of my pussy brought more pressure on my clit from Kyle's thrusts and I blasted into an orgasm that shook my whole body.

Kyle came next. Then Allen.

My pussy throbbed with heat as it was drowned in all three of our juices.

I had lost count of how many dicks I'd had in me that night, but Kyle's and Allen's were by far the best.

Spent, we lay panting, tangled and cuddling, beneath the fresh breath of the night air. The three of us, who'd hooked up by chance, yet danced the edges of ultimate fantastical pleasure on a daily basis together. How had we arrived here? I dared not assume we were meant to be, but being together now made all that not even matter.

Chapter 14

The flashbacks from the previous night pelted my brain, making me smile, raise an eyebrow, and snicker. It all felt so surreal now. Like it was a dream, or I was playing a part in a movie rather than living an epic event in my own life. I'm still not sure I'd do it again. Maybe. I've never orgasmed so much in such a short time, though, which is a huge plus. My brain swam, processing it all. But the amazing thing is it's not bad feelings, they are all good. I guess I just like sex.

The grass was long in my yard, like wading through a wild field. The boys had been promising to mow, but they'd been busy, so I'm taking the reins and just doing it. It had been a challenge for me to learn to drive the mower, but I'd done it. The fear of tipping it had been what I had needed to overcome. After a few times, I realized I was adept at it. The garage was sweltering and the trees outside were not moving, so there'd be no relief of a breeze under the blaring sun other than the wind I'd get from the slow mower ride. I was clad in a tube top and short shorts, so I was ready. After fucking some of my neighbors last night, I glanced at the homes of the men that were nearby. I wondered if they'd be watching me out their windows, wishing they could come and fuck me, bent over this mower. The thought thrilled me. I straddled the mower, ready to rub one out as I rode, but when I turned the key nothing happened. I turned it again.

Dead.

"Fuck. Now what? It's always something," I muttered as I slid off the mower. I walked around, assessing "Humpf. What the fuck?" I recalled a time when the boys were young and they'd turned the key and the mower went dead. Maybe someone had left it on, or maybe it needed gas.

I glanced at my car, wondering if I should go get gas. I'd left my car outside last night because Alex and Jasper had parked inside. Who knows why, but I just didn't care, so I left mine out. But my car looked odd. Curiosity got me. I cocked my head, foregoing looking at the mower gas gauge, and walked towards my car.

I gasped as I approached. My driver's side tire was flat. "Oh my God," I muttered as I eyed it up. "Well, damn. This sucks. I can't mow and now I can't go buy gas."

I wandered into the house with the intent to look for the boys' keys so I could use their car to get gas and a note on the counter caught my eye.

It was from Mark.

It read:

I'll be back to pick you both up at 4 pm so we can fish. Love, Dad.

So, this was new. I hadn't seen this note here earlier. A horrible thought flooded my brain. I shook my head in horror. Mark turned on the mower and slashed my tire?

I can't assume this but, clearly, Mark had been here to drop the note recently. Anger boiled in me and it took every ounce of my resolve to not scream. That fucker. I bet he did this. I know him. He lives to frustrate me, to make me think I'm crazy and incapable. This is just the kind of thing he'd do. I put my elbows on the counter and cradled my head. All the emotions of the last twenty-four hours flooded my body and the urge to cry took me over. This note also meant he came into the house again uninvited.

I couldn't say I was upset, but here I was crying. Not even understanding myself, I filled a glass of water and grabbed a slice of watermelon. I planted my butt on the swivel deck chair and pulled out my phone to text Allen and Kyle.

Me: Having bad things happen. I think it's Mark.

Kyle: what happened?

Allen: you ok baby girl?

Me: my mower is dead and the tire on my car is flat. And I'm crying eating a piece of watermelon on my deck.

Kyle: Fuck. That bastard.

Allen: Geez. Baby girl I'm so sorry. He's not there now is he?

Me: no I'm alone. But he dropped a note off for the boys so he was here. It was on the counter so I'm betting he came in without permission again. Doubt the boys would save a note. They are going fishing later.

Kyle: I'll mow for you. I was planning to do ours anyway.

Me: Mandy won't like that. But thank you.

Kyle: idgaf

Allen: I can come change your flat to your spare. Are your boys home to help?

Me: Yes. Both are in their rooms. I'll ask them once I stop crying.

Allen: I'll be there in fifteen minutes.

#

Watching Allen working with Alex and Jasper was actually fun, to observe him teaching them was a special treat. He's such a good man and father figure. It's so good for them to see this example of a man as young men themselves. Not that I expect a man to take care of me, I'm not a fucking diva, but it's nice to be taken care of at the same time. Mark would have either tried to get out of dealing with my tire or made me feel guilty for his taking his time to do it for me. And if he had done it, he'd have reminded me several times for more validation of 'his efforts'. It was amazing to have both Kyle and Allen insist on helping me, without the constant fishing for strokes to ego afterward. My years with Mark still left a stain, though, and guilt crept in on the edges even while I struggled to keep it at bay. I feared his influence wouldn't ever fully leave me, but I was accepting help, and feeling wonderful because of it. And that was a start.

In no time they had it swapped out and the boys were heading out with my car and flat tire to see if was repairable.

"How did you get my boys to offer up their services to bring my car in?" I asked, flabbergasted. This was no small feat. My boys were helpful, but this was above and beyond.

"I just talked with them about caring for you. Helping take care of you. And they were more than willing."

I blinked several times. "Wow. They really are growing up." And not taking after Mark, thankfully.

"Yup, they have a good mama." Allen pulled me into a hug and kissed the top of my head.

It wasn't wasted on me that we were in the driveway as he did this. He never shied away from public affection, which was shocking, considering Miranda.

He smiled down at me. "I guess I'm showing the neighbors more than I should, huh? Just can't resist holding you." He kissed me again. "You are irresistible."

The drone of a riding lawn mower grew louder as Kyle came near. He saluted us before turning the mower back in the other direction. He was shirtless and gorgeous. Such a succulent body he had on him. My hormones jolted. I wanted to fuck.

I was just about to pull Allen inside for a quickie when he got a text.

After reading it, he said, "It's Miranda. I gotta go, baby girl. I'm sorry."

Phooey.

"It's okay. But thank you so much for coming to my rescue. It's really a turn-on, if I'm being honest."

His grin enlarged. "I like the sound of that."

I'd heard on a sexuality podcast recently that everything not sex in a relationship was actually foreplay. They weren't wrong.

I watched Kyle for a moment, admiring his body as he rode the mower. Just for a split second, I pretended we were married. Dangerous territory, but him on the mower, me on the porch was like real, just for a speck of time, and I loved it. I yearned to dwell in that moment for a lifetime instead. Would we still be a threesome relationship if Kyle and I were married? I loved to think so. The whole idea was a dream.

I glanced across the street and noticed my neighbor, Melissa, staring at my house. She probably was wondering why I was lounging on my porch while Kyle was mowing my lawn. It wouldn't have been weird if a teen neighbor boy was mowing my lawn, but a grown man probably raised suspicions in her. I could hear the neighborhood rumor mill creaking. Soon someone would be saying Kyle and I were having an affair. I smiled, hoping the rumor took off. I didn't mind one bit if it did. But it might cause problems for Kyle, and I didn't want that. We both know he's stuck in a marriage he'd love to flee from, but that's just not in the cards. He's a solid man who honors his commitments. What a sad reduction of a marriage that started out on love, but true, nonetheless.

Kyle had opened up to me the other night and I was still a bit shocked that he and Mandy only had sex like four times a year. Four? Oh my God. That's literally insane. At that point, why even bother? And he'd said he was always the one initiating. How could a woman only want sex four times a year? This was unfathomable to me, considering I'd be interested in fucking four times a day on some days. Did the woman at least masturbate? She seemed like the type who wouldn't dare masturbate because she'd think it was taboo. She was all about putting on a show for others. Kyle had confided that he got tired of being turned down, so he stopped initiating, so that lead to sex so infrequently for them. She hadn't stepped up initiating herself, so their marriage was about as sexless as a screen porch was warm in Minnesota, only a small portion of the year.

I watched as Melissa still kept glancing my way as she was pulling weeds. Her husband was pretty fucking hot, and she was a rather large woman. Not that it mattered, but they were not what I'd call a match. She was nice enough, but a bit haughty. She'd be one to start a rumor too, so I braced for more dislikes in the neighborhood. The big neighborhood BBQ was happening tomorrow at the Melak's and I'd know by the disdainful glances at the party if my name was being further dragged through the mud. My Daddies had spread the word that I was giving head to all takers on the sly at the event. My jaw wasn't as ready as my libido was, but I was both scared and turned on by the idea of sucking cock in semipublic. The thrill of getting caught was a delicious fact and highly possible.

I waved at Kyle and then went inside.

Chapter 15

Alex and Jasper walked in the house with huge grins. They had takeout bags in their hands.

"We made dinner," Alex said with a proud expression while holding up a bag.

I clapped my hands. "Seriously? You guys take care of my tire and buy dinner? You are the best sons in the world!"

"Jasper's idea," Alex said with a raise of his eyebrow. "I'm not that good."

"Thought you needed a cheering up, Mom." Jasper handed me my car keys. "It was a nail in your tire that did it."

"Really? I wonder where I ran over a nail?"

"Could be anywhere really," Alex stated as he untied the food bag. He pulled out the cartons. "We just ordered a bunch of different things and thought we'd just share them all."

"That's perfect." I was honestly thankful it wasn't another sabotage, but a legit organic issue instead.

"Did either of you forget to turn the key off on the mower? It was dead."

Alex shook his head, which made his thick hair flop. "I know for a fact I turned it off last time."

"Huh, weird." I tried to stave off suspicions of foul play, but I wasn't doing as good of a job as I had thought because I was suddenly worried. What if it had been Mark, after all?

"See any kids playing around it? You know how kids like to sit on mowers. Maybe it was Max or Devon from next door messing around." Jasper pulled out three plates.

"Could be. But I've never seen them come in our garage." I shrugged. "It's clearly possible though. When you two were young you'd sit on it and mess with it."

Alex cracked up. "Dad would get so mad. Jasper, remember that one time when you dared me to turn it on, then I did. Dad was so pissed!"

They both laughed. I joined in. He always overreacted about things the kids had done. Not unlike how he is now to this day.

"What time are you guys going fishing?"

They both looked at me abruptly.

"Fishing?" Alex asked with a confused look.

"Yeah, fishing." I reached for the note and held it up.

"Mom, we don't have plans to go fishing with Dad today."

A chill crept up my spine and left an unsettled feeling along my torso. "You don't?" It somehow didn't register, even though he'd said it plain as day.

"No. We don't."

"Is this an old note then?" I examined it and realized it didn't really look like Mark's handwriting either. Panic began to rise in me, but I'd tried like hell to remain calm.

"I don't know. I've never seen that note before." Jasper took it from me and looked at it. "Want me to take it to the police for fingerprints?" he asked with a joking look on his face.

"Yes!" I laughed at him, but I wasn't really kidding. Who would do this? Was Mark playing games? Had he put the nail in my tire and turned on the key to the mower? But if he left this note, then I would suspect him, so that didn't make sense either. And, if it wasn't him, who would be weird enough to do this? To come into my house and place a fake note on my counter was definitely an odd thing to do. I mean, obviously, I'd find out it was fake.

"Someone broke in and gave you a fake note. That's just freaky." Alex scooped a monster mountain of rice on his plate. "Anything taken?" he asked nonchalantly.

A desperation rose in me. "I don't know. Not that I've seen." I wasn't sure what bothered me more, wondering if it was Mark messing with me or someone else. And why would they? Mandy? Miranda? Mark certainly had his moments where he had tried to make me think I was crazy, and he'd even say I was, but this was a series of odd events, all on the same day, and it made me very nervous. Maybe a neighbor knew what I'd done at the barn dance and she was getting back at me. Maybe it was Mark, and he was just up to his usual hijinks, especially with all the damage to my flowers and the hostas.

I scooped food on my plate, but the worry had taken my appetite. I kept going, though, because I wanted to share a meal at the table with my boys. This time was fleeting, what with the end of high school approaching for both of them. I'd often loved having them only a year apart. The phases they went through over the years had been similar as a result, so they both were often into the same toys, shows, and fun, so as a result they became such good friends. But now it felt scary to know that soon, both would be off at college and I'd be alone. It wasn't that I minded being alone, I just loved having them around. I was going to miss them terribly. Motherhood was definitely bittersweet. I loved watching them grow and soar, but I missed all the stages we'd gone through together. They were gone and I'd never get them back.

"You two are the best, you know that?" I let too much emotion flavor my words.

"Ah, you're the best mom," Jasper said jovially as he made a sappy face.

His joking helped lighten the mood and we sat down to a nice dinner I hadn't had to prepare. It was pampered me day and I was loving it.

I grinned big at my boys. "And it isn't even Mother's Day."

"Every day is Mother's Day," Alex said in an ultra sappy voice.

The food was good, the company was better, but my heart was at a level of serious unease. I couldn't shake the strange events of the day. And they weren't just strange, they were possibly malicious. Yet they seemed innocent and possible. It was a very calculated set of moves by someone, or pure coincidence. The previous had Mark written all over it.

#

In the morning I woke with a clit boner. I'd learned this was a thing. It wasn't just men who woke with boners. I peed, then grabbed my favorite clit sucker and popped it on my clit. I chose a threesome porn video online and came in less than two minutes. Refreshed and exhilarated, I got up and strolled to the shower. I flipped it on to warm it up as I washed my sucker toy. The big orgasm had left a smile lingering on my face. I had loved the porn video. That was on the list to try with Allen and Kyle. They absolutely loved it when I found a new thing from porn that I wanted to try. With two dicks and four hands they pleasured me to the brink of heaven on a routine basis.

I hummed as I slipped into the shower. The day ahead was full of possibilities. It was the day of the BBQ. The day I'd give more head than I ever had across my entire life. I wasn't really good at giving head, but messing around with Allen and Kyle, while they held no specific expectations, had really allowed me to expand and try new things. I'd never be one of those women who gagged on purpose and found it hot, but I had learned to enjoy it more. I'd either hate giving head or love it more by the end of the day, that was for sure.

I was so curious how they planned to accomplish this at a public neighborhood party. It wasn't at either of their houses. If it were, that would be easy. I'd have likely been planted on my knees in a bedroom for the duration and shrouded by the protection of four walls. But this was not going to be a simple thing to hide. And as far as free for all, would they have already asked men? Or would they ask them at the party? And how did they know which men to ask and which would be utterly offended? Was this like some kind of secret male talking or code? Did all men think getting head was okay? It wasn't like sticking cock in a pussy or ass. It was my oral orifice, but it wasn't like actual sex. At least not how I defined intercourse sex anyway. This was more like ... foreplay sex. Maybe that's stupid, but whatever. I'm pretty new to all this shit.

My mind spun further as I scrubbed my hair. The scent of the shampoo was lovely. I couldn't quite place the scent, but it was very pleasant and soothing. The water was hot and surely making my skin beet red. What if someday we did a different event like role play prostitute? I laughed, wondering what they'd offer, because money seemed too risky. Mowing my lawn? Wow! That would surely start a rumor mill if many men took turns mowing my lawn. I laughed out loud and it echoed in the shower stall. Maybe handyman work? The thought of me owing them sex for them doing something for me or me owing them for work around my house was definitely on the fantasy list. Something to talk about with Allen and Kyle. They loved dreaming up these scenarios for me and directing them. I delighted in being their sexual muse.

I dried off as I pondered my outfit for the BBQ. I definitely wanted cleavage showing. The men looking down at my exposed cleavage was a very arousing idea and I wanted to take full advantage. I couldn't wait to see if I'd be able to pop out a tit to show them a nipple. I hoped one of my Daddies would suggest a sex toy in me and control it. I had loved that last time at the gangbang. I squealed and did a jump. It was like sexual Christmas day.

I snagged my tube top, my new white one. I liked how my hard nipples easily poked out the fabric and, being white, the wrinkles and bumps of my hard nips beneath were even more obvious. I wished I could have it be wet as I sucked their cocks. Instead of a wet t-shirt, I'd have a wet white tube top. Why hadn't someone made a thin t-shirt tube top? That sounds like a very sexy idea. Wet tube top contests, now there's an idea!

I slipped it on over my head and selected my black shorts leggings. I gave myself a once-over in the mirror. I felt sexy. I couldn't wait for the day to progress. I had pondered bringing knee pads, maybe then switching to a dress. I'd decide on an outfit at the last minute before I flew out the door, no doubt. The men would surely get a kick out of knee pads, but I wasn't sure how I'd smuggle them into the party unnoticed, or how I'd remove them quickly enough if someone were to catch us mid-bj. I didn't want that to be a giveaway. I snickered, thinking how funny that would be to be caught with knee pads on at a neighborhood party. What a naughty, delicious string of thoughts! I was so turned on that I wanted to grab my clit sucker and make myself come again, but I also wanted to be hungry for big O's so I'd come while I gave head today. I scurried downstairs to grab breakfast so I wouldn't be tempted to fuck myself again. I needed a distraction.

I popped a cup in my coffee maker and hit brew. The scent of the dark coffee grounds filled the air. I enjoyed the aroma. Such simple joys as an orgasm and a coffee in the morning always made the entrance into the day easier. It was going to be a very good and interesting day indeed.

Chapter 16

I arrived a bit late, but Allen and Kyle had instructed me to make a later appearance. They had said it would be easier to hide our shenanigans when a larger crowd was present. All my neighbors were there, for the most part. A few of them glanced my way as I approached with my crockpot of meatballs. Only two had a nasty scowl, the rest were friendly enough. Their judgment of me would be vehement if they knew about the planned sexual escapade, but I was of a different opinion. Sex was about sex and pleasure, and nothing else, unless the parties involved wanted more. I could separate the two, which many people could not. I saw sexual pleasure as no different than enjoying a chat with someone, if mutual. We each took our bodily pleasure from the interaction, then moved on. Jealousy wasn't a part of it either. The focus was my pleasure, which my Daddies took their pleasure from. And they not only rewarded me for doing what I wanted, but also for what they wanted. All was negotiated and agreed upon.

It was bliss. It was heaven. It was what I wanted.

I loved them being in charge of my sexual self. I thrived on it. I got off on them wanting to get me off, and they got off on it all. We had become symbiotic, both feeding off of each other and feeding each other mutually. They may have held the power, but I gave them the power and dictated what would happen. And, in turn, they never pressed me past my stated boundaries. There was constant discussion and debriefing. There was never overstepping boundaries or assumptions because we had talked about it all up front. Consent was fluid and ever-changing and no one took the stance that consent was assumed either. It had to be in the moment, could be revoked at any time, without any explanation needed. We'd talk about it later. We all knew where each other stood on everything.

People were smiling, talking, eating, and looking around at each other. It was a pleasant enough looking party. I was not a snake in the grass, I was there to give and receive pleasure, which was mutually desired. There were no obligations. It was just oral sex and nothing more. I never believed one partner should limit another, and that's what was wrong with most of the marriages; they exerted themselves on each other rather than accepting each other. No one was truly happy, not many. Miranda and Allen were one couple who seemed to have figured that out. They made room for each other, allowing, and even celebrating, their differences. I admired them for accepting and still loving each other. In that kind of situation, love can flourish rather than die or get choked into a sexless roommate marriage. The majority of marriages ended in divorce, and I believed this was why.

Religion and culture had a way of killing the long-term relationships that they fought so hard for. It was actually massively fucked up when I stood back and evaluated it all.

To me, sexual pleasure was no different than enjoying a strawberry. What was different, and sacred, was the intimacy with sex. That I had with my Daddies. And I couldn't have had it with anyone other than them. Sex with them had all the pleasure, and so much more. It left the other acts lesser, but still highly enjoyable, and honestly their presence during the acts brought the intimacy for me. It was about my pleasure. They wanted me satisfied, satiated, and turned on because it benefited them, then me back in return.

Several people were tipping back beers, and many women had the low-cal seltzers, which were all the rage these days. Counting calories while drinking was tricky.

Miranda was biting into a brat when I first saw her. She was so sexy, in such an easy way. She never had to try. She was just naturally sexy. I found myself fantasizing about her joining Allen and Kyle. I really needed to work on her. Maybe she needed my permission to feel comfortable joining us. Or maybe she wasn't into women, which was fine, but I'd still love to watch Allen fuck her. That would be a massive turn-on. I'd love to fuck Kyle in the same bed where Allen was fucking her.

"Whew!" I muttered under my breath. It was hot out and I was getting hotter. I smiled. A foursome on the bed was great fodder for getting me aroused to suck lots of cock under the sunshine.

I desired to be desired. It was almost a kink with me, which really was at the heart of my enjoyment of being used. That was what today's event was exploring for me. It wasn't that I absolutely loved sucking cock, I was getting closer to that, but it was more about the joy I gave them. It was about the control I had in giving them pleasure. I was in the driver's seat, and if they took the reins, it was because I decided to give it to them. I'd learned my sexuality was mine. I owned it, and it was mine to give away how, when, and if, I desired. It wasn't Mark's, which he tried to exert on me. It wasn't about ownership in that way, not the way I viewed relationships, not the way I viewed life. I shared what I wanted with whom I wanted. I was in charge of me.

I spotted Allen and Kyle talking to Mike. I knew he'd be in the blow job lineup. He was a delicious man, well, they all were. Another thing I'd noticed about the evolution of myself, I really celebrated men for their sexuality without judgment. They let me into their inner chasm of sexuality a bit when we interacted, as I gifted them entrance to mine. I was less judgmental now than ever before in my life. This made me immensely happy and free to be me as well.

My life had made me who I was, all the sexual influences, the cultural, the religious, and I had been learning to use all that rather than be scared of it. I wasn't trapped by it, or tortured by it, I was liberated. I was like Pavlov's dog. I couldn't unlearn some things that were so primally ingrained in my brain. Reflecting on my life, as a young person, I had been a sponge. I soaked up the bad along with the good, the intentional, and the unintentional. I took it all in. My experiences molded my sexuality without me even realizing it. I couldn't make those old pathways disappear, but I could use them how I wanted.

I meandered over to the three of them with a saucy look on my face.

Their eyes all flared with a passionate appreciation and excitement, which fed my lust and arousal. Lust wasn't bad, as long as it was consensual.

"Hi," I said with a little knowing smile.

"Hi, baby girl," Allen said, giving me a side hug.

"Hi, sweetheart. How are you feeling before we start this train?"

I released a big sigh quickly. "I'm ready."

Mike looked like he was ready to enjoy the biggest donut of his life. And I took pleasure in the anticipation of being that donut for him.

"Hello, Alexa. You are looking ravishingly beautiful today."

I'd take all their compliments, I'd been starved of them, so they were water to my deeply dehydrated affirmations. Not that I needed them to feel good, but feeling sexy was a thing a girl wanted to hear. It made the sex hotter.

"Hello, Mike. Nice to see you." I glanced down and he already had an erection. He followed my gaze and nodded.

"I'm number two."

A confused expression consumed my face. "Number two?"

"Okay, so baby girl, this is how it's going to work." Allen took a swig of his beer.

I was excited to get the pre-scene set up. I'd been dying to know exactly how they were going to pull this off. I needed details.

Allen glanced around, then spoke. "Every man has a number. When they get texted their number, they will come to you. They all know you may stop at any point, and they will just be out of luck, so you do you, babe. No obligations here with this. It's meant to fulfill your fantasy and your fantasy alone. When you are done, you are done. You decide, as always." He widened his eyes at me and went silent. After a few seconds he asked, "Do you agree? I need your full agreement on that before we continue. This is your show and your show alone."

A slow smile spread across my face. This was something I was fully beginning to understand and internalize. My sexuality was my own and I did get to decide. There were no obligations, and I was truly free to begin and stop at my own whims. It was thoroughly freeing and liberating. It made me more turned on than ever before to suck cock.

"I understand and agree." My nipples were hardening, and my clit was responding as this discussion of consent was sexy.

"Good," Kyle piped in. "And Mike has agreed to help this happen. He's going to be an extra lookout for us to make sure no one strolls in on you unexpectedly. So, Allen and I will be watching you too. I'm going to be watching only you, though. Allen will be oscillating his gaze between you and the surrounding area."

I nodded as I smiled at Mike. He smiled back even bigger. "I got you, Alexa."

I couldn't keep my eyes from drifting down to the erection pushing out his pants. I'd never wanted a cock in my mouth more, other than Kyle's or Allen's.

There was something sexy about him helping me achieve this fantasy. I guess it was because he was acting like Allen and Kyle, and that was very yummy to me.

I shifted my thighs. My pussy lips were wet. This was all still a bit of a surprise to me. I never thought I'd put this sexual act on my list, but I was surprising even my own self these days. Sexuality was meant to be adventurous, not stagnant, repetitive, and dull. Well, maybe nothing was meant to be that. I laughed inside as I observed Kyle and Allen nonverbally communicating with their eyes.

Allen took a deep breath. "Okay. Baby girl. We've got twelve men, which is more than you expected. Is this number too overwhelming?"

I took a step back as I gasped, my hand flew to my throat. "Twelve?" I croaked out. "Oh, my Gawd," I drawled. I silently mouthed the word 'twelve'.

All three men chuckled.

"That's a lot of cock!" I glanced around, realizing I said that a bit too loud. Before anyone could say a thing, I declared, "Well, I guess I'm going to be busy."

Both Allen's and Kyle's faces shone proudly. Not that I thought they'd have been disappointed in me if I'd said that was too many. We were beyond that. Instead, they were just awed, amazed, and delighted by me. I was the caster, star, and director of my own destiny. I was the boss.

"Excellent," Allen said with pleasure.

"That's my girl," Kyle replied with a quick narrowing of his eyes and a raise of his left eyebrow. "Let's get started." He paused. "But do you need a drink or snack before you eat?" His smile was full of jovial humility and teasing.

I grinned, appreciating his jab at what I was about to do. "Oh, I had a snack and two glasses of wine this afternoon. I'm sufficiently stuffed and lubed for the moment. I may need refreshment during. Bring a bottle of water." I hadn't thought about how long this would take until now. Could I really handle that many cocks visiting my mouth in a short time? I was both terrified and electrified at the thought. The cultural taboo nature of what we were about to do was intoxicating all by itself. My heart beat faster than I could breathe. My body felt alive and, at the same time, I had the desire to rush into this and flee. I wasn't changing my mind, but this was like committing to a marathon of sorts when my training hadn't even come close to the destination planned.

I puffed up my chest, extended my chin, and said, "Show me to the garden of cocks."

All three men busted a gut as I followed them toward the patch of hedges on the edge of the property.

Chapter 17

Full of freaked anticipation, I followed them to the shelter of hedges. The house owners had likely imagined they had made a little garden maze to frolic in. But to me, this was a natural house of cock worship. I'd instructed Allen and Kyle that there would be no face fucking. I'd save that for trying with them someday, if I decided that was somewhere I wanted to go. This time, I'd be fully in charge. They could touch my head and do a tiny bit of thrusting, but I wasn't going for full thrusts, nor for them jackhammering my throat. I knew I'd do some gagging, because that was my natural inclination, I couldn't not at times, but mostly I'd be mouth massaging cockheads and my hands would be masters of their shafts.

I couldn't calm my nerves. I wanted to scream and shout and run away, well not really, but part of me was scared. I had to admit that to myself. I comforted myself that these feelings weren't that odd about something I'd never attempted before.

The hedges were thick and well taken care of, so there weren't large gaping holes on the sides of the big bushes. Instead, they were confluent and plush. There was a patch of multicolored lilies between the far hedges, and hydrangeas and rose bushes populated the space between the other hedges along the backside. Beyond the garden were fields of corn, their tall stalks swayed in the slight breeze. Their tick-tocking back and forth was hypnotic.

The aroma of flowers was thick, and it made for a lovely feeling washing over me. This was primal and natural, and being outdoors for it added to the sensuality of what I was about to attempt. No one could have prepared me for this, not even the many fantasies I'd had deep in my bed with five sex toys and floral lube at the ready at my side. This was likely to blow my mind.

"This is so raunchy, and I love it," I said in a breathy, sensual voice.

"It is very raunchy, baby girl." Allen held my shoulders. "You know the signals. I know I'm being annoying, and you know all this, but this checklist is for me too."

I nodded. "Yes, Daddy. I get it." It might be ritualistic of him to dictate to me, but I appreciated it, even if it did annoy a part of me. We'd talked about this almost ad nauseam. But I also understood that they felt in charge of this and they had to make sure I was as safe as possible. They didn't want me traumatized in any way. It was a real concern of theirs, and I felt their love because of it. They'd managed to make me feel more special than any other human on the planet.

Kyle spun me around and hugged me. "You. You be careful out there on this wagon."

I laughed. "It's like you are sending me on a journey no one has gone on before. Uncharted territory into space!"

He joined in my humor as he chuckled. "Well, it is for you, and for us. And for all these men."

'All these men' rung in my ears on repeat like an echo. 'Twelve' chimed in several times next.

Jordan, from down the street, appeared from behind the hedge near the bench. I imagined at some point I'd have a man sit on that bench as I sucked his cock. I wanted to christen every inch of this garden. I imagined a plane flying overhead and the thought thrilled me. They'd likely hover and be shocked, curious, maybe even turned on. I liked imagining it that way anyhow.

Jordan was a neighbor who was rather shy. He was of average height and looks, nice and polite. The fire and passion in his eyes was a surprise though. I'd never seen him so energetic.

"Alexa," he said with very obvious desire.

Seeing him this way excited me. I immediately loved this expression on his face and wanted to intensify it.

Kyle's face took on a serious tone as he prepped me with his instructions. "Alexa, Jordan wanted me to express his thanks to you and convey his appreciation. He hasn't ever had his cock sucked by his wife. This will be his first time. He didn't want you to expect too much out of him."

I cocked my head at him with a smile. A virgin blow job at his age? That's a damn shame. "That's okay, baby love. You do what feels natural and you will be just fine."

His face reddened, and a sheepish guilty thought clearly took over his brain.

"Now, none of that. If you come in three seconds, so be it. It will be my honor to be your first, regardless."

He walked towards me and his face thankfully turned back to its previously aroused state. This was much more of a turn-on.

"Come," I instructed. My heart beat so hard and I was panting so much that I could barely talk. I played with the hem of my dress. Allen had instructed me to wear a sundress, so I'd changed out of the tube top a minute before I left the house. He'd been right, of course. I loved the feel of the breeze up my dress.

When Jordan reached me, I touched his face, then dragged my hand down his body and pressed my fingers against his erection beneath his beige Bermuda shorts. The pleasure on his face was something I'd never seen there before. It was a thing of beauty.

Kneeling on the plush grass, my dress draping my thighs, I suddenly wished I could be naked to do this. However, that was too risky at a party. But then, if someone walked in on a blow job, that was already shocking enough, so what harm would being naked add?

I rocked back on my heels and yanked my dress off quickly over my head. I was braless and commando underneath, so I was fully nude in mere seconds. All my indecision about what to wear suddenly didn't matter now that I was bare naked.

All the men groaned out.

Jordan exclaimed, "Holy fuck!"

I smiled as the true goddess I was and massaged my breasts and hard nipples.

I could have burst into the sky for how powerful I felt as I leaned into his groin. I kissed the bulge in his shorts and gripped his hips as I mouthed his cock through the fabric. I pressed my teeth gently into his boner.

"Oh, dear God," he muttered, his breathing rate increasing rapidly.

I snagged his zipper with my teeth and pulled it down with the help of my hands holding the fabric taut.

His hands shook as he slowly moved them to hold the sides of my head. His breathing became faster yet and was steadily increasing. He was going to climax fast. The look in his eyes was almost pleading. In many ways, he was so eager it was sweet, and most definitely a turn-on.

He pulled my hair into a ponytail and held it, which I always appreciated and found hot.

I licked his frenulum and he gasped, his body startling at the light touch of my tongue.

"Oh, fuck me," he whispered with so much appreciation that I figured his blow job alone would satisfy me, and I had eleven more to go, and that didn't even include if I blew Allen and Kyle after the gangbang blow job event was over.

I was not an expert at this, like at all. But after today, I wondered if I'd at least be decent. Both Allen and Kyle told me such thoughts were stupid. That any straight or bisexual man would love a woman's mouth on his cock on any level. And 'a blow job couldn't be bad, no such thing'. Which I did understand, but l also knew from experience that cunnilingus could be very, very lacking when a lover was not into it. But likely cocks were different since they were just bigger and more accessible than a clit. A woman's clit is something to search for and work on. A cock was just in my face.

I consumed his cockhead in my mouth and sealed my lips around it. He gasped so loudly that I wondered if nearby people had heard him. I bobbed my head on him as I stroked his thick shaft with my hands. My clit did a twitch as he let out a low growl. His hips were doing tiny thrusts, which seemed out of his control and more a of reflex than anything intentional, which was also adorable.

I yearned to suck him dry and give him an experience he'd never forget.

Jordan gripped my hair tighter when I stroked his balls and, when I applied gentle pressure around his right ball, his body jerked, and he cried out.

He pulled his cock from my mouth, and I recoiled as his cum splattered across my face.

"Oh, fuck, Alexa, I'm sorry," he gasped out.

I wasn't sure if he was sorry about the cum on my face, or for coming so quickly, but either way, I took great satisfaction in having made him come.

"You did perfect, Jordan," I smiled up at him as he took a staggering step back.

The look of lament switched in a flash to bliss.

"There, that's the look I was going for," I said as I wiped his cum off my face and spread it down my right breast, ending with a pinch of my nipple.

He grinned appreciatively as I spread his spunk all across my nipple.

"I'm wearing everyone's cum to the party afterward." It was something I had thought long and hard about and I didn't care if someone smelled cum on me. I'd delight in it. No one would dare say a thing, but I had certain people I wanted to stand by to make them wonder. It was rather wicked of me, and I loved it. Twelve loads on my skin, maybe fourteen, and maybe we'd get another to make it a nice round fifteen.

I sat back on my heels and rocked as Allen ascended upon me. He handed me a vibe.

"Well done, baby girl. Now slip this inside you. Mike is up next."

Allen switched the vibe on and I moaned.

I nestled the stem of the toy along my clit and rose up on my knees as Mike approached.

"I've been watching your crotch, and your bulge hasn't gone down one bit. But I'm going to destroy it now," I said in a seductive voice. The power I'd have over him in a minute was intoxicating. I'd get to move him along, edge him, or decide to obliterate him.

He pressed his covered erection in my face. "Hungry?" he asked with a smirk.

"Tease me," I pleaded, "more."

He bumped my mouth with his erection and bounced off of it several times. My body jerked back each time he gently tapped my face with his covered dick. A few of the onlookers cackled, and I smiled at them. It turned me on to be their toy, but only because I'd decided it. I was in control. I loved letting him play with me.

He thrust his pelvis against my face several more times and Allen ramped the toy inside my pussy to full blast.

My lust raged and I grasped the waistband of his shorts and yanked them down. I had his boxer briefs to his knees in the next second. One of the men hooted softly as I attached myself to his cock like a mongoose. My hair flopped as I pumped my mouth on him. His hands flew to my ears, and he squeezed my head between his hands.

His grunts grew more frequent as I sucked, then I slipped off his cock and gazed up into his eyes. A one second edging was all I got. The want in his eyes was too delicious to not satisfy so I took his cock inside my mouth again and sucked as hard as I could. I pressed my fingers behind his balls, attempting to somehow activate his prostate gland. I cupped my hand around his ball sac as I stroked his shaft with my other.

The toy inside raged me up my orgasm hill and I teetered over the edge.

Kyle was to my left and he said, "Good girl, make him cum."

Him telling me was so hot that it launched me into my first orgasm of the blow job onslaught. My body curled around Mike's cock and my moans came out muffled around my stuffed mouth.

Mike lost it. His cock twitched and cum started to fill my mouth. He quickly yanked himself out of my orifice and spewed his ejaculate on my bare tits.

We were both panting heavily as we rode back down that climax hill.

Neither of us moved as our heightened bodies began to settle, until Allen intervened.

"Awesome, so happy you came, baby girl. Mike, good work." Allen patted Mike on the back.

He looked so satisfied it was another notch in my confidence to blow a man to coming. Perhaps I was being too hard on myself. Men came fast often after all anyway, so my Daddies were right. There was no such thing as a bad blow job, other than a nonexistent one, or a duty suck. Obligation wasn't hot unless money was involved.

I smiled up at Allen. "I want to stroke someone while I blow the next man. I want to service two cocks at once."

He beamed at me with a salacious smile. "That's my girl," he said with approval.

"Thank you, Alexa. That was the best head I've ever received," Mike told me.

Jordan still looked shocked, but very happy.

I widened my eyes at him but simply said, "I'm so thrilled you enjoyed it, Mike. I did as well."

He scoffed. "That will be spank bank material for me for life. And honestly, this location really ramped it all up." He glanced towards the bushes that camouflaged the party for us.

I had to agree. I bit my lip as he saluted me and then walked back to his lookout post.

My neighbor, three houses down on the left, Sean, appeared from behind a hedge next. I adored Sean, but I was a bit surprised he was partaking in my mouth. His wife was always bragging about their sex life, so I figured he didn't need the use of my mouth. But then, maybe she was lying. Or maybe she didn't suck cock either. What was with all these women who wouldn't suck cock? Unless it was because their husbands didn't eat pussy, then I'd totally understand. I'd withhold sucking cock myself in that case.

He grinned at me. "Surprised?" he asked.

"I could ask the same thing of you," I snickered as I rose up on my knees. I was thankful for the slow progression, so I had time to come down off of my last orgasm.

Sean had on a t-shirt that read 'F*ck off, Mitch'.

I laughed. "I love your shirt, Sean."

He chuckled. "I know, right? It's fucking hilarious."

"It really is." I didn't know who 'Mitch' was, but it was funny nonetheless. I sucked my lower lip into my mouth as I pushed my chest out. "You have a nice juicy cock for me to enjoy?"

"Oh, do I," he said as he patted the mound. "Nice and fat today."

"Awesome," I slurred as I shook my breasts for him.

"Oh, fuck yeah. Nice tits, by the way. You have the most perfect breasts. I always figured you did."

To be appreciated by so many men and told sexy compliments was such a gift. There had been times I hadn't felt sexy at all in my life, and them gifting me their true thoughts of me as sexy was oh so satisfying. To be desired was a kink of mine, and they were delivering on that so nicely today. Maybe Allen and Kyle had prepped them, but at this point, I didn't give a fuck. I was enjoying.

"I've always wanted to see your tits bare. You don't disappoint at all." He grinned deeply. "My cock just got even harder."

"Mmmm," I said as Allen moved the mode of the toy up higher from the low hum he'd set me on after I'd come the last time.

"I hear a hum. You got a toy in that pussy?"

I spread my legs and showed him the little pink tail of the toy pressed along my clit.

"Oh good, I always think a woman gives the best blow jobs with a toy up her cunt." He pushed his swim trunks down and his cock swung out. "I loved that little orange bikini you wore at the last pool party." He shifted his hips, which made his cock swing in my face. "Now I'll know what you look like underneath it."

"I will enjoy your leering looks next time around the pool." I leaned closer to him and clasped my hands around his cock. My mind swam with thoughts, wondering if he and his wife were swingers. I'd love a round with him and his wife, Jessica. She had nice tits too. I almost asked him, but I was overcome with the desire to have him inside me.

I shoved his cock in my mouth too hard and I gagged. My eyes watered and I shook my head, but looked directly into his eyes.

He had a slight chuckle residing in his gaze as I grabbed his ass and squeezed.

"Aw, fuck yeah," he said with a sigh. "Nice, Alexa. Real nice."

To my left, a cock appeared. I glanced up and saw it was Manny from down the street. Manny was an Asian man with a wide face and thick body. I grabbed his cock, which was slicked up and smelled of coconut oil. That, I knew, had to be Kyle's idea. He loved coconut oil, and it was something I could consume as well, so when it came to Manny's turn to be sucked, we'd be good to go.

"Don't make him come, baby girl, just edge him." Kyle gave my bottom a light tap and I groaned out.

Both of the men snickered. They liked Kyle bossing me. In truth, so did I. He was in charge of my sexuality because I'd given it to him, but they didn't likely know that.

I sucked cock while I stroked cock amidst hearing all the party guests chat, shout, hoot, and holler. The music blared as I rode both men to near climax.

Manny stepped back and, since my hand was now empty, I wrapped both of them around the cock in my mouth and I rode him hard. My hands slid over his firm flesh nicely from the coconut oil.

His grunts were low and guttural, burgeoning on primal, and I could tell he was fighting the urge to face fuck me. His body was twitching, but he didn't do it. He followed the preset rules and let me finish him off.

He grunted loudly, and said, "Fuck."

That was it.

He tore his cock my from mouth and I whimpered, which was odd of me. I should have expected he was about to come after his exclamation. His cum landed on my chin, my left breast, and the grass below.

"Whoa!" I spewed. "That's a lot!"

His face was spread in pure ecstasy. I was triumphant.

My knees were starting to hurt, so I sat on the ground as he zipped up his pants.

"Thank you kindly. You can suck my cock anytime you want, Alexa." His expression was gloating, but since I put the expression there with my sucking him off, it made him sexier.

"Jess won't mind?" I asked coyly, fishing for more info as I seductively squirmed on the ground beneath him.

"Nope, she and I swing. We do this kind of stuff all the time." He shrugged like it was no big deal. Which it wasn't.

"Oh, I wish I had known while I was blowing you, that would have been hot to know. We should all play sometime." The neighborhood sex secrets continued to surprise and delight me. I lived in the sexiest neighborhood around and, for years, I had no clue. "You should have brought her along to watch."

"True. I should have. But yeah. I'm definitely in to play with you guys sometime. I'll talk to Jess." He nodded and slipped away between the two biggest hedge shrubs.

"Ok, whose big beefy cock is next?" I was hot and ready for more.

I blew cock after cock until an idea occurred to me. What about blowing two men at once?

"Kyle, Allen ... Daddies," I said seductively, but with the full confidence of a woman empowered. "I want to have two at once. Can you text two numbers this next time?"

Chapter 18

I swayed to the music dreamily as I heard Mandy cackle loudly and then screech. I ducked, pretending the evil witch was about to descend on me when her voice hit a disturbing peak. She had such a shrill way of losing her shit and it came out of her mouth in such a cringy way.

"Damn, she sounds close." I loved the exhibitionism, but I really didn't want to be caught by Mandy, of all people.

Kyle laughed and nodded as he ticked his head to the right. He said in a hushed voice, "Yeah, I think she's very close. I keep hearing her voice too."

I was surprised at how calm Kyle looked. But I suspected he was starting to not care.

This was beyond risky, and it made my heart race. What we were doing was likely illegal and I could get arrested. Likely no one else, but I was the one naked in public. It's easy to slip a dick inside pants. Plus, they could claim they were taking a whiz. Me sans clothes alone would get me in deep hot water, let alone performing a sex act in public. I had no legit reason to be without clothes on. I rested my hands on my hips as I licked my lips.

I was hungry for more. "Is the next man here yet? And do they know I'm doing double? And that their cocks will touch?"

Allen piped in, "Yep. I texted a second number per your request so he should be here shortly. And I texted them all that information too. They are both in." His face showed he liked this very much.

I couldn't wait to see who the two men were. I danced about as the few remaining onlookers watched. I adored their eyes on my naked flesh. I was a goddess of sex, a breather of life into lust, a beacon for sexual expression and satiation for myself and for these men I was servicing. It rather felt more like I was servicing myself, though, because I was making all the choices and decisions. My Daddies were more the facilitators, and they might slip in a few commands, but their main role was as the protectors. I was the main director.

Allen ramped up the toy inside my pussy as my older neighbor from down the street, Henry, rounded a hedge. His gray hair was styled into a nice, sophisticated man 'do, like he'd been to a stylist this am. His eyes were bright and excited, and his cock was pushing out his trousers. It was delicious to think I'd have my mouth on his cockhead in mere seconds. This was a blessing in my eyes to be able to give, and he could receive.

"Henry, so nice to see you visiting my little garden of lust." I was instantly curious about all these men. Did they live deprived sex lives getting blamed for having a normal healthy sex drive, and mislabeled as sex addicts just for having a libido? Were they sex starved? Not all, clearly, but some of them most definitely were likely lacking at least on some level, or they wouldn't be here.

I simply couldn't resist. I reached out and touched Henry's hair because it looked soft and flowing. He snuggled against my touch as our eyes met.

The other man who was up for my mouth was Jason. He was a father of five kids. Their family was known as the religious fanatics of the hood. But, clearly, he was a bit malleable when it came to sex. If there's one thing I'd learned since I started swinging, it was I could just never tell what a person was in to, and my preconceived notions were not always right. I'd been surprised and wrong about many of the people I'd encountered, but they were also the least judgmental and most accepting people I'd ever met. Yet, the world judged them back at least quadruple as harshly. Through it all, I'd learned to not make assumptions.

"You are an angel," Henry said under his breath. "My cock hasn't felt the lick of a tongue in twenty-five years."

I widened my eyes at that. "Wow! Geez. I'm so sorry, Henry." I immediately wondered if his drought included penetrative sex too. It was a damn shame. He was a sexy man.

"Same," Jason said, a look of weariness left his face as I touched his cheek. Clearly, he'd had penis-in-vagina sex recently, his kids were the proof. Well, not necessarily, but several looked just like him, so it was a sure thing.

I fondled my breasts as their grins grew wider. "All I seek is gratification, for you, and for me. Just pleasure, plain and simple." The donations of my mouth I was offering were not only hot, but desperately needed.

With my skin already loaded with dried and multi-fragrant bathings of cum, I dropped to my knees. The mix of young and old definitely made this double blow job sexier. My mind reeled, assessing how I thought they might react to this. Some men would try and push their luck, as some penis owners do, but others were happy with what I was willing to give. Those were my favorite.

I massaged both their groins through their clothing. I'd learned how my clit swelled and, now that I'd learned that my own sexual organ also did what men's penises so obviously do, I could sense it, and even felt my clit swell and push a toy when I was near peaking. It was involuntary and delicious. Both Allen and Kyle had sat listening to me describe it under the moonlight in Allen's backyard the other night. We'd just finished fucking, Miranda's bedroom light had been on, and I had secretly hoped she had watched us, then gotten off herself.

"Oh my," Henry said with amusement as I rubbed my face around on his erection.

I did the same to Jason and he moaned out. Jason's expression was of pure want. No amusement graced his face.

"Do you come when you give a blow job?" Henry asked with concern in his voice.

I loved his touching words, hoping I'd get off too. I nodded as I spread my legs open. "Yeah, I do. Allen is zapping me."

Both men chuckled and I grinned with deep humility, my cheeks flushing slightly. I celebrated that I had no shame in showing them I liked to get off as much, or maybe even more, than they did. "He's gotten me pretty damn good today too."

"Oh, I'd love to see that," Henry said with deep desire. "Can I ask for her to climax?" His eyes were almost pleading with Allen. "It's important to me. I can't come if you aren't enjoying it too." He looked sheepish, but held eye contact with me.

"I love that Henry," I said, enjoying every little nuance of his expressions. I'd become convinced older men made the best lovers.

"You got it, my man. A man after my own heart," Allen said with a reassuring nod. Allen reached down and pulled the toy off my clit. He gave me several hard clit spanks as I moaned and writhed against his slaps. Allen knew this was a surefire way to propel me toward an orgasm. He chuckled. "I'll get her closer to climax for you."

Both of the men groaned appreciatively as I reacted to Allen's touch.

"Thank you, Daddy," I slurred out in a soft, mewling voice.

Allen replaced the toy nestled inside my cleft, securing it against my clit.

I turned my seductive gaze to the two men and lunged at them, making my tits swing as I flew toward them. They started to pull their pants down, but Kyle stopped them.

"Let her do it. She's in charge and it gets her hotter." Kyle's voice carried and a small sliver of worry grew in me. If we didn't keep it down, we'd surely get exposed. I'd have to move out of the neighborhood most likely in that case. I'd get stoned by the vanillas on my way out.

Both men froze their actions. They were in complete alignment with it all as I kissed both their cocks through their clothes once more. I grinned up at them and grabbed the waistline of both their pants. I slid their pants down in unison and their cocks swung out in tandem.

I squealed with delight and their faces showed how much they appreciated my adoration of their cocks.

I pulled them closer to each other and whispered, "I'm so excited you two are both down with this, I mean, your cocks touching and all. I think it's hot."

Henry's expression turned to absolute giddiness. "I'm just happy to get a female mouth on my cock. I'd do just about anything."

Jason was much more somber than the jovial Henry, but he nodded and muttered, "Same. Totally."

Their drought was something I understood. Not as a man with a dick, but that deprivation of sexual expression, both giving and receiving, that killed a marriage's potential. I felt for them, and I was savoring the idea of being the woman to bring them their long-awaited oral sex climaxes. It was a badge of honor I'd wear when their cum adorned my skin as well.

I gently joined their cock heads together and licked both heads. Their verbalizations were already delicious, and I hadn't even taken their heads in my mouth yet. I lavished my tongue all around both their cocks, tasting their salty precum and dragging it around their cockheads. I realized I was mixing their juices, but neither protested, so I kept going.

I stroked both their shafts as I attempted to get as much of both their tips in my mouth. It was an epic failure, but I grinned up at them regardless before trying again. They both had a hand on my head, playing with my hair.

I groaned as I played with their hard dicks. Allen's clit spankings had hurled me up the orgasm hill pretty far.

"Fuck," I whimpered as I licked each of their frenulums. I stroked their cocks hard as I opened my mouth and dabbed them all along, taking a turn to suck first Henry's head in full.

He yelped out so loudly as his hands pressed my skull. He thrust a tiny bit into me, and I held his ass cheeks firm.

"Fuck," he slurred with great effort.

I stroked Jason as I sucked Henry, then I switched. Jason's body jolted as I sucked him. I knew he was fighting off coming too soon.

I pressed their swollen heads together and licked and sucked their packed flesh. I released Jason to let him come down off the high a little bit. I didn't need to make his turn too short by pushing his limits. He needed the chance to savor.

So, I focused on getting Henry off first. I grunted as I took him in my mouth. I sucked him hard as I fondled his balls, slightly squeezed, then rode his shaft hard with the dollop of lube Allen had so generously squirted in my palm. The toy's vibrations on my G-spot and clit were maxed out. My orgasm was coming for me like a fighter jet on magic fuel.

"Good girl. Yup. That's it. Good Girl," Allen murmured, gently coaching behind me as my body lost control.

My orgasm consumed me. It was a big one—one of the biggest of the day so far. My body went rigid, and I almost lost my ability to keep Henry in my mouth as my body took over. My torso twisted in torsion as contractions reamed through my vagina and beyond.

Henry groaned out, "Oh, God. Yes!" He released my head and I fell off his cock. He lost his balance as he began to fall back, but Kyle caught him and pushed him forward so most of his cum streaked out across my face and chest.

He was panting and gasping. I was heaving as I crawled swiftly to Jason. I was shaky from coming, so he helped me get his cock in my mouth. The orgasm had made me weak and woozy. Staying upright was a struggle, but I garnered strength when I noticed Henry still had a raging boner.

I motioned him over. Ecstasy loomed. "Again," I said excitedly.

I either wanted them both to come in my mouth or on each other's cocks.

I sucked each meaty head, taking turns singly, then with both fat tips pressed to my loosening and tightening lips. My body was getting weary, but I wasn't done. Not by a long shot. The thought of both of them bursting their seed right into my mouth made my clit twitch with an electric jolt. My post-orgasmic, hypersensitive bean juggernauted me into another monster of a climax. I kept sucking through my peak, but Jason lost it, then Henry. It was almost perfectly simultaneous.

Jason yanked his ejaculating cock away from my mouth. He continued stroking his cock to milk out all his cum on my face and hair. Henry copied Jason.

I licked my face to taste their combined juices, just like a slut I'd seen recently on a porno. Not that giving head was slutty, but I was sucking on many cocks in one day, so I certainly fit the bill.

Jason heckled devilishly as he pressed his messy tip to my lips. It was so fun watching him unravel out of his stoic demeanor throughout all this. I licked him and reconsumed his cockhead because he was still hard. I kept sucking harder and his exclamations grew too loud, but I was too in the moment to care.

I reached under him and squeezed his balls, because he had clearly liked that earlier, and his cock jerked as he came again. This man was a coming machine! This time I reigned in the strength to keep myself on him and I swallowed his cum. It wasn't much, and I hadn't planned to do this, but here I was, taking it down my throat.

The sounds he made would have made me come while I masturbated. I'd be back to this memory to replay them in my head, no doubt. Today was another day of delectable memories to add to my spank bank.

I laid on the ground panting, listening to Jason's breathing begin to slow. Henry appeared to have recovered and was smiling so big it warmed my heart.

"Oh, fuck. I've never had that. Holy fucking shit, I … " Jason was at a loss for any more words, but the look on his face said it all. He was flabbergasted, but happy.

The whole BBQ blow job event had been raunchier and more dizzying, epically world spinning on steroids, than I had expected. A dream couldn't have been better, nor a fantasy. This was real and it was fucking sex magic.

I'd broken through so many previously held sexual barriers that I could feel the far-reaching impacts of all of this on my sexuality bleeding stealthily into my future. There was no telling where I'd go next on my opened-up sexual journey.

But I needed a break. Hormones had flooded my body and were taking their sweet time dancing around my insides. It was glorious, but I was exhausted.

"Water," I managed to say from my makeshift bed in the grass. My nipples were still hard, and my womanhood was both throbbing and tingling. Thankfully, Allen had put the toy on low.

Allen produced a water bottle for me. "Baby girl, how are you doing?"

I chugged half the bottle of water before I scooped the cum off my face and spread it down my tits. "I'm out of breath," I said through my panting. "I'm exhausted. But fucking unbelievably amazing!" I laid flat and my breasts spread apart. "But I'm not stopping."

"You are totally incredible. I knew you wanted to do this, but honestly, I'm floored. You are kicking ass at this, babe." He stroked my hair and looked down at me with love in his jovial gaze.

"I wasn't sure I could do this either, to be honest." I drank the second half of the bottle. "I know I came across confident, but I was actually rather terrified."

"Do you want to continue, or are you done?" His worried face took over and I wanted his in-charge Daddy Dom facial expression back. "You are in charge of this, and you owe no obligations."

"I know. But I'm good. And I'm finishing, even if the last man only gets a single lick, I'm finishing this cockstand line."

Drinking cum was something I'd never done until I'd started fucking Allen and Kyle. I wasn't ever much for it, but there was something exciting about making them burst inside my mouth that turned me on something fierce. I loved the tease of it, the dance of bringing them to the edge, then pushing them back, then full-on making them lose all control. They'd brought me to so many new places sexually that I'd be forever grateful, no matter how long we kept up this threesome. The thought of it ending sent a wave of panic through me. I quickly dismissed that horrible thought and smiled again.

Allen cackled an appreciative laugh. "You are a goddess, baby girl. A true goddess."

"What number are we on?"

"We have only two left. Then it's time to join the party." He released a sigh. "Miranda knows we are doing this, but she's getting impatient for me to join her."

I immediately wondered about Mandy. She was the more demanding of the two women. She must be hopping mad by now with Kyle not by her side.

"Okay, let's get them in my mouth and spurting then." With the finish line in sight, I had renewed energy. I scrambled to sit up and hopped on my knees.

"You are truly an inspiration, Alexa," Mike said with a nod from his post.

"She truly is that and more," Kyle said with a sweet, loving expression. More and more I felt Kyle and I drifting towards each other. It was a pipe dream to marry him. But it was my pipe dream. And I'd hold it hard to my heart no matter what.

"Bring them forth." I felt like a queen when I said it, as if I were summoning my subjects. Which, in some ways, they really were.

Next came Dan, and he came faster than a shot of Tequila is jarring without lemon and salt. The thought made me giggle.

Peter was the last of the cocks to cop a squat in my mouth. His dick was short and thick and a true challenge to suck. I just couldn't get his big black cock very far in, but that didn't stop me from making him make a cum bath of tits. I smeared his cum all over my dried sticky skin, realizing most women would have abhorred this experience, to be marked by so many men. In my past, I may have been the same, but now, and in my future, sex had become a realm of pleasure that I'd let nothing confine, unless it was truly something I didn't want. I was open. I was free. And no one could send me back to that worried, meek woman. I was roaring to the world my goddess-ness and those who I chose would get to see it, and live it, right alongside me.

Chapter 19

Wearing all the men's cum beneath my sundress, I was the last to saunter out of the garden. I was exhausted, and a bit sour that I didn't get to suck Allen and Kyle as a part of this whole experience, but I knew they'd be up for it later. I had to accept that they had obligations.

I caught Kyle's vision as he dutifully stood next to Mandy. She was gesturing and highly animated. Kyle shot me a goofy face, then pretended nonchalantly to strangle himself. Then he made a laughing face and I laughed outright.

"I couldn't have done it." Miranda handed me a cup of dark red punch. "This is spiked."

"Oh, thank you." I grinned at her. It was delicious that she knew I had done it, and she wasn't even mad.

"I bow down to you. I couldn't have taken that many. You are a fucking goddess."

Her eyes were wide, but her compliment was affirming. The woman didn't hate me after all. In fact, her words were scrumptiously validating, not that I needed that, but it was satisfying to hear, nonetheless.

I shook my head. "You never know what you can do until you try. I'd have said the same thing about myself before I actually did it. I'm not huge into blow jobs, but Kyle and Allen have changed my viewpoint on that quite a bit. And today, well, that changed my opinion altogether. I never fully appreciated the power that comes with a blow job. I pushed and pulled them from the edge so easily. I found a way to make blow jobs good for me. That made all the difference. Owning it, ya know?" I laughed. "Honestly, it was really quite fun."

"Allen told me it all. I hope you don't mind." Her sheepish grin didn't match the spark of intrigue in her eyes.

"Mind? Hell no, Miranda, I'd have loved it if you had watched."

Her face shifted from worry to an expression of enjoyment. "Really? Seriously?"

"Yeah, for sure." I downed the entire cup of punch. "I need more. I'm parched, and I'd love a nice buzz after all that cock in my mouth." I had said it under my breath, but my neighbor, Jack, seemed to have heard me, and a look of shock, followed by a smirk, drifted across his face. I wondered how many men my daddies had approached. I made a mental note to inform them about Jack's reaction. Maybe next time, Jack.

"You are a damn queen boss bitch." Miranda shook her head. "I just don't think I'd even want to try to do what you just did, though."

"I amaze myself these days. But I tell you what, I feel so free, so satiated, it's like a state of elation I've never experienced before in my life." It was time. I needed to go there with her. "You really should join us sometime, Miranda. I'd honestly love it." I hesitated, but then plunged in deeper. "I'd love to play with you myself. You are hot as fuck."

She took a step back as her face fluttered from confusion, to shock, to surprise as she stumbled backward further.

I reached for her. Grabbed her arm to steady her as her eyes met mine.

"Me?" The look of being absolutely flabbergasted flooded her face, and not only was it cute and sweet, but rather yummy. She looked so innocent, I just wanted to make her come, corrupt her little vanilla experiences, and immerse her into the world of sexual eroticism and pleasure. Every woman deserved to go there. I'd give anything to usher her into it, to pop that vanilla cherry of hers.

Did she not realize how sexy she was? That needed to change. And now. "You do get that, right? I mean, you are the hottest woman in our neighborhood." I snorted. "In town!"

Her look of deep confusion returned. I was confused too. I know how Allen is, and no doubt he's the same way with her as he is with me. He makes me feel sexy, special, and hot every single day. The same treatment, or more, must happen to her. How could it not?

"I don't know."

"Well, you are. And I'd enjoy it if you decided to join our fun sometime. I know Allen and Kyle would be into it too."

She shook her head and walked away.

Oops. I had gone too far. Well, fuck. I sauntered over to the punch bowl and refilled my cup. I had to try with her. If Allen hadn't succeeded in helping her open up sexually, I had to try. I didn't want to kill our budding friendship, but this was too important to not address. Miranda was not free to explore her sexuality, and it was clear she herself was the roadblock. It certainly was not Allen.

The sun was hot and the aroma of cum was thick on me. I wondered how many people were noticing, and that thought thrilled me. I filled up my plate with food as I smirked. Who knew sucking that many cocks would make me this famished? I found an unoccupied table and sat by myself. No sooner than I'd taken one bite of food and Miranda appeared and sat with me.

"I'm confused." Her face proved her words even further. She looked lost.

"Okay, then ask." I shoved a piece of cheese in my mouth and chewed it heartily. "Mmm. Damn, I was so hungry."

"You don't want them all to yourself?" Her innocence was fresh and sexy.

"Them? You mean Kyle and Allen?" I think I was beginning to understand the wall she was facing. "No, I'm not like that. I'd love to share. And, if I may be honest, I find you extremely attractive. Honey, you're hot as fuck." I shoved a carrot in my smiling mouth and finished chewing as I watched her face flit through a myriad of emotions. I'd never known I was a seductress until now. And this was fun.

Her expression turned sheepish again, but there was a flicker of interest. "I had no idea."

"Well, we've even talked about it, me and the guys. They'd love it, Miranda. I'm not sure if you have any curiosity about being with a woman, but I'd help you figure that all out, and with great pleasure." I smiled at her as kindly as I could. "See. I understand feeling limited. I'd have never said that several years ago. I didn't know how limited and trapped I was until now."

Her chest was rising and falling quickly, so I knew she was either anxious or getting turned on. "Trapped," she repeated.

I continued. "I've come to such an open place with my sexuality. And honestly, I got stuck in being mom mode for many years. It was like I had forgotten to be a woman. My full identity got usurped for a while. Then Mark didn't help that at all either."

At the mention of Mark, her eyes widened. She remained silent, but I saw a glimmer of a twinkle burgeon further in her eyes. This was working.

"You can just think about it for as long as you want. But know that we all want you to do it."

"You really smell like a cum factory." She wrinkled her nose, but then giggled. "I should have snuck over. I just felt I didn't belong, so I stayed away."

I guffawed. "Well, that's a true shame. If you had desired that, you should have asked." I deeply lamented her not speaking up. She needed help. Clearly, she was keeping her desires to herself. "It would have been extra hot if I had known you wanted to watch and then did. I have a feeling you aren't sharing what you truly want sexually with Allen, are you?"

She squirmed in her seat and dropped her head in her hands.

It hurt to watch her look uncomfortable, but it was clear she was hurting.

"No," she said in a voice so meek that it didn't even sound like her.

I reached out and wrapped my hand around her wrist and stroked her skin with my thumb. "It's okay. It can be hard to do. And we aren't cultured as women to feel comfortable speaking about our sexual desires. It's encouraged in men, but not us. I get it, honey. I've been where you are, and I can help you."

"I don't deserve your help." She was almost sobbing.

"Oh my God, Miranda. Please stop." What was this about? Deserve?

She sat up and pulled her arm from me. "I don't. I really don't."

"But what if I want to help you?"

She stood up and fled.

"Well, now I feel like a shithead," I muttered under my breath.

I searched for Allen to check if she was fleeing to him, but he was talking to several men, and she was nowhere to be seen.

Feeling defeated, I finished my plate and scanned the crowd for a friendly face to go chat with, but a buzz on my phone stopped me just as I was about to reach Laura, one of the few women in the neighborhood who didn't seem to hate me.

I drew my phone out of my handbag and read the text.

Miranda: Please come to my house. I need to tell you something and I can't do it at the party.

I waved at Allen, who was watching me. I pointed towards his house, and he nodded. I mouthed 'Miranda', and stole off across the backyards. My heart was pounding as my brain flipped through the possible things Miranda might tell me. I instantly hoped she wanted to try something sexual, but then I chastised myself. I couldn't think of sex when she was clearly distraught. It couldn't be about sex, this had to be something else entirely. All I knew was I wanted to help her feel better.

My heart still raced, though, as I recalled all the changes her face had gone through as we were talking. The demon that was terrorizing her was big.

I entered her house without knocking. It was cool and refreshing after being in the hot sun for so long.

"I'm in the kitchen," she called out.

I didn't see any kids, which was quite impressive considering their gaggle of boys.

She was at the table, with two glasses of dark red wine. One was in front of her, the other was in front of the empty chair next to her.

"Are you okay, honey?" Seeing her in pain hurt my heart.

She shook her head and looked again like she might burst into tears.

"Aw, I'm so sorry I've upset you." I instantly regretted all I'd said.

I sat next to her as she burst into tears and covered her face.

"Aw, sweetie," I said as I stood up and pulled her into my arms.

After one second, she pulled back. "I don't deserve your kindness. I had made you out to be a monster, and you aren't one." She sobbed heavily. "I'm a bad person." Her body shook as she cried and gasped.

I reached for her. "Let me help you feel better."

She jumped back from me like I'd tried to hurt her. I cringed.

"No." She scrubbed her eyes. "No, no, no." She shook her head several times, then hugged herself. "You will hate me, and you should."

Hmmm. This was so odd. I frowned. "Why would I hate you, Miranda? It's quite the opposite. I like you. A lot."

"No, you won't when I tell you."

Something wicked pierced my heart. "Whatever do you mean? Miranda, you can tell me anything. I'm the least judgmental person these days. I've shed that baggage of being judgy of others. I hate being judged, so I've positioned myself differently around that and I don't do it to others, or myself. Who am I to assume I know what another has gone through? And I can't begin to guess what you've gone through in your life."

"I'm the monster."

Her body bent over and her despair jackknifed my heart to the floor.

"Aw, honey, please talk to me. I hate that you are berating yourself so harshly here."

"I am an awful person. You have no idea. I'm a disgrace. An abomination." Her eyes were pleading and full of remorse. She cried and she belted out in desperation, "It was me. All those horrible things." She gasped between sobs. "It was me." Her words came out louder with each admission, and full of increasing exasperation. "It. Was. Me."

My mind scrambled to grasp what she was confessing to. I'd only seen kindness, generosity, and friendliness from this woman, and here she was acting like she'd hurt me.

"I'm so sorry. Truly I am. I think I went mad with jealousy." She kneeled in front of me and almost touched my knees, but pulled her hands back as if my skin were hot. "You are a good person. I should have never attacked you like that. It was immature of me. I didn't even recognize myself, but when I saw what you three had, I … " A look of scorn covered her pretty face. "And I'd never want to hurt you, honestly. I think I just went a little bit insane. I'll replace it all. I promise."

A horrible thought flickered into my brain. I didn't want to voice it, let alone think it, but I had to ask, even though I didn't want to know the truth. "You were the one wrecking stuff at my house, weren't you?"

She nodded, then cried even harder, collapsing to the floor in a heap.

I froze as it all hit me. The broken pots, the chopped lilies, my hostas, the crippling fear I felt that Mark had walked inside my house, invading my safe space. It had all been her! I shook my head in disbelief. This sweet, kind woman had terrorized me? It didn't make any sense at all.

"See. I'm horrible. I'm a horrible person. And I pretended to be your friend. And that makes me even worse." She gasped deeply as she struggled to speak. She shook her head aggressively. "Wait, that's not true. I am your friend. I like you, but I hated you. Will you ever forgive me? But I don't expect your forgiveness, I don't deserve it." She wept in her hands.

It was too hard to process it all and be the kind, understanding person she needed right now. I needed to move. I stood up and paced the floor. I'd never been so grateful for a glass of wine in my life. I stopped and took several sips. It was a juicy full wine with plum accents. I hung my head and then met her gaze. This was not Miranda. No way.

"This is a lot to take in, Miranda." I wanted to hate her, to blame her, and scream in her face, but I also saw a hurt human being, one I cared about as a friend, and had so often hoped for more than just friendship from her. It was my turn to take a leap. "But I'm going to try." In some ways, I saw myself in her, the me I was before I embarked on this healing journey.

"You can hit me, scream at me, call me names. I deserve it all. You should. And it might make me feel better if you get mad at me." Her face fell further, and her shoulders drooped.

I sighed deeply. "I'm not going to do any of those things, Miranda."

I continued to pace back and forth, stopping for sips of wine. After about ten minutes, I sat down. I patted her seat. "Sit. Tell me everything, and don't hold back. You can tell me it all."

She sat down carefully, as if she were trying to find a cool spot to sit on hot concrete.

"If you want to beat my butt with Allen's paddle, I'll let you. It might make us both feel better." Her face was one of someone who had lost her best friend.

I'd never thought such a thing, but I smiled. "I'm not really a dominant, but if you want that sometime, I'd flip into that role for you. But now is not the time for such a thing." I smirked. "And then you can call me 'mommy.'"

Thankfully, her face slipped into amusement as a small chuckle left her lips.

"Now that's better." I took her hands in both of mine. "Talk," I demanded.

Her eyes were full of fear before she spoke. "I guess it all started because I didn't want to stifle Allen. We get one life, and for me to tell him he can't have certain sexual experiences felt wrong. I didn't want to do certain things, but I didn't want to stop him from experiencing them." She shrugged. "He got pleasure from other people in other areas of his life, like having fun with the boys going to a baseball game. I didn't have any interest in going to a baseball game, but that didn't mean he couldn't enjoy that with other people. I began to see it was the same with sex. We were committed in our marriage, our family, so I was okay with him playing. It was like outside of us. My original opinions were that of our culture and constructs of interpretations of the Bible. But those are just opinions and interpretations, and I realized I could conclude my own." She paused and toyed with the napkin. I was happy she wasn't sobbing anymore. "I won't lie, though. At first, I was shocked. I worried he'd get bored with me and leave. But then when I realized he wasn't going to leave me, that he really loved me, I was okay with it. I mean, some of his fantasies turned me off and I didn't want to do them in real life. Like I'd never do certain things, like ever. But who was I to say he couldn't have them?"

"Yeah, that makes sense. It's like we are okay with our spouses doing things with others in different areas of our lives, but when it comes to sex, we get all weird about it. If two people are committed, it's actually intimacy-inducing because you care more about the person's pleasure and satisfaction than your own selfish needs and grasping at ownership."

"Right. Just because he and I are married, it doesn't mean we own each other's sexuality, basically. That was a hard lesson, but I finally got it."

"You're enlightened and it freed you. But, I get it. Yeah, our culture is weird." I cringed and shook it off. "I had it even worse with Mark. Like he'd get jealous if I even talked to another man. God forbid I was friends with one. It was just so bad. I felt so watched everywhere we went. He'd look at who I looked at, who I talked to, and I didn't even feel free to smile at another man without him getting suspicious about it. It was like I couldn't even respond like a normal social human anymore. It was also a total turnoff to me." I paused and screwed my face into a painful expression. "Then he would try to turn my friends and own sister against me. He'd use things I'd told him against me. I realized I had a choice. And I didn't have to stay with him and be miserable."

"He was trying to isolate you." An understanding flickered in her eyes.

"Yeah, I finally realized that." I sighed. "Thankfully, I had a few friends he didn't know about to bounce things off of to anchor me."

She nodded with an understanding look in her eyes. "That's paramount."

"It was. And it made all the difference in the world."

Her eyes clouded and she suddenly looked exhausted. "And the other thing is, I don't want another person to be responsible for taking care of." I wanted to wash the guilty look off her face.

I fluttered my eyes as I processed what she was saying. "But, Miranda, you have that the wrong way around. They will take care of you."

She gazed at me like what I said was a foreign language.

As she remained silent, I made the decision to press her. "As Daddy Doms, they would take care of you. Your pleasure would be the topmost important thing, and they'd want you satisfied. You wouldn't be the Dom. A Dom is the leader, but they only do what you give permission for."

She clearly didn't get what I was saying because she snorted and laughed. "Yeah, right. They would want everything their way, then I'd have more people to try and do for."

"It's not like that, Miranda. Not if you enter into this type of relationship."

"Even if you are right, Allen and I already have our relationship. We have all the history. We can redo it and somehow remake it. It is what it is. Yes, Allen has been a wonderful husband and very supportive, but it's different than with you. I can see it. He's different."

I touched her hand and caressed it. "I bet it doesn't have to be that way, Miranda. You guys could negotiate this. He might need your permission, is all. To hear what you want."

"Negotiate? Even that sounds like too much extra work. No thanks." She looked worn out.

"It's not. I promise. And it's just conversation, it's not doing anything but talking about it all. And the benefits you will reap, and Allen will reap, will be huge."

"I don't know. It sounds impossible. We are what we are, and I can't erase the past." She raised both hands as she said it.

"You wouldn't have to. You just make a new chapter."

She still held that skeptical look on her face. "They do what you want?"

I nodded. "And only what I want. We have boundaries. And, Miranda, even I don't want to do everything they want to do. We aren't carbon copies of each other, no two people on Earth are. But we respect our differences and don't confine each other to them. It's about being able to play in a world of freedom. Look, I knew from the beginning that you and Allen are committed to each other. That was a clear boundary, and I knew I wasn't going to try and take him from you and the boys. That was never my goal anyway. And well, he and Kyle came to me, but it was never a part of my plan to break up any marriages. He was happy. And I wasn't going to take that from him." I smiled and raised an eyebrow. "If he hadn't been happy with you, I may not have been so complacent to not try, but he was happy with you, that's obvious. And he made it clear that he wasn't leaving you, he was just playing."

She slowly nodded as what I said seemed to percolate to the understanding part of her brain. "So, what about Kyle then?"

I flushed. Kyle was a different story. But I was still not going to take him from Mandy. "Kyle is different. He's not happy. But also, he makes his own choices." I shrugged. "He's trapped, to be honest. He feels stuck and he's miserable. Even she's not happy. He hasn't brought up divorce, but he's talked with me about how he thinks they are too different and they'd both be happier separately."

"Wow. That's a hard pill to swallow. But I get it. Allen and I are committed, but we talk about everything, but I haven't told him what I just told you." She sighed. "I'm scared too, to be honest."

"Why? Miranda, you should. If he thinks you are resisting joining him in sexual exploration because you feel like you will have to take care of others, I predict he will dispel your fears and prove you wrong. Give him a chance. I predict he'd help you see you wouldn't have to feel like mama to anyone who didn't once live in your pussy." I smirked. "Unless you wanna role play step mommy or MILF or some other taboo shit."

Her face cracked from the misery that had been holding it stern, and blissfully, she smiled. Then she laughed. It was like sunshine. "Oh, that's rather funny." She chuckled heartily. "Though I think Allen wouldn't mind living in my pussy, or at least part of him."

I joined in her laughter. "I know, right? No lie! The man is pussy obsessed."

"And feet," she smirked.

I nodded. Oh, we both obviously knew that quite well. "The man knows what he likes. And wants."

"I'm glad we had this chat. And I'm sorry. I really am. I feel like a heel, a child that I did all those mean things to you." She shook her head. "Really was super uncool of me. Unforgivable, really."

"It's okay, Miranda. It's refreshing to be in a relationship with someone who admits what they did and apologizes for it."

"Yeah, I can't believe you lasted that long married to Mark."

"As I said, I was taken in by the cycle of abuse, and I didn't see it until a friend started talking to me about it. Then once I started reading about narcissism, I understood, and I saw it laced everywhere in my marriage. Those were some very dark days." Those feelings started to rush in, but I put up a wall. Not going there right now. Miranda needs me.

"I bet. But at least you are free now."

"Yeah, and I'm not sure if I'd ever want to be married again and be trapped like that." At times, the thought of being married again made me feel as if I were choking.

"Makes sense. Like I would. Like, if Allen died, God forbid, I'd want to marry again. But then, I've had a good experience being married, so we are different there."

"Yes, we are. It gives me hope, though, to see you and Allen and how you two are together. I need to find me an Allen!" I pointed in the air to emphasize it.

We both laughed. I wouldn't bring up how I'd fantasized about us both being Allen's wives. That was another taboo thought for maybe another day, or never.

"So, I have to ask, would you ever consider playing with us? It will really blow your mind, and your orgasms sky high." I was hopeful the look in her eyes meant she'd agree.

"No, I just can't do it. I mean, Kyle is sexy as fuck, but, I don't think this setup is for me."

"Well, don't expect me to stop trying." Maybe it was me she wasn't attracted to. "In any case, you look better. Do you feel better?"

She nodded slowly and her eyes told me she did. "Yes, I really do. It's a load off confessing my atrocious secrets to you." She scrunched up her shoulders. "I'm really not a mean person, I promise."

"I know you aren't. You were driven by jealousy. And that emotion can make a person do crazy things."

She stood, walked across the room, and pulled a block of cheese from the fridge. "I need a snack. I didn't eat much at the party, just wasn't hungry." She sliced the cheese into several slices and placed it on the table between us. "I'm avoiding carbs, but do you want crackers?"

I shook my head. "I should be avoiding carbs too, so no."

"Tell me what it's like, though, to be loved on by two men at once."

The pique of interest in her was delicious to observe. "Oh, it's unbelievable. It can get overwhelming, but it's a good overwhelm. They make me feel like a goddess and I'm their focus so they get off on making me come. I started reaching the highest number of orgasms in a single encounter and I can't tell you how incredible it makes me feel. Like it's true euphoria. I haven't done drugs, but it feels like what others describe feeling while doing psychedelics. The good parts though." I frowned. "But Allen must do that for you, right? The whole multiple orgasms thing? I can't imagine he doesn't."

"No, he does, but it's just usually me who puts an end to it. Maybe I'm a fool."

"Well, I'd say next time you two have sex, don't stop, go full bore. You will feel exhilarated beyond your wildest dreams. Have as many as you can possibly handle."

"And the other thing I'm jealous of is you. You getting to fulfill all these fantasies. I mean, I'm not sure I'd even remotely be into anything like you did today, but, I do have desires I've never been able to actualize in real life."

I gave her a super slow nod. "And, Miranda, I guarantee they will help you achieve those just as they have for me."

"You wouldn't see me as encroaching? I mean, you are the center of you three as you say, if I join, you'd have to share that."

Oh, sweet baby yes, yes, yes. She's considering. "I'm not worried about that one bit. Plus, I'd love to help you live out those fantasies in any way I can too." I was fishing for her sexual interest in me. I was on pins and needles wondering if she was bi-curious at all.

She said nothing but shoved cheese in her pretty mouth. "I'm not so sure how Allen would feel about another dick in me either."

"Ask him."

She pursed her lips as she cocked her head. "Maybe."

We finished off the bottle of wine and the block of cheese talking about our boys, the weather, our summer plans, and all that normal small talk crap, but underneath, I saw her brain working on what we'd talked about, and I couldn't resist holding hope.

Chapter 20

My conversation with Miranda felt unfinished. She wasn't reaching her full sexual potential and it hurt to see that she was limiting herself. It wasn't much of a leap to believe she was partitioning off her sexuality because of her own fears and that, deep down, it's not what she really wanted. I could sit and speculate all day, but Allen and Kyle were coming over and I had to get ready.

I was ready to fuck. All evening after the BBQ party I kept remembering moments that would seize me and throw me into the fires of lust, but I didn't want to masturbate. I wanted to wait for them, so I tossed and turned all night. They'd chastise me. I knew they would tell me I should never ignore the desire to masturbate. Allen especially got mad when I did that. He'd likely spank me to get me to submit to his plan. He hadn't yet, though. The thought didn't turn me off, it only made me hornier. I wasn't sure I was going to last before they got here anyway.

They were sneaking in because my boys were home. We generally never did this when they were here, but since I hadn't got to suck my Daddies' cocks yesterday, I was feeling desperate. Super dumb considering how much dick I'd had in my mouth yesterday, but who was I to argue with my libido? I'd learned by now that I certainly could not. I'd eventually lose.

I grabbed my phone with the intention of being demanding.

Me: Bring Miranda.

Kyle: Oh I'd be all over that. I'll beg.

Allen: I've tried. I can't get her to do it.

Kyle: What would it take? I'll do it. You name it.

Me: Same

Allen: She's being stubborn

Me: I tried yesterday

Allen: I know. She told me. Thanks for trying. I'll be there soon.

I wondered if she also had told Allen about all the nasty acts of destruction she committed against me. I was determined to shove them to the side, though, and proceed with the new version of our friendship.

Kyle: I'll be there sooner. I'm out the door.

Shit. I hadn't showered yet. I flew into the bathroom and stripped. I took the fastest shower I could, but when I came out, Kyle was on my bed, naked.

"I laid in bed too long," I said sheepishly.

"Drop the towel," he demanded with a smile.

I obeyed.

"Good girl." He stroked his thick cock. "I'll watch as you get ready. I love watching you."

He did love to watch me, which I loved. I'd hated it when Mark would watch me, but his version of watching was entirely different from Kyle's. His way had made me want to hide, where Kyle made me want to flaunt myself and show him everything, even things I should keep private, like inserting a tampon. Kyle had this unconditional way about him that made me feel not only shameless, but sexy in areas I'd never expected to feel sexy in, such as brushing my teeth. Once he'd come up and caressed my ass with his hard cock and pelvis while I brushed my teeth. Who knew brushing teeth could be a part of foreplay? Well, Kyle did. He made everything foreplay outside and inside the bedroom.

I wondered if he realized how sexy he was. I mean, he knew what a fool Mandy was, but did he really understand his own appeal? He was off the charts sexy and I, for one, planned to always show him that truth.

"You need to brush your teeth to suck cock, you know," he teased.

"I don't plan on that being the end of my morning of sex, though."

He laughed. "Um, hell no, it's not."

It was Sunday and I knew the boys wouldn't be up for hours. They tended to sleep in, and both had been out late, so I felt secure in the fact that they wouldn't hear us, as long as no one was screaming, which I couldn't guarantee.

I considered texting Miranda. Maybe she just needed an invitation. I reached across the bed for my phone, but Kyle pulled me into an embrace.

"I've been waiting too long to touch you. I need you. Want you." He collected my body to his in a quick snatch and our mouths collided.

We kissed deeply for a minute before I leaned back. "I want you. Damn, you taste so good."

His dick was extra fat today.

"I need you in me, Kyle. Please, I'm so horny, I can't wait," I begged breathlessly.

There was a knock at the door.

We both froze. I hopped up and was about to open it for Allen, wondering why he didn't just come in as usual.

"Mom," Jasper said.

I froze in place as I shot Kyle a look of terror.

I covered my breasts instinctively. "Yes, Jasper? What is it?"

"Miranda and Allen from down the street are here to see you. Should I tell them you will be right down?"

I gasped and mouthed 'fuck' to Kyle.

"Um, yes. That would be great. Thank you, honey."

I swiveled quickly and dashed into my closet while Kyle dressed. He'd have to stay here until I saw the boys weren't around to see him leave my bedroom.

"What is he doing up?" I hissed. "He came home at 1 pm. How is he already awake? Fuck!"

"I'll stay hidden." Kyle dressed quickly and covered up his waning boner.

I mourned the quickie fuck we were likely about to have and slipped out the door. I'm sure my boys would wonder why I shut my door, because that wasn't a common thing.

I ran down the stairs to find Miranda and Allen sitting on the couch in my living room. I gave them a confused and expectant look.

"Did you get caught sneaking in?" I asked them in a whisper.

"Nope. We came to the front door." Allen looked very happy, and Miranda looked very nervous. "We thought we should talk instead of doing this morning."

My heart began to race.

Miranda hopped up and started to leave. "I can't," she said.

"Miranda, please, stay. Talking doesn't make you obligated." I'd make damn sure she was as comfortable as possible in this.

She slowly turned, giving us a three-hundred-and-sixty-degree view of her curvy, lush body, which looked particularly yummy in her magenta workout outfit. Her breasts alone were enticing, but she had this curve to her thighs that made me want to run my hands over her. I'd never wanted to touch a woman more in my life than how much I wanted to touch Miranda. I yearned to tell her this, but I also knew we had to move slowly. She was cagey as a newly caught panther around us.

"Okay. That's true, I guess." She made her way back to the couch and sat next to her husband. They held hands.

"Perfect. I'm thinking we'd better go to the basement, so my boys don't overhear us." My heart pounded with anticipation of what they were going to say. I stood up and checked around to see if my boys were in the kitchen. Once back in my living room, I said, "Go down. I'll make sure the coast is clear for Kyle to leave my room, then we will head down." I skipped a few steps and Miranda laughed at me.

"You are in a giddy mood." Her voice came out lighter than the last time she spoke.

"Well, you're here. That's a good start." I smiled at her, and she returned my smile.

My heart skipped a beat as I skedaddled up the stairs. Both of my boys' doors were shut, so I opened my bedroom door and motioned for Kyle to come out.

"Basement," I whispered.

Without a word, he slinked out of my room and bounded down the stairs. I followed him at a rapid speed.

I pulled the door closed behind us before we descended the basement stairs.

Miranda and Allen were still holding hands, and Miranda didn't look so scared anymore.

"Hi, Miranda," Kyle said. "Allen. How goes it?"

I sat in the lounge chair closest to the tv while Kyle took the one closest to the couch.

"Well, I'm dying to know what brings you both to my house this morning." I folded my hands under my boobs. "Dang, it's chilly down here." I popped up and grabbed a blanket. "Anyone else want one? Miranda?"

She shook her head. "Nope, I'm good."

I felt all their eyes on me as if I were on a stage, and it felt yummy.

Allen cleared his throat. "So, after much discussion, Miranda has decided to watch us. We wanted to talk about this first because we need to talk about everything to be clear. To set expectations so no one suffers disappointment over this. How do you two feel if she watches us?"

I snickered. "Well, everyone knows where I stand on being watched. I find it extremely hot, and I'd love it."

Kyle grinned as deeply as I was. "Same."

Miranda released a big sigh. "Shit. I can't believe I'm going to do this."

I immediately worried she'd get jealous again and maybe even scream at us, throw things. But I needed to trust her decision, I couldn't control how she'd feel watching us, and it wasn't my responsibility anyway, so I shed the anxiety.

"The question is, where will we do this and when? We need to not have kids around, so that's the tricky part." Allen looked horny.

I shifted my eyes back and forth as the realization that I wasn't getting fucked this morning hit me. "Right, that's the tricky part." I sighed. "I expected my boys to still be sleeping. I mean, we could sneak up now, or we could just go at it right here, but I don't have a lock on that door." I pointed toward the stairs.

"Right, plus, we won't have a relaxed environment worrying about being caught. We need a more controlled setting. So I propose a hotel." Allen had clearly thought all about this.

"Oh, hotel sex. Yes! I'm so in!" I was so eager that it came out rather loud.

Both Kyle and Allen delighted in my outburst and Miranda's face lit up.

"Yeah, that's a great idea." Kyle let out a big sigh. "Only I will have to come up with a legit reason to be gone."

"Hey, Kyle, want to go fishing up north with me next weekend?" Allen had all the great ideas.

Kyle's face lit up. "Why, yes, Allen. I would love to. Thank you for asking." He pulled out his phone to check his calendar. He typed something, then looked up. "All scheduled."

It was the perfect setup.

"Oh, my Gawd, I'm so excited!" I clapped my hands as my brain started a list of which sex toys to bring. "Miranda, you won't regret this, I promise."

"I'm having a new thought. How about I look for a cabin rental on a lake for real? Then you could even fish," Miranda piped in. "My friend has one they are just starting up, maybe it's open. I'll ask." She pulled out her phone and began to text.

I shot her a thrilled look. "I'm so thrilled you are a part of this, Miranda. You always have the best ideas."

"That would be totally ideal," Allen said in agreement. "Is it Laura's? The one in Aitkin?"

Miranda nodded. "Yup, and it's not too far. They were just getting it set up for renting last time we talked, but I don't know if they've actually started booking yet." She opened her phone. "She's texting back. I'll find out right now." She smiled. "She said to call her."

She called the number and went to stand in front of the sliding glass door.

Her friend picked up.

"Hey, Laura, it's Miranda."

Silence.

"I'm really good. How about you?"

More silence.

She chuckled. "Nice! Say, I won't keep you, you are busy with the girls, but I was wondering if you have the cabin open for renting yet? Allen and I really need a weekend away."

She was quiet. Allen and Kyle exchanged happy glances. This was going to be epic. A sex weekend at a secluded cabin, just the four of us. No potential for any kids to catch us in the act. No chance of Mark coming into my house uninvited. We'd all feel so free alone up at a cabin. It was perfect!

"Seriously? That would be amazing, and perfect. We are open next weekend."

Holy fuck. I raised my hands in the air. The stars were aligning.

Miranda said her goodbye and turned to face us. "I guess we are cabin bound next weekend." I loved that her hesitancy was now gone and her body visibly relaxed. "We can do what we want without the threat of kids coming in."

"Oh, this will be so fun! Miranda, let's plan the menus. We can make some awesome food too. And you guys could maybe even fish for real, like Miranda said."

"Wow. Can't wait." Kyle was beaming. He winked at me. "Sex, fishing, food. My ideal weekend. Raincheck on what we were about to do, Alexa?"

I knew he only had a short time before Mandy duty started, and we couldn't stop this discussion. It was way too important, and some serious fucking progress.

"I'm here all day, sexy. We can make it work later," I assured him.

I ushered them to the patio. "Anyone want a cup of coffee?"

"I'll help." Miranda followed me into the house and up the stairs.

It hit me how we all needed some hangout time together to make this work between us. We needed bonding time as a foursome before having actual sex together. Miranda was going to just watch, but I saw that little spark flickering in her eyes that had appeared yesterday. It was stronger today, though it was switching between that and nervous gazes, it was still there. It existed. She'd join us at some point, of that I had no doubt.

Chapter 21

The week was agonizingly long. We'd all decided to not fuck for the week in preparation, and I was so sex-starved I thought I was going to die. I allowed myself masturbation at my whim, at my Daddies' insistence, but I wanted cock in me, on me, around me, and I missed their skin on mine most of all. It would be a spectacular event when we finally fucked again, and I was convinced Miranda wouldn't last on the sidelines. She'd want in like a lion to a bowl of steak in about three seconds flat of watching the three of us engage in sexual activity.

I'd started sending short little sexy texts to Miranda as a teaser. She'd been pretty responsive, but even in text, she held onto hesitancy. With some of her responses, I'd wondered if she would change her mind. Which I'd hate for so many reasons and feared it would completely cancel our trip if she backed out. The idea of being at a cabin with my Daddies was the most delicious fantasy, and I couldn't wait. Add in Miranda, and afterward, I think I could die happy. I still had yet to check the female sexual experience off my bucket list and I pleaded with God and the universe that Miranda would be my tool to reach that this weekend.

My boys were all set. I'd grocery shopped to the max for them, and Mark was going to check in on them, not that they needed that, but, whatever. I'd told them I was going to a cabin with Miranda and Allen and another neighbor. It was totally the truth, and I was feeling so good about going.

I'd started packing. I slotted all the sex toys inside the suitcase, all cradled in clothing to protect them. I devilishly grinned as I had taken a pic of them all packed up and texted the pic to Miranda. I declared I'd share with her and show her new sexual heights with them, to which she only texted back a big shocked O-face emoji. It was a buzzkill.

I assured her I'd blow her mind, and that was just me. Allen and Kyle would literally blow her mind, as they had mine. She had no idea what pleasures lay ahead for her. Likely, she couldn't even fathom it. I hadn't. So, coming from experience, I knew where she was at in her mindset. Not entirely, because I'm sure Allen had brought her pretty high on his own, but Allen had informed me she was quite timid when it came to sex toy usage.

I fully intended to send her to the moon and back a zillion times. She'll be screaming and jerking her way through orgasm after orgasm all weekend long. The idea of it drove me wild.

Miranda and I'd planned all the meals, bought the food and booze, and we were ready to leave at 7 a.m. Friday morning. I had a few things to finish up for work in preparation for being off, but otherwise I was ready to head out in the morning. Secretly, I hoped we could start on the drive with some road head, some pussy to tongue tickle action from Kyle to me in the back seat. Maybe we could set a good sexy example for Miranda to give Allen road head in the front seat. I smiled wickedly as my plan of attack formulated in my head.

Miranda texted.

Miranda: Do we really need all those toys you packed? I can't imagine what all of them are for and why we'd need so many. Don't they all do the same thing?

Me: I sent her a few laughing emojis. Oh, you of little knowledge, you will be on your phone ordering more sex toys before the end of the weekend. They will blow your mind, and your orgasms to the sky

Miranda: Doubtful

Me: Absolute

Miranda: If you say so

Me: I do

Miranda: Do you think I should bring lingerie? Are you?

Me: fuck yes! And you'd better!

Miranda: K

Me: That's an absolute must. I am proposing a fully naked day on Saturday.

Miranda: She sent a shocked face emoji

Me: Why not? We will be seeing each other anyway

Miranda: Well, you all may not see me but I'll see you I guess

Me: I have high hopes, Miranda

Miranda: At any rate, I'm excited for the weekend. It will be so nice to get away from the obligations of being a mom for a few days. I need this.

Me: Yes you do. I'm really excited too. Can't wait!

\#

I woke up horny, as usual. I resisted my natural normal inclination to rub one out and rose out of bed, blue-balling myself.

"This sucks," I muttered. I'm not used to restricting my masturbation. Allen and Kyle rarely restrict my pleasure, they may withhold it to edge me, to get it to build to the highest level possible, but then I get to come. "Phooey," I said, feeling like a brat. "I want to come."

I sighed and turned on the shower. It was 6 a.m. and we'd leave in an hour. The water felt especially good, a poor substitute for an orgasm, but I'd still take it. It was very lovely and luxurious. The promise of reduced parenting tasks and zero work obligations, plus the looming orgasmic heights, was very satisfying. I felt free already.

I dried myself off and slathered hemp seed oil all over my skin. Feeling very luxurious and pampered already, I slipped my new tube top over my breasts, opting for braless so Kyle could play with my tits on the drive. My clit twitched as I envisioned Miranda looking back at us and seeing my naked boobs. Then her watching Kyle molest them was an even hotter thought. Would she look away? Masturbate herself in the front seat? Or just smile? I was dying to know.

I was so happy Mandy didn't put up a stink about Kyle leaving. Maybe she liked the idea of being alone. I always had. The stark difference always had become obvious within seconds of Mark leaving. I was free. It was a bit shocking how free I felt. But I got that feeling all the time as days went on. His pull on me got less and less with time and I was thankfully losing the mindset of feeling watched every second of every fucking day. It had been jail. I couldn't be me.

I sighed as I left a note for the boys and headed down the stairs. The plan was I would drag my suitcase through the backyards. With my car home, Mandy might think I'm home too. I'd already dropped off all the groceries I'd bought at Miranda and Allen's. This way, my sneaking through the backyards would be smoother and easier. I'm not sure I could have handled the food and the suitcase at once anyway.

My suitcase bumped along through the yards, bouncing in and out of dips in the ground. My heart was pounding as I hoped no one was looking out their windows at 6:49 a.m. on a Friday. I knew it was a long shot, but it could happen.

I entered Miranda and Allen's garage through the back service door. It was dark inside. Someone grabbed me and whirled me around, my suitcase fell to the ground.

I squealed. "Oh!"

Kyle wrapped me up in a bear hug as he swung me.

"We are free!" he said with joy. His relief was obvious in his voice, and it was so lovely to hear.

"Yes, we are. All go okay with Mandy?" I didn't mean to darken his joy, but I was nervous for him. Mandy was a suspicious and controlling bitch.

"All went okay. I'm just so excited about this weekend. Why haven't we done this before?"

We both connected our gazes and said "Miranda" at about the same time. She was most definitely the turnkey for this weekend. Her being in opened this new door for us.

"Bless her heart. We need to make her come lots this weekend," I said, nodding.

"Yes, yes we do." He kissed me on the lips, then pressed his tongue between them.

We kissed deep and long as his erection announced itself like a red flag against my torso.

"I'm thinking road head for that." I leaned back and pointed downward toward his crotch.

"You've read my mind." He smiled as a snicker pelted out of his lips.

Miranda and Allen emerged into the garage, arguing.

"Uh oh," I whispered to Kyle.

They approached us as we separated.

"Hey, guys. Everything okay?" Ignoring their spat would not have set the tone right for the start of our fabulous weekend.

Allen sighed. "Yes, we are just arguing about one of the kids. They will figure it out. We are mostly checking out for the weekend and our oldest two are in charge. So, we need to let them do their job. Let's go." He motioned towards their SUV. "All aboard the fuckmobile."

"Oh, I want in on that!" I said as I grabbed my suitcase and wheeled it to the back of the vehicle. "I hope there's still room for this."

Allen followed me and chuckled. "Barely, as usual, Miranda packed everything but the kitchen sink."

She gave him a nasty face, but then switched to a pleasant expression. "And every time we use everything I bring."

"She's not wrong," Allen said with humility.

He nestled my suitcase into the almost completely full back area and pulled me into his arms. He gave me a kiss.

"You okay with showing this affection for me in front of her?" I asked in a whisper. "Is she okay with it?"

"Well, I'm pretty locked into it now." He released me and I caught Miranda's eyes.

I smiled. "Miranda, give me a hug. We need to start this out right."

I pulled her into a hug and her eyes lit up, then became soft.

"Yes, we do. I'm going to try really hard to be open." She shrugged. "It's not like I didn't know that's been going on." Her smile was small, but genuine.

It was the first time our fronts had been fully in contact with each other. She felt as voluptuous as she looked. I couldn't help but become even more aroused, especially since she was seeming on board now.

"This will be awesome. Epic. Mind-blowing. But remember, you have to be honest with us, and you have to speak up for it to be the best it can be."

She nodded. We'd had a few group discussions over the week in preparation for the weekend. All three of us had told her firmly we wouldn't be disappointed in what she decided to do or not do, and that she had to speak up to prevent trauma from settling in. It was of paramount importance, like success or failure importance.

"Let's get on the road before one of the kids sees we are still home and decides he needs something." She pointed to the vehicle and was the first to hop in.

She wanted out of there and I couldn't blame her.

The drive started out nice and calm, with a swing through the coffee shop drive-through. With soft music playing we set off out on the road. The talk was pleasant, small talk like we aren't really going to a cabin to fuck each other's brains out. Once our coffees were gone, though, Kyle and I started to eye each other up.

"You know, being in the backseat means we should be making out," Kyle said in a deliciously seductive voice.

I shot him a suggestive look. "My thoughts exactly."

"Oh dang, if you two do that, I might have my eyes glued to the backseat and make us crash." Allen heckled himself. "I'm easy to arouse, as you all know."

Miranda reached across and placed her hand on Allen's crotch. "Yep, you are. You've got nice morning wood going." She glanced back at us. "I'm game if you two are."

"A round of road head!" I announced.

Both Allen and Kyle cheered.

"This might be the best idea we've ever had," Allen said as Miranda unclasped her seatbelt and situated her head above his lap.

"No shit," Kyle said appreciatively, as I did the same to him.

"Tandem blow jobs on a road trip," Allen said in a raspy voice as Miranda already had his cock head in her mouth.

"It's already a trip for the memory books," Kyle pet my hair as I unveiled his hard cock.

I took Kyle's cockhead in my mouth as he played with my breasts.

I sat up. "Miranda, we should be topless too."

Our eyes met with all the raunchiness we could muster. I was so excited she was on board with it, which escalated the hotness level to super delicious. Plus, Kyle and I would get to see her bare breasts for the first time. It'd been a long, agonizing wait.

Miranda hesitated as she eyed us up. She glanced between her husband and us as he nodded vehemently.

"Do it, baby, it will be so hot." His voice came lusty and full of anticipation.

Miranda cocked her head to the right, shrugged like it didn't matter, then pulled her top off. Her breasts spilled out of her bra like it was a bit too small for her bosom.

Kyle groaned.

"Spectacular already," I said with a sigh.

She reached behind her back and undid her bra.

"She's got killer breasts, guys, brace yourselves." Allen chuckled as Miranda beamed.

I loved that she was enjoying this.

Like she was unveiling a delicious meal, she let her bra fall, revealing the most gorgeous tits I'd ever seen in my life.

Kyle whistled.

I moaned out, "Oh, wow, Miranda! You are just beautiful!"

Allen chuckled. "I've always told her she should have been a nude model, she'd have made a killing."

Her face flushed. "Aw, you guys are too kind."

"Just honest," Kyle said with a release of a big breath. "Stunning, Miranda, you are just absolutely stunning."

Allen cackled. "Wait until you see her pussy."

Miranda smacked his shoulder, but her grinning like a cat with a mouse said it all. "Oh, stop, it's just a regular pussy."

"It's not, babe. Alexa has a pretty pussy too. Wait until you see hers." Allen sighed heavily as his wife leaned down. "Pussy heaven abounds."

"Goddam," Kyle said as Miranda's heavy breasts hung down. "I'm not going to last long this round with you two women."

I removed my shirt and leaned over Kyle's lap. I quickly took his cock in my mouth. Listening to Miranda's mouth sounds on Allen's dick and Allen's groans made me ready to bust an orgasm too. Wishing I'd thought of a toy for the road trip, I reached down and molested my clit.

I moaned with Kyle's cock tip in my mouth as he made deep and lush appreciative sounds. The pleasure apparent in the SUV reached extreme heights in no time. Allen took the next ramp off the interstate.

"Fuck, I can't drive like this." He released an exasperated guffaw.

The car jerked and I almost toppled to the floor, but Kyle gripped me to him.

Allen maneuvered us to park somewhere. I couldn't see where because all I saw was Kyle's lap and belly.

He pinched my nipples and played with them.

In the front seat, Miranda and Allen were making such delicious vocalizations, which hiked me up my orgasm hill fast. I was about to tip off the edge.

But Miranda beat me and she moaned. Then she released a sound like she was climaxing.

I lost it. My body jerked as my pussy contracted.

Allen yelled out, "Fuck!"

Then Kyle made his usual climaxing sounds.

We all sighed as things seemed to simmer down.

"That was fucking crazy," Kyle said. "We literally all almost came simultaneously. That just doesn't happen."

"Oh, it was unbelievably awesome." I sat up, making my tits bounce.

"Well done, ladies. Good girl." Allen cupped his wife's face. "Very very good girl." He glanced back at me. "You too, Alexa. Good girl. You both outdid yourselves there. That was hot as fuck."

We all laid back in our seats, slumping as we came down off our highs.

"I'd say let's fuck again, but now I'm starving." I glanced around for a restaurant. "Anyone else hungry, or is it just me?"

"Famished," Miranda said. "And that was way hotter than I thought it would be."

"Good," I said, smiling at her. Perfect. "Now let's go eat. Miranda, let's go in braless."

Kyle squeezed my thigh. "I love you, babe. Do you know how much I love you?"

Miranda physically startled at Kyle's declaration, but she busied herself putting her shirt back on, which hugged her breasts nicely. Her nipples pressed out the fabric beautifully.

We exited the car and entered the café Allen so graciously chose to park near.

Chapter 22

We pulled into the cabin driveway, and it was such a pleasant surprise. It was a dream location with a sparkling blue lake just beyond the cabin and a grassy lawn ending at a sandy beach. There were six multi-colored Adirondack chairs around a bonfire pit on the beach. There was a volleyball net in the yard and a trampoline, plus a basketball court off to the edge of the lawn.

"I think we've arrived at heaven," Allen said, clearly voicing all our thoughts as we sat in awe in silence for a few moments.

"It's amazing!" I said as I scanned the single-floor log cabin. The structure spanned about half of the grassy area. A peek of the deck on the lakeside was visible.

I eyed up the hammocks near the water and the dock with a pontoon boat and a ski boat.

"This place is a gem! It's like literally perfect." I opened my door and slid out.

"Yeah, they will be making their money spent fixing this place up in no time. He told me it was really nice, but that's an understatement." Allen cleared his throat and motioned to Kyle. "Let's get the groceries in first and then they can set up the kitchen how they want, and we'll finish the unload."

Miranda and I took one load towards the cabin.

"Wow, this place is just gorgeous, it's like my fantasy cabin." I ascended the steps up the front porch.

Miranda followed me. "Yes, and apparently the inside is amazing too, I hear." She joined me with the door key in her hand. "And she just told me they had the hot tub installed on the deck."

"Oh, seriously? I didn't know about a hot tub."

"Yep, they put a rush on it just for us. It wasn't scheduled to go in until next week."

"Oh, how generous of them!" I followed her inside. The décor was rustic and cabin-like, as expected, with lots of wood surfaces, decorations of nature made out of wrought iron, and even a chandelier of antlers. The couches looked comfy, with red overstuffed cushions, beige and dark blue pillows adorning the corners. A set of four lounge chairs were positioned to face the large-screen tv and the lake.

"Yup. Heaven! We've found it!" I exclaimed as she set the bags on the kitchen counter. "I love the open room concept. How many bedrooms does this place have?"

"Four. But only two have king-size beds. The other two have double beds, and one has a bunk-bed in addition." Miranda smiled at me sheepishly. "I really enjoyed that in the car. I never knew it'd be so hot to do next to another couple."

"Yes, and I've never done that before where two blow jobs were going at once. The sounds they made, oh my Gawd, it was delicious." I pulled out the groceries and placed them on the island.

"It really was. I loved hearing Kyle react. Plus, when I'd glance your way, I was so extra turned on."

I loved that she had been watching us. "That's really hot, Miranda." This surely was a very good sign that she'd be all in. I had hope.

Miranda and I set up the kitchen and the groceries where we wanted them as the afternoon sun blasted through the lakeside windows. The sky beyond was a brilliant blue and the lake surface sparkled, doing the bright sun justice. The lush lawn was a healthy, succulent green, and plush and looked like the best place to fuck under sun or moon. The property was also private, with only the roofline of the next cabin to the right visible through the trees, and on the other side was a thick forest.

"I think if I lived here, I'd never move. Damn, would I love to live in such a place." I settled back on the couch with a glass of wine in my hand as Miranda joined me.

The men had been busy for a while doing something they were keeping secret.

"I am so curious about what they are doing," Miranda said as she folded her shapely legs beneath her.

"I'm telling you, those two are a force of sexual nature. They create these amazing scenes and experiences. They are quite gifted in sex and giving the best sexual experiences. They are a dynamic duo." I chuckled. "Though, not gay."

She almost spit out her gulp of wine. She managed to swallow the mouthful, then laughed. "Allen has no gay bone or cell on his body."

I wanted to tell her about the double vaginal penetrations they often did on me, but decided it might be better for her to observe the full extent of the three of us slowly, so she didn't go into some kind of paralyzing shock. But doing that didn't make either of them gay, it was just a sexual act. But still, it was dick on dick.

"Yeah, Kyle too, but you just never know what they might try." I sipped my wine, holding all my secrets as I gazed around the room. "They must have had this place professionally decorated. It's got interior designer written all over it."

"Yeah, they did. They really went all out. Their hope is to pay it all off, then retire here. So it won't stay as a rental forever. Maybe like ten to fifteen years, and then they will move here."

"Sounds like a good plan to me. I'd do that."

The men appeared in the hallway to the left, coming from the bedrooms. The house was shaped like a J, with the great big room and kitchen at the top, and the bedrooms swinging down the bottom of the J. The master bedroom suite Kyle and I gave to Miranda and Allen. It was situated at the bottom of the J overlooking the lake with its own porch off the sliding glass door.

"What have you two been up to?" I asked with great anticipation in my voice as I ran a finger around the rim of my glass. I couldn't wait to sleep in the same bed as Kyle and wake up in his arms. I hoped we would fuck during the night, in the morning, and take full advantage of sleeping in the same bed for once. It wouldn't come again for an eternity.

"You will just have to wait until later." Kyle placed a hand on my head. "But you will like it. A lot."

"No going into our suite this afternoon, until we invite you two in." Allen had a stern, fatherly look like he'd spank us if we didn't listen. The look always made me wet. "Got it?" he asked in a reinforced dominant tone.

"Yes, Daddy." I watched Miranda watch me, her eyes big. "If I sneak in, will you spank me?" I snickered with my eyes lit up. "Please?" I laughed harder as Allen grinned big.

"Oh, that will happen, little girl. Don't you question it. We've worked hard on this, so don't ruin your surprise." He meandered to the kitchen. "Kyle, beer?"

"Yes, please. I'm dying to have one." He reached for my hand to help me rise. "Let's take our drinks down to the beach."

"Oh, good idea. I want to get my bikini on first, though." I rose and let Kyle take me in his arms.

"You'd better." He gave my ass a single swat as I turned away. I loved this setup, like Kyle and I were a real couple, just like Miranda and Allen. It was fun to pretend that anyway.

"Oh, good idea." Miranda stood up. "Oh, but my suit is in the room."

"Allow me. You can get dressed in the living room like real strippers." Allen laughed at his own joke. "No one will mind. Plus, now they've seen you. So, no hiding your beautiful body anymore."

Miranda blushed and it was cute. "Well, I guess you are right." She began to strip, a gloriously sensual expression on her face. She clearly felt very free here.

My mind went to yummy places as I imagined Miranda stripping on a stage. Dang. She was really getting into this body sharing as she seductively began to dance. She pulled down her short leggings with a hip shimmy to reveal a shaved smooth mound. She swiveled and her perfect bubble butt swung into view.

"Well, fuck," Kyle said. "I'm not sure I'm going to last until after dinner."

"You can do it, my man." He pointed to the lake. "Head out there so you aren't tempted to start anything. I'll be joining you in a split second for the same reason."

He nodded. "I think I'd better." He grabbed the speaker off the counter and headed outside.

Miranda, Allen, and I strolled across the lawn in our swimsuits, the sun bearing down on us. Kyle had already reached the beach and was messing with the chair arrangement.

"Whew! It's hot. I might need to swim in a bit." The grass blades were plush against my soles. My pedicure had been a good idea.

Miranda had perfect feet too. The woman should have been a model. Maybe Allen could get her to do a Fans account. They'd make a ton of money.

I made a mental note to suggest it to her after the weekend, if all went well. I was getting to realize my full sexual potential, as should she be able to.

Kyle was seated, lounging in a chair with his shirt off. I hadn't noticed he already had his suit on when we were at the house. He looked scrumptious. I couldn't resist, I sat on his lap. He grinned deeply as I settled into his body and we kissed. I leaned back on him, and it was so natural, so right. I dared not let my heart wish for more, but it was too late.

"I'm enjoying being with you like this," I said in a whisper.

"Oh, me too. This is like a dream come true." His eyes showed me how true that really was for him. He was happy. And it made my heart swell to see him that way.

"It really is." I played with his chest hair. I wanted to tell him my desires for us together for the future, but instead, I poured more wine down my throat. It wasn't time.

"What's on the menu for dinner?" Allen asked as he laid back in the chair, sunglasses adorning his nose.

Miranda was perched on his lap.

"Steaks. Salt and vinegar potatoes. Salad. Bread. Wine." Miranda ticked off all the items we had planned for tonight's meal. "And chocolate-covered strawberries for dessert."

"Oh, that sounds wonderful. Your recipe for the strawberries?" Allen asked hopefully.

"Yep, and Alexa planned a delicious berry and walnut salad with a lemon vinaigrette dressing." Miranda leaned back and I resisted the urge to take a picture. We'd all agreed on no pics this weekend, just in case the wrong person saw them.

"This is unbelievable, amazing. I'm definitely getting in that water soon, though," I said as I savored my skin on Kyle's.

"Same," Kyle said. As he shifted, I could feel his hard shaft beneath my thighs.

"Oh, damn, what's that I feel?" I asked coyly.

"The effect of you on my lap, that's what." He made no secret of it.

I couldn't stand it. I jumped up and grabbed his hand, set down my cup and his beer on the table beside his chair, and I pulled him towards the lawn.

"I need that cock in me."

He stopped dead in his tracks. "No, baby girl. We have plans."

I pouted. I'm so not used to him saying no to sex. I didn't like it. I reached for his cock.

His face clouded. "Alexa, we have plans."

I massaged his cock.

"Bend over," he commanded.

"Yes, Daddy," I said in a barely audible whisper.

We'd talked about this, and my lust salivated as the anticipation of him showing his total dominance over me solidified in my mind. I had told him I wanted him to exert it fully over me.

I gasped. This is usually Allen's role, though.

He pulled my bikini bottoms down and landed a smack on my ass.

"Who in charge?" he demanded. He spanked my ass hard again. The shock wave of the spank reverberated through my throbbing clit, and it made me even hornier, but I knew I wouldn't get to satisfy it yet.

My heartbeat raged as I realized Miranda and Allen were watching him spank my ass in broad daylight in an open space.

I'm so stunned I didn't speak. So he spanked my ass again, hard, forcing my body forward. I winced and released a whine.

"You are, Daddy," I said in an obedient, yet sensual, voice. His spanking and taking control of me turned me on even more, and I knew he wasn't going to even fuck me. The whole thing totally backfired on me. Yet him putting me in my place with him as the leader this way was a fantasy I'd been waiting to live through.

"Who tells you what we will do sexually?" His voice was harsh and commanding, which raged my turn on even more.

He spanked my ass three times in a row, sending my cheeks flopping. The last one really stung.

I was close to saying my safe word.

"You, Daddy," I said meekly.

He spanked me one more time and it really hurt. "And who else?"

"Allen."

He pulled me upright and hugged me, caressing my spanked cheeks. "Good girl. Who are we? And what always happens?"

"My Daddies, and you are in charge. Always."

"Good good good girl." He stroked my hair as he snuggled me to him, his aftercare affection overflowing.

I was embarrassed by his dominating me like that, but the absoluteness of it was delicious. I'd enjoyed the humiliation a little too, which I'd have to reflect on before discussing it with them. I'd pined for this complete control to be brandished upon me. I grinned. "I'm supposed to be punished, right? But that really turned me on."

He grinned as he rubbed my sore backside, then pulled up my bottoms. "I know it did. Why do you think I did it?"

"To dom me." I jerked slightly as my suit slid across my spanked skin.

"Well, that too. I am in charge, baby girl. Don't you forget it."

I couldn't really wrap my head around it yet, but I loved it too. "It's not very often you say no to your cock in my pussy." I pouted slightly as I glanced at Allen and Miranda, not more than fifteen feet away.

"Nicely done, Kyle," Allen called. "I would have done the same thing."

Miranda's face was hard to read. She looked perplexed, yet not upset. It was a lot to process for her, no doubt.

Kyle grabbed my hand, and we walked back to the bonfire ring. "As I said, we have plans. And you need to obey."

"I guess he showed me," I said with chagrin to Miranda, my cheeks blushing. I wondered if the whole public spanking display had anything to do with him showing Miranda how we rolled. Either way, it did put me in my place, and had the double effect of showing Miranda my place. A place I loved to be. I wanted them to dominate me daily, to be in control, and to live out this fantasy in real life, and in front of people, was so satisfying for me.

Miranda's face lingered in an expression I couldn't quite figure out. It wasn't outright disdain, but a mix of confusion, shock, and maybe a bit of interest. Maybe she had a bit of a submissive in her too. I couldn't wait to help her figure it all out. Be her guide.

She remained speechless as I sat down. "Ow, that hurts, Kyle." I smiled. I wasn't mad.

He guffawed. "Daddies are in charge, baby girl. You needed a reminder." The lust in his eyes was the reward for it all, though. I could see his desire to fuck me, and he was holding off, which was hot.

"Well, I always want to please you two."

"As we strive to please you, baby girl." Allen leaned forward and pulled his glasses down his nose. "But make no mistake, we are in charge."

My cheeks flushed again. The shame in being spanked in front of others was something I'd been curious to explore. I'd never really expected to tick my lust up higher, but it most certainly had.

"Well, I'm certainly even more turned on for tonight now." I couldn't stop my heavy breathing.

Kyle reached for me and placed me back on his lap. My spanked cheeks rested on his hard-on, driving me crazier.

I needed to move, I was super antsy. "I think I need to cool my buns in that water. I'm on fire." I raced towards the water and plunged in. The cool water soothed my buttocks as I glided in it. I dipped underwater and swam a few feet before I popped up. "Aw, that's better." I swam around as the three of them made their way toward the water as well.

"Good idea," Miranda said as she sank into the water with a sigh.

We played around in the water, kissing, caressing, and getting each other amped up for later. Miranda and I still had not interacted much sexually, but I was set on letting her make the first move.

We enjoyed each other all afternoon, getting drunker and more turned on by the minute.

Chapter 23

Miranda and I prepared the food in our bikinis. Allen and Kyle kept glancing our way as we worked. They were playing cribbage at the table. It was fun to be turning them on as they attempted to play the game; they weren't succeeding very well at it. I loved being their distraction.

Kyle grinned big at me. "I love this weekend. We get to drink beer, look at our gorgeous, sexy, hot women, eat good food, and fuck all we want." He shook his head. "Heaven!"

"Well, not all we want. You denied me this afternoon." I was still a little bitter. Not about the spanking, but him denying me sex. I couldn't ever deny I loved him controlling me sexually.

"Need a round two?" Allen piped up hopefully. "My lap and spanking hand are at the ready, baby girl." He laughed because he was getting drunk.

"Oh, don't I know it." I glanced at my backside. "Is my ass still red?" I asked Miranda.

"Only slightly. I see a bit of a handprint, though." She wrinkled her nose above her smirk.

"Yeah, he got me good." I laughed while I blushed. "It actually turned on me hardcore, though. I love them dominating me." I shuddered. "It just drives me wild."

"I have a hard time wrapping my brain around it," she admitted as she prepped the steaks. "I mean, Allen has given me a few spanks during doggy, but never like a means to punish and control me like that."

She said this, but her eyes told me she was a bit intrigued. "Did it turn you on at all? Just asking, 'cause it would be hot to me if it had."

She shrugged. "I don't know. I've always been a strong independent woman, so I might not handle that very well."

"Oh, I am too. Don't get me wrong. It's not like that. To me, it's the letting go and granting permission for someone else to decide that I think is so sexy. It's the ultimate passionate high to be so desired and told what to do. But it's only with sex. I could never do that 24/7 total power exchange thing. No way in hell."

She laughed with a trail of a high-pitched sigh. "I don't even know what that means."

"It's where the dominant is in charge and tells the submissive what to do every second of the day, both in the bedroom and out."

"Um, no thanks. I'm not into that either." She shook her head vehemently.

"People can be submissive to one person and dominant to another, or it can even be situational. You could be one way with Allen, and another with Kyle. Or even me. It's very fluid."

I looked up. The men hadn't said a peep in a few minutes. They were intently watching us with amused expressions.

"Oh, don't mind us," Kyle said nonchalantly. "This is fascinating, please go on."

I smiled at him because I can't ever not smile back. With great humility and reverence, I said, "I want you two to control me sexually in every way. Not that I won't try to get you to play, though, as you both know."

"Yeah, I want you to initiate babe, you know that." Kyle pressed his hands together. "Please do. But today, we have big plans I didn't want to ruin."

"Oh, I totally get it. And a maintenance spanking is what I needed. I was being a demanding brat."

"I love you being a demanding brat," Kyle said. He was getting drunk too and his loose, aroused expression showed it. "And it's my deep pleasure to satisfy and punish that brat."

"Yep, I know you do."

"I haven't gotten to do that in a while. It was delicious."

"It was." The truth was, he'd never gone quite that far before. I pointed my finger at him. "But you just wait until I get you in that bed tonight."

Allen busted out with boisterous laughter. "You say that now, but after this evening, I predict you will be out cold, asleep for a good eight hours, baby girl."

"Well, that excites me! I'm so in!" I started the salad as Miranda and I met our gazes. The wine was loosening her up, but I wondered how much it would put her in a mindset to fully enjoy. I had told her earlier in the week to totally surrender to her hidden desires this weekend and it would honestly blow her world up in the best way possible and definitely change it.

We finished the prep work for the dinner and handed the steaks off to the guys. We high-tailed it to the beach with plans to enjoy a plate of cheese and crackers together with our wine while they grilled the steaks.

We all enjoyed the amazing dinner on the deck as the next stage of the night had us all ready to fire off. We were loaded, cocked, and ready to go. The food helped us all stave off being too drunk, but we decided that dessert needed to be a part of the sex because we were all too damn full to eat another bite.

"So, do we get any hints, or do we just have to wait until we walk into the bedroom?" I couldn't help asking, even though the sting of Kyle's domination was still fresh on my ass, and he might decide to remind me again. It was worth the risk.

"We will wait. A half-hour to let our food settle. Then we will usher you two to the room." Allen tapped his plate. "And Kyle and I are doing the dishes. We want to pamper you too and make you feel like queens. So, relax and enjoy. Your night of leisure, pleasure, and intense orgasms is about to start."

They cleared the table and my mind drifted to Miranda's thoughts. "So, how are you feeling?"

She leaned back and sighed. "Amazing. Utterly amazing. And I haven't even had an orgasm tonight yet."

"I know, I literally can't wait. I am also excited to watch you experience them. They are totally amazing in action together, Miranda." I held her hand and squeezed it. "Do you think you will engage, or are you just planning to watch us tonight?"

"I don't know." Her face told me otherwise, she knew. "We'll see." She bit her lip. "But I'm very interested in completely letting go, whether it's just with Allen or ... more." The 'more' came out shaky, but suggestive.

I took it as a promise because I wanted to.

We continued to chat about the kids and neighborhood goings-on until Allen and Kyle appeared in suit and tie. Each man had a silky dress hanging off their arms.

"Your attire for the evening," Kyle said with a twinkle in his eyes.

"You mean for the moment? These won't be on long!" Allen's jovial nature beamed brightly on his face.

"Ah, true my man, true."

"Oh, you two are the sweetest! New dresses too!" I squealed.

Miranda hooted. "You guys know how to butter us up."

"You have no idea. This is just the beginning," Kyle said as he gave me a cheesy eyebrow raise.

The men led us into the living room where a bottle of champagne was chilling in an ice bucket. Four sparkling champagne flutes surrounded the ice bucket like they were the watch guard.

"Oh, we should have the chocolate-covered strawberries." Miranda started for the kitchen, but Allen stopped her.

"Babe, I've got them in the room already. We'll take our champagne there soon and enjoy them." He held the dress up. "I want you to relax. You aren't responsible for anything but your own pleasure tonight."

Miranda's face blossomed from bewildered into the biggest smile I've ever seen grace her face. She needed this. She needed it badly.

I stripped first down to bare skin as Kyle slipped the dress over my head. He smoothed it down my body. The act of him dressing me was also seductive and I gave him my fuck me eyes to prove it.

"Perfection. You look smoking hot, baby girl. And since I put that on you, I get to be the one to take it off." His lust was evident in his eyes and words, so much so that I was caressed, cupped, and stroked from them alone.

I glanced over at Miranda, and she was naked and in Allen's arms. They were looking deeply into each other's eyes. It was such a surprising and moving sight to see the two of them like that, so entranced by each other that I gasped and made eye contact with Kyle.

He nodded and pointed to them. "Yeah. Wow. Look at that," he whispered in my ear as he shook his head.

I sucked my lips into my mouth and whispered back, "It's awesome."

Kyle poured champagne into all four glasses.

After Allen slipped Miranda's dress over her head, they joined us.

"I had to copy you, that was a slick move, my man." Allen held Miranda around the waist.

They connected their gazes, as did Miranda and me. So much was getting said through our eyes, we could write a book.

Kyle held up his glass. "Cheers to friends, and friends who fuck, and cabins on lakes that might as well be a dream they are so perfect."

We all clinked glasses and took a seat. Kyle and I sat on the couch, Miranda and Allen took the love seat.

We chit-chatted for a few minutes, but I was antsy, so I had to ask, "When are we getting to the fucking? I mean, honestly, we've been doing this kind of thing all day, let's get to the joining of the parts!"

Kyle let a laugh burst free. Allen nodded with a giant smile, and Miranda scoffed.

"Wow," she said, but was smiling.

"Guess I'm the brat once again," I said with chagrin.

Kyle stood up. "Who are we to keep a horny woman waiting?"

"True," Allen declared. "Certainly not me." He rose and held out his hand for his wife's. She placed it in his palm, and he closed his hand around hers. "My bride, are you ready to be astounded, astonished, tickled, pounded, wowed, and pleasured into the nether-spheres of sexual pleasure?" His chivalry was hypnotic.

She slowly nodded with a look of apprehension on her face. Despite this, she said, "Yes."

I raised my hand. "Oh, me! I'm so ready too!"

Kyle bent down and snatched me, throwing my body over his shoulder. He took off, running down the hall like I was just a sack of potatoes, as I squealed and screamed in delight.

He carried me into the suite. I was instantly titillated by the magical land of sex they'd created. There were groupings of toys scattered about the room, plus there were candles, flowers, rose petals strewn about, and Christmas lights hung about the walls.

"Whoa!"

He set me down and I swiveled, taking in the whole room.

"We've got stations set up."

"This is like the sexual prom!" I exclaimed as I dragged my gaze from the BDSM station to the sensual station, to the sex swing hanging from the bathroom door, the dildo section, the vibrating clit toy section, and the refreshment station. Then to the bed that was covered in rose petals.

Kyle chuckled as Miranda and Allen entered the room. Miranda's eyes were open wide.

"Okay, we have a series of stations set up. And this is also in reverence to Miranda, who is new to some of this stuff. We thought it would be fun to allow her a chance to taste some of this stuff with her body. Try them out, so to speak, and this was the best way to do it."

"We have rules in place. Rules you both must follow." Kyle shot me a commanding look, reminding me to follow their rules.

My cheeks flushed slightly as it aroused me.

"Or there will be consequences," I said sheepishly.

Kyle grinned wickedly as he gave me a feather-light tap on my right buttock. "You got that right, Baby Girl."

I watched as Miranda squirmed in place. She'd figure it out for herself, I had confidence in her.

Allen instructed, "It will be your choice which stations you visit. I will follow Miranda at first, and Kyle will follow Alexa. Then we will switch if all are okay with that. If you do not choose a station, we will choose for you. You can redirect us from a station or get us to stop any action or talk by saying the safe word of the evening, which is coffee."

Kyle spread his arm across the room. "We will first take a tour so you can think about what you'd like to try and have done to you, or do."

Miranda looked nervous. "So, we don't all play together? It's just me and you, then me and maybe Kyle?"

"Baby, it's whatever you want. We set this up as a way to ease you in and allow you choices rather than shove you into a scene, or even watch a scene."

That all made a lot of sense. It met her at her comfort level. She had the liberty to get used to us watching her and Allen be sexual, or she could all-out engage as she desired. It was brilliant!

She released a big sigh. "Okay, I get it." The look of ease and comfort in her eyes was sexy.

"I'd like you both to pick stations for me," I said. "I love it when you tell me what to do sexually."

"Figured you would, baby girl." Kyle pulled me into a hug and passionately kissed me. "I love that you want me to dominate you, baby girl. You turn me on like no one else ever has."

I melted into him and shuddered with jubilation. "Take me, Daddy, I'm yours."

"I'm going to fuck you hard, my whore." He grabbed my wrists and clasped them together.

He dragged me across the room to the sex swing and released a sexy man growl that made my clit twitch. His cock was pushing out his dress pants like a raging beast trying to get out. I glanced at Miranda and Allen. She led him to the sensual station, but I didn't get to watch for long because Kyle bent me over and fitted my body into the sex swing, facing the bathroom. I wished they'd had it face the room so I could have watched Allen and Miranda.

"Mmm, this is so sexy. I've always wanted to try out a sex swing."

Kyle fastened me into it, for which the eroticism was further enhanced by him pressing his erection against my backside. "Allen bought it special for the weekend. He has hopes Miranda will love it and they can use it at home. If not, I guess it's yours."

I don't care either way. I am obsessed with Kyle fucking me in it and that's all that my brain had room for at the moment.

Kyle lifted my dress off my bare butt and planted a kiss. "Still a bit red. I guess I went a little too ballistic on your butt."

I snickered. "Yeah, I'm not really feeling like adding to the damage by getting spanked by a paddle again tonight."

"We don't need that," Kyle said. "Neither of us is that sadistic. I'm going to drive you crazy, though, and make you come more times than you can count tonight. Then I'm going to fuck you in the morning, and tomorrow, and every chance I get this weekend. You are mine."

"I am yours," I repeated his yummy words in a sensual voice as I glanced back at him. Declaring it out loud made it even hotter.

He unzipped his pants but remained in his suit, which was so sexy, like all those Dom pics I'd seen on social media. A man dressed up with only his hard cock out, and the woman naked or in something scantily clad with straps or lingerie. Her ass oftentimes was bare or her boobs. The images always had aroused me.

Kyle scooted my dress up and I raised slightly so he could slip it off. "Told you this wasn't staying on long."

It was like he read my mind.

"Thank you, Daddy. This will be better." I laid forward as he maneuvered the swing around. I was his puppet in the swing, and I loved it.

There was soft music playing that I hadn't noticed at first, but it became more prominent as a heavy metal song came on. It had a good rhythmic beat to fuck to.

Kyle massaged my clit and lapped at my slit as I writhed gently in the swing. My clit was doing its job responding to Kyle's touch and I was raging into massive arousal. He poked his tongue into my pussy and pussy-tongue fucked my hole.

I moaned as he shoved himself up my juiced cunt. Hearing Miranda and Allen's moans added to my excitement, especially as it sounded as if Miranda was coming already. I was dying to know what they were doing.

Then I heard loud smacks, which had to be her getting paddled. Fuck, I wanted to watch. She shrieked out as he laid a few more slaps. Those sounds and Kyle eating me out pushed me right to the very edge of my ability to control my orgasming.

"Can I come, Daddy?" I asked breathlessly.

He pulled his tongue from me. "Not yet, baby girl. Don't you come yet."

His breath alone hitting my aroused parts almost made me come. I pouted because Miranda just got to climax. I kept my mouth shut because he was then gifting me his cock as he pressed his thick, swollen head at my pussy.

"Please," I pleaded with desperation.

I hungered more for him, even though he had pressed himself deep inside me. My nipples hardened as he shoved his dick all the way up in me, both basting and barraging my G spot. I wanted stronger clit stimulation so badly, but I couldn't seem to release my hold on the swing because Kyle was rocking my body so severely.

Kyle spun me in the swing and presented his cock to my mouth. "Suck my tip, baby girl."

I was enthralled with the fact that it was so easy for him to spin me, to control my body with minor movements of the swing. And now, facing this way, I got to watch Allen and Miranda as I sucked Allen. What a fucking turn-on!

I consumed Kyle's dick into my mouth as far as I could, which wasn't far at all. I was bombarded with the taste of both of our precum fluids. The taste of our sex was so good. I rode his cockhead, then he gripped my skull to thrust into my mouth gently. I relaxed and allowed him to use my mouth. I savored it. As his sounds ramped up, he pulled his cock from my mouth before he peaked.

"Let's move on." He unstrapped me from the swing and led me to the next station, which was the BDSM toy station that Allen and Miranda had just vacated.

As far as I could tell, Miranda was the only one of the four of us who had come.

"I really liked that swing. That was so hot!" I spilled it out like someone who had just tried the scariest, most thrilling ride in the park.

Kyle pulled me to him and our bodies touched all along our fronts. His solid shaft disappeared as it was sandwiched between us. He kissed my forehead, my nose, then my lips. "Me too. We will have to get one. Keep it at our house for when the boys are gone."

"Perfect. I'll get shopping tomorrow, but I really liked that one. Especially the tent-like fabric of the swing part."

"I almost came," he admitted.

"I know."

Kyle reached for the handcuffs. "It's time." He smiled like a devious demon. "I'm going to eat you out. I need a cool down or I'll spew."

"On fire still, huh?" I smiled, loving the fact that I didn't have to worry about that. Being a woman, I could climax as many times as I wanted.

"Yeah, I admit, you got me pretty fucking aroused today. And then us setting up this room, I had a boner the whole time." He ran his hands all over my body and I danced along his touch as I hummed softly.

He pointed to a pile of pillows. "That's your landing spot, but stay put."

"Yes, Daddy." I loved saying that. It never got old. I beamed at him as he swiveled me to face away from him.

He collected my wrists and then slapped the handcuffs on. He disappeared and I waited for him to return. It was pure agony. He returned and slipped a blindfold over my face. "Borrowing this from the sensual station."

My heart raced. "What are Miranda and Allen doing? It really turns me on to know," I whispered. "Tell me, please."

"They are using the sex swing."

Just then I heard the skin smacks of a doggyfuck starting and then Miranda's moans.

"Oh, fuck. That's really hot."

"I know, it really is. We've never gotten to do this before, four people. It's insanely erotic."

"It really is." He tightened the blindfold and shoved me forward, so I hit the pillows hard. The rough aggression made my clit twitch.

"Oh, Daddy," I murmured into the pillow. I breathed and my slit flared open.

Kyle spread my legs and shoved a pillow, then another under my pelvis, so my hips were raised, and my ass was tilted up.

"Ass up," Kyle said. "As you should be."

I started to raise my hips higher to obey him.

"No, just rest on the pillows, babe." He pressed my body back down to rest on the pillows.

"Okay, Daddy." It was so satiating to be obedient to him, to submit. But only because he was who he was, and with the history we had. I couldn't even imagine doing this with anyone other than Kyle or Allen. Maybe a fuck, but full submission like this? No way.

He slipped two lubed fingers into my pussy and began a fast finger fuck. Within seconds I was all-out screaming.

He pulled his fingers out and ate my slit, his nose dabbing between my ass cheeks as he reached my clit. He tickled my most sensitive part, then gripped my thighs, effectively pinning me to the pillows. He then began full-bore sucking my clit. I screamed and thrashed, squirming to get away from the extreme sensations, but he had me clamped down.

His breath on my skin sent shivers rippling through my body, which also lit up my clit. "Now, just come when you feel the rise, baby girl. Come for your Daddy. I want to taste your cream on my tongue. Give it to me."

His words alone almost made me climax. He clamped his mouth upon my clit and sucked hard as I tried to buck him off. I screamed into the pillow and my body raged into a massive orgasm.

As I came down off the high, he attacked me once more. The intensity was magnified. I pumped my hips against his mouth, trying to get away from the heightened sensitivity, which was almost unbearable.

Then he slipped away.

Confused, I tilted my head to the side. Through my panting, I asked, "Daddy?"

My heart was pounding stronger as I heard a buzz. Someone touched my buttocks, but the touch was very light and gentle.

"I'd like to try a toy on you," Miranda said softly. "Are you okay with that?"

Oh my ... "Miranda?" I asked, aghast.

"Yeah, it's me. I've never tried these kinds of toys, and I'd like to see how they work, but not on me yet. Can I play with you with one or two of them?"

I gasped. "Can you? Oh, fuck yes, please do! I'd love that." I'm brimmed with joy.

"Can you flip over?"

"Yes," I said as I struggled to flip myself while still being cuffed.

"Allen, Kyle, can you get these off of her?" She fumbled with the handcuffs. "I can't seem to find the release."

"Yeah," came Kyle's voice as he removed them. "You got it."

Miranda removed my blindfold, and our eyes met. Her eyes showed excitement and were full of mischief.

"So, I just press it to your clit region?"

I nodded, smiling. "Yes, and you can vary the pressure, and also pop it on and off. My clit will get sucked in, sometimes it swells and fills up the hole."

"Really? Wow!"

"Miranda, I can teach you so much about sex toys. And so can the Daddies."

"The Daddies?" she repeated it as a question, gave me a skeptical look, then wiped her face of anything negative. "Get ready to scream, Alexa."

I laughed jubilantly and settled back against the pillows, making eye contact with Allen and Kyle as I did. Their eyes were charged up with appreciation and lust as they both stroked their cocks behind Miranda's raised butt.

I enjoyed the wet sounds of them jerking off as Miranda pressed the toy to my clit. I adored that she initiated this all on her own. It was a beautiful thing.

She pressed it gently to me.

"You can go a lot harder, I like really strong pressure. That's what makes me come."

"Okay, I don't want to hurt you."

I laughed. "Are you kidding me? It takes a beating from those two and I come like a hose on full blast!" I stared into her eyes. "You can't hurt me. It's not possible. I like it hard."

She chuckled. "Oh, ok. Well then, in that case."

She transformed. A tenacious look overcame her face as she pushed the toy to the max level and pressed it on me with force.

I jerked and cried out from the intensity.

"Oh, wow, this is powerful," she said in a sensual voice. "Play with my hair," she pleaded.

I recognized that look in her eyes. I'd harbored it myself. I grabbed fistfuls of her hair and yanked as I tried desperately to make eye contact with her with my half-closed lids.

"Oh, fuck," she said.

But she didn't squirm away, there was no repulsive recoil. To my delight, she was into doing this. I seriously thought she'd be with Kyle sexually before she did anything with me. In all our talks, she hadn't voiced much interest in me. It was more about the men and the potential interactions of all four of us. This was pure bliss anyhow, the only thing better would be me making her come.

I thrashed and traversed my orgasm course, which was ever-heightening, listening to the men react to watching us.

"Oh, my fucking fuck," Kyle said. "Shit. This is like my dream to watch."

"Oh, fuck yeah, I've wanted her to try something like this for our entire relationship." Allen chuckled.

It was extra hard for me to zone in on exactly what they were saying as they whispered more.

Allen continued. After something I couldn't quite catch, he said, "I know she's listening. I know she's not doing this for me, but she knows it's one of my turn-ons to watch women be sexual together in any way. I'm in heaven here."

"I love it too." Kyle groaned and I rose higher. I was going to come and soon.

I focused on myself and Miranda, tuned them out as my orgasm charged on full force. I lost it. I yelled out, then fell silent as the orgasm snatched me.

Miranda said, "Good girl, Alexa. Come for Mommy."

Oh, I was now the little here, I surmised, chuckling inside. My body jerked in response to my contractions. My shoulders curled and my legs drew up, then my head fell back as I crested fully into the euphoria of a second orgasm, then a third before it settled.

"Big big big big," I chanted in a barely audible voice.

"Nice, Alexa," Kyle murmured.

"Fucking fantastic," Allen said with a slur. He'd likely been hitting the champagne station some more.

I smiled. "Wow," I whispered with my eyes closed.

"That was big," Miranda said as she laid beside me. We embraced like lovers.

The silence in the room was natural as I floated down. My arousal didn't go down to baseline though, that was impossible with Miranda's naked body pressed to mine. Her breasts were smashed against me and the scent of her pussy musky and temptingly strong.

"Oh, fuck, that was amazing, Miranda," I whispered in her ear.

Her breathing was rapid as she positioned her face a few inches from mine. My heart did a flop as she leaned in for a kiss. It was just a peck at first, then she deepened it and we French kissed, our tongues slid along each other's for the first time ever. I'd imagined it many times, but my imagination hadn't even come close. This was delectable. Her curvy body was something I couldn't resist. I caressed her back as we kissed, my hand traveled down to feel up the gorgeous curve of her hip as it tapered to her thigh. I'd dreamt of touching that spot on her for a long time.

"You feel amazing," I murmured.

She cupped my breast, and I moaned in her mouth as we continued to make out.

"Oh, damn. Fuck this is so hot." It was Kyle and it turned me immensely to know my Daddies were watching this.

It was both of our firsts, tasting a woman sexually, and Miranda had not indicated she wanted this, but clearly, she did.

Our groping of each other's bodies led to me to wanting to finger her pussy. I dragged my hand down her belly and pressed my fingers to her plush mound.

"Yes, Alexa, please," she said softly as she kissed my neck.

The only pussy I'd ever touched was my own. My breathing turned heavy as I fingered her clit and pressed it, then I played my fingertips along her lips. She moaned and sighed, and it drove me wild. Knowing what I liked as a woman made this easy to do with Miranda. I pushed two fingers into her sacred hole and she groaned out. Just inside her entrance it was wet, warm, and textured, just like mine. I worked my fingers around to decipher where her G spot was by her responses. I had determined I'd found it when she cried out.

She quickly reciprocated and tickled her fingers along my pussy.

Soon we are both moving rapidly as we finger fucked each other hard simultaneously.

The men's sounds were hot, and hotter as we continued.

She broke our kiss.

"I want cock in my pussy. You?"

I nodded with great exaggeration. "Yes, I do," I agree.

"Allen, get over here and fuck me into oblivion." She motioned him to come quickly.

"I don't need to be asked twice," he said eagerly.

I motioned for Kyle to hurry over.

Kyle and Allen approached us, hard cocks swinging.

I smiled seductively at Kyle. "I want you, Daddy, Fuck me, please," I pleaded. "Need you inside me."

They fucked us side-by-side. All the pleasure sounds, the skin smacks, and the ability to glance at them fucking right next to Kyle and me sent me into a series of climaxes that was one of those plateau orgasms with peaks, and as I finished the sixth peak, Kyle exploded inside me.

"Holy fuck," I managed to say.

Miranda and Allen were already cuddling, their climaxes over.

"Wow, wow, wow, wow," Miranda repeated softly. "That was way better than I imagined it would be. I'm so in guys."

Allen hooted loudly through his panting. "Fuck yes, thank you, Gawd!"

We all chuckled together, and I for one was thrilled by her revelation too. I just knew if she tried it, she'd find it both exciting and satisfying. A foursome going forward, I couldn't ask for more. It was the ideal situation.

"And I can't wait for tomorrow." Miranda giggled.

"That's my girl," Allen said in a dominant tone.

"I'm starving, dang. All this has left me so hungry. Do we have any of those strawberries left?" I rose with the intent to gather them and bring them over to the pillow area where we were all lounging.

"I got it, babe, you stay. I want to take care of you." Kyle hopped up and grabbed the strawberries.

Allen followed and brought over the champagne. "Post duo fucking treats."

We all enjoyed the strawberries and beverages.

After indulging our taste buds, Kyle began to play with my nipples.

We fell easily back into sex as did Miranda and Allen, and it was tandem side-by-side sex once again. Round two.

Chapter 24

I woke in the morning, and I was still cradled in Kyle's body. A smile took over my face. It felt amazing to wake up in his arms. I had woken at 2 a. m. to find myself in bed with Kyle. Apparently, he must have carried me unconscious to the bed because I sure didn't recall walking to it. The images and emotions of last night flooded me. The whole evening was overwhelming, delicious, exciting, and intense as fuck.

And Miranda! Oh, my Gawd, Miranda! That was such an amazing, thrilling, and fun experience. My first time with a woman blew my fantasies out of the water. Nothing compared to really doing it.

I loved snuggling in Kyle's embrace. What I wouldn't give to have this every day. I was starving, though, but leaving the comfort of him was hard to consider doing, but my hunger won. I slipped out of his grasp and pulled my tank top and shorts on. Out in the hallway, the sunlight was just starting to flood the house from all the windows. I'd call this the house of glass if I lived here. It was so open and with all the windows, I almost had the feeling like I was outdoors.

Miranda was on the deck with a steaming cup of coffee in front of her on the table. The first rays of the sun were shining off her, making her look as if she were glowing. Or maybe it's just my groggy eyes, or her orgasms saturated in her body. I definitely had drank way too much wine last night. But she looked gorgeous in the early morning sunshine.

I fixed up a cup of coffee for myself and placed a blueberry muffin on a plate. As I opened the door, Miranda smiled at me. She looked happy, but a little guilty.

"Hi," she said a bit sheepishly. "I had way too much fun last night." She looked so sexy in her pink silk robe, open slightly so I could see her cleavage and her toned tummy.

"No such thing as that."

She shrugged. "Maybe you're right. We are consenting adults." Her expression went giddy. "We kissed. And I made you come." Her hand flew over her mouth as she exuded exuberance.

I laughed, copying her energy. "Yes, yes you did, and it was amazing. It was really hot. I'm thrilled you decided you wanted to."

"I did. It's not something that was easy for me to talk about, but the mood of the evening made it possible for me to let go and just try it."

Agreeing, I nodded as I settled into the seat next to her, realizing I was frozen in place for a few moments, just taking in all her words before I got fully comfy. "It was amazing, Miranda. I hope you enjoyed it as much as I did."

"Yes, yes, I did. And I'd like to explore us more."

Her salacious smile turned me on, and my mind started to fantasize about us tribbing. My goal for the night, if she was willing.

"Whew. Damn, did I sleep really hard? I woke in the bed. Kyle must have carried me."

"Yeah, that's one of the last things I remember. You had fallen asleep with him on the ground after you came."

"I came hard too. I remember. I am shocked at how many orgasms I had. I must have had twenty or thirty."

"Same. I'm pretty sure I hit thirty. I'm a bit shell-shocked, to be honest." She took a sip of her coffee and then swirled it slightly. "That was more pleasure than I thought I could handle, and more pleasurable than I thought it would be."

"That's just the beginning, Miranda."

She smiled at me so genuinely it tugged at my heart. What a sweetheart. "I really enjoyed all our fun too."

My whole being flooded with joy as I recalled our entanglement. "It was so hot. And if you never want to do anything again, I'm not offended, okay?" I raised my hands in emphasis.

She swallowed her gulp hard and coughed. "Are you kidding me? That was epic! I'm in! I also got so turned on when the men were reacting to us. That was seriously so fucking hot, like off the charts!"

"I know, that got me going pretty hardcore too." The memories descended upon me like an ecstasy bath.

"And you were right. I somehow feel a little different with Kyle, like, I think it's getting easier to let him dominate me. I'm not sure how Allen will react to that, though."

"You know, it is what is. And give it time. Your relationship will iron itself out. You two will feel around for a mutually enjoyable spot you are both ok with." I paused. "And you know, it's likely because of your history with Allen. And all the little things that might influence you, both negatively and positively. Like Kyle is more of a blank slate, you know?"

"Yeah, that's a good point. Not that I'm not willing to explore more with Allen, but it might just take more time and discussion. I guess we have long-term marriage baggage to handle." She cracked up. "I did find it intensely arousing at first when he used the paddle though, but then it just hurt, and I was out."

"Oh yeah. I know what you mean. There's a fine line between pain and pleasure sometimes, and often one or the other takes over and wins."

She fell silent and I let her dwell on it as I watched the birds fly around and sing. I savored the fresh burst of sunshine as it finished up the sunrise.

"I know you have feelings for each other, all three of you. I don't want to be a fourth wheel." She stared at the table.

"You aren't, I swear you aren't, Miranda. We all want you here with us doing this. We want you joining in. Every time you desire to, you are more than welcome. I'd love it, in fact. I'm being honest." I'd said this so many times over the week, I had hoped that after last night it had finally sunk in. I touched her hand, and she met my eyes.

"You love Allen." It came out of her mouth as a matter of fact, but she stared at the table again. I sensed a bit of sadness as she returned to meet my gaze. "I can see that, and he has feelings for you."

There was a deep vulnerability in her eyes that I felt the urge to fix. So, I jumped on her with a quick response.

"Miranda, I'd never try to break you up. You two are really amazing together. Please know that. No matter what we do going forward, I want you to understand that."

"I'm mostly over the jealousy, but I know it's bound to come back. And again, geez, I'm such a child. I'm so sorry for what I did to your pots and plants, your lovely garden." She dropped her head to her hands and shook it back and forth. "I'm a fucking moron. I didn't even recognize myself."

I wished she'd let the shame go. "Hey, I bet it helped you process that anger. I get it. I've been pissed before. I'm not innocent. I've done stuff I'm not proud of. Especially with Mark."

"Yeah, but he likely deserved it all," she piped in with a snort. "You didn't."

"Well. True."

"And I know you won't try to steal Allen from me."

"I wouldn't do that, as I said." I raised my hands and shook my head exaggeratedly.

"And I also know you won't, because you love Kyle." She raised an eyebrow.

I nodded slowly as I contemplated taking the first bite of my muffin. "I do."

She gripped my hand, which prompted me to look her directly in the eyes. "Alexa, you don't just love Kyle, you're in love with him."

The words struck my heart like a bludgeon. The realization hit me that others were now noticing what I'd barely voiced inside my own heart. I was in love with Kyle. Like really in love with him. Hearing her say the words out loud made it even more real to me. I smiled a slow, sappy smile. I sighed as I maintained our mutual gaze. "It's that obvious, huh?"

"Blatantly. And he's clearly in love with you."

I squirmed in my seat as I kept my eyes on my muffin. "But married."

"Yes, but she's a cold, crazy bitch who treats him like shit. I've always wondered why he stays with such a fake plastic hoe."

I gasped out a guffaw, her calling out Mandy lightened the discussion. "Yeah, that's all very true. But he's a man of obligation. His vows."

"I'd think he'd rather be happy."

I'd asked myself that question five hundred times at least. "I know. It's a tough situation. And honestly, about Allen, I'm just so thankful you share him with me. He's an amazing man. And if you two ever stop swinging, I'd totally understand."

"I've seen him through different lenses this weekend. And I must admit, I am amazed. I also now realize we have lots of ground to explore together. I kind of thought we'd been there and done it all after decades of sex together."

She shrugged. "I admit, sex has been a bit ho-hum. But last night," she paused to giggle, "oh my Gawd, it was unbelievable!"

"I love that you feel that way. It's so true. You've got to experiment with it all. Experience as much as you can. And remember, just because you don't want to do something now, you might change your mind, so remain open." I finally took the first bite and chewed it slowly. "Mmm, this is really good. You made these?"

She nodded. "Yup. It's the favorite blueberry muffin recipe of the whole family."

"How's your blog coming along?" I asked as I savored another bite of muffin.

"Really good. I'm starting to make money. I'm considering making a cookbook. I've got sponsors for the website too. I'm getting better and better at photography, so I'm considering a book."

"That's awesome, Miranda! I'm really excited for you!"

The men slept in and, around 9 a.m., we saw the smiling face of Kyle appear. The first sight of him awake today and all that Miranda said circled inside my head. She wasn't wrong.

I raised my mug towards Kyle and shouted, "Coffee!"

He chuckled and we join in with his laughter.

"Not that kind of coffee. That was a good safe word choice for the evening, though," I said. "But after that sleep, I'm fully rejuvenated and ready for more sex, though, in case you were wondering."

He sat next to me and placed his hand on my thigh. "And that's why I love you, baby girl. And yeah, I'm in. I'm ready any time after I eat something. You both wore me out. I never sleep this long, and I'm famished."

"Well, sleeping after being fucked into a sex coma is certainly my choice way of falling asleep." I caressed his face as Miranda's words about us being in love still circulated in my brain. What are we doing to do? How will we proceed? We can't ignore our love for each other forever and live a lie. But nothing seemed doable or easy.

"I threw in that quiche, so it should be ready in like ten minutes." Miranda stood up and her robe fell open. She didn't fix it. "I should go make sure it's not burning. I'm not familiar with this oven yet."

"Nice view," Kyle said as I nodded in agreement. "And I'm not talking about the lake." He made direct eye contact with her.

"You wake up beautiful, Miranda," I said in agreement. "I thought that earlier but didn't say it."

Her cheeks flushed. She smiled at us and then scurried into the cabin without a word.

"She's pretty humble, isn't she?" Kyle took my face in his hands, and we kissed. His eyes were so full of love and happiness. "How are you this morning, beautiful? You had quite the evening."

"Amazing. I feel exhilarated, free, and like I just got my brains fucked out." I glanced at Miranda. "You know, I think maybe she's forgotten how sexy she really is, being super mom to all those boys. We need to help her re-realize her sexuality."

"We can certainly do that. I think our union will be really good for her, and their marriage. From what Allen has shared with me, anyway."

"Yup, agreed." I held my hands over his, resting on my thighs as he kissed my lips. "Last night was epic. It blew my mind, and I didn't think that would happen with Miranda, so that was a very pleasant surprise."

"Oh, it was. It all will happen, I think. And I intend to blow your mind on a regular basis. Anything you didn't like?"

"No. I really loved the sex swing." I watched his face, acknowledging in my head that I was indeed in love with him. It was a noticeable shift admitting it to myself, and I liked it.

"Me too, I'm getting aroused just thinking about it. We might need to go wake up Allen and take a round in it."

"Oh, that sounds fun. I'm in."

Miranda appeared with the quiche and four plates. "It's ready."

I hopped up. "I'll help."

Miranda shook her head. "Why don't you let us do this, Alexa, and you go wake up Allen with a blow job?"

Both Kyle and I dropped our jaws at her bold suggestion.

"What?" I asked, as if I didn't hear her.

"Yeah, then maybe Kyle and I can bond a little bit. We are never alone."

Well, that made sense. She needed some prep before sex with Kyle. "Well, I don't need to be told that twice."

"This quiche needs to sit for at least ten minutes before I cut it. The timer is going, Alexa, you'd better hurry. Ten minutes and counting. Go." She pointed inside the house.

Her telling me what to do aroused me and my feminine energy twitched. "Oh, it won't take that long," I said with a snicker.

"I'm wishing I was still in bed," Kyle said jokingly. "But, honestly, I'd love some time with you, Miranda. Maybe we can take a walk later or go out on the boat and do some fishing. Do something just us."

I zoomed into the cabin and tore off down the hall, loving the idea that Miranda just told me to go suck her husband's cock.

Chapter 25

I snuck into the bedroom and Allen was still snoring. Perfect setup. I slithered under the comforter. As I made my way down toward his groin, he stirred slightly. He was naked, and I was super grateful for that. His cock was sporting a nice solid morning wood.

As I lifted his hard cock, he squirmed.

"Mmm, Miranda."

"No, Daddy, it's Alexa. Miranda gave me an order to wake you with a blow job."

"Oh, wow," he murmured sleepily. "I love this." He paused, then slurred, "Order?"

I stroked his hard shaft, and he flung the comforter off of us.

"I want to watch you suck me, no blankets," he commanded, sounding more awake.

"Yes, Daddy." I took his cockhead in my mouth.

He placed his hand on my head. "No, Alexa. You need to be naked."

I sat up slowly with a smile and removed my clothes.

"Good girl," he said.

His words excited me.

"Suck my cock, babe."

His command made me hotter. I loved complying with his demands, but only because he was who he was, and because he had done what he had done. I smiled as I relished our history.

I sealed his cockhead inside my lips and sucked hard while stroking his shaft. It was extra hot following Miranda's direction. I could see our power exchange roles were already forming, and I was landing at the very bottom of the hierarchy. Suited me just fine. Their dominance only happened as a trickle-down from my decisions to submit to them. I chose them, and they complied with direction and leadership. And I felt taken care of and cherished. It was ideal.

I sucked his cockhead as he played with my hair. He thrust into my mouth, fully using my orifice to come quickly, with a giant groan. I swallowed his load.

"Ah, fuck. Nothing better than waking up that way. Thank you, baby girl. That was amazing, just what I needed. And I was missing playing with you last night. I needed to focus on Miranda."

I wiped my lips as I savored the taste of his cum on my taste buds. "Yeah, I totally get it. You definitely needed to."

"I hadn't expected her to do it. Though she had told me earlier this week she wanted to."

"Oh, she did? See, she never said it to me, so I had no clue she was even attracted to me, or women for that matter."

"I think she's bicurious, but she definitely finds you attractive. She told me so."

"Good, that's really wonderful to hear."

"It is wonderful. I completely agree, and I will enjoy watching you two evolve."

I snuggled into his open arms with a sigh. "I missed you last night too, so I'm super glad I got to give you waking up head." His body was warm and soft. We'd never had such an aftercare morning moment together as this, just us cuddling together in a warm bed after he came.

"Can I return the favor? I'd most certainly like to."

"Nope, Miranda gave me a timeline. The quiche is out. I was given strict instructions to suck you off in less than ten minutes."

"Oh, we'd better listen. She's a drill sergeant when it comes to being at the table on time for meals." His voice was garbled as he chuckled.

"Got it. Well, I don't need any spankings at the moment, so let's go."

He heckled me as I slid out of the bed to dress.

"This weekend is even more fun than I expected," I said as I pulled on my tank top.

"Yeah, it's proving to be better than I thought it would be too. And that has a lot to do with Miranda. She's doing a great job at being open. This is all so new to her. I mean, she knew I was with others, but for her to do it is another thing in her mind."

I nodded as I hugged myself, feeling so loved. "Oh, for sure. I remember my adjustment period when the three of us first started. It's definitely a thing to get used to and process it all."

We held hands as we walked down the hallway. Kyle looked really, really happy.

"I gave him head in the kitchen," Miranda blurted out as she stood up. "I didn't plan to, but then, as I thought of you two doing it, and I couldn't resist."

Allen and I each released surprised laughs.

"It was fucking amazing too," Kyle said as he pulled up his pants with a giant grin.

"I basically attacked you, though." Miranda's face was flushed with excitement.

"And I loved it. Do it anytime you want." Kyle touched her face. "You are very sexy, Miranda. I think you don't know how sexy you are."

She blushed and busied herself getting the fruit plate ready. "Thank you," she muttered, as if she wanted to dismiss the comment as quickly as possible. "Let's eat. It's all done."

"Well, we are starting this morning off quite nicely." Allen kissed Miranda on the lips. "Thank you, babe, and good job."

It wasn't wasted on me that Kyle's cum might still be on her lips as Allen kissed her. And that was a very hot thought.

She nodded and they both grabbed food plates. I scooped up the coffee pot and creamer, and Kyle the croissants.

We ate in the morning sun, discussing our plans for the day. The men wanted to fish, and while I didn't like fishing very much, I wanted everyone to have fun. Plus, Miranda and Kyle needed some more time together. She was warming up to us as a foursome, but more time couldn't hurt. And I loved time with Allen, so we headed out on the boats to fish. Miranda and Kyle took the fishing boat, and we headed out to the lake on the other.

Giving Allen head in the boat with a fishing pole in his hands, in broad daylight, and with boats not too far away from us, was super-hot. Two blow jobs in one morning, he was making out like a bandit. But he stopped me before he came, and he insisted on eating me out. Then we fucked on the boat. It was so damn good, and I couldn't wait to share the story with Kyle and Miranda, and hear about if they indulged in any boat sex as we did. I was really hoping they did, so the four of us could fuck tonight and christen the weekend right.

Back at the cabin, we all enjoyed an early happy hour on the beach as Miranda and Kyle spilled their sexual escapades on the boat. Allen and I shared ours as well. Every one of us had huge grins across our faces. Miranda was even glowing as she situated herself on Allen's lap.

"Well, fishing as a swap worked out fabulously," I said with glee.

"It really did, and I'm feeling really more comfortable," Miranda said with happiness in her voice. "Kyle is really amazing." She glanced at Allen. "I can say that, right?"

"Of course, you can. As I said, I want you coming and satisfied, and if at times that's with another man, so be it. I just want you orgasming as much as possible, baby. We both might feel twinges of jealousy, but we don't own each other. Things get dangerous when we think we own a person."

"Yeah, and you take the person for granted too." I wanted to change the subject, though. "So, the plan tonight is dinner, sex, and more sex, then sleep. Then sex, then eat."

"Eating and sex!" Kyle declared with a raise of his hand. "I'm in! My favorite things to do in this world. Stuffing my face and fucking!"

We made a delicious meal of grilled chicken, cold pasta salad, asparagus, homemade rolls, and brownies and ice cream for dessert, which we ate naked on the deck.

"Naked dessert. This is now a thing," Kyle said lustily.

"Indeed. I love it. Delicious brownies, Miranda. I think I'd gain ten pounds living in your house with how you cook." This whole scene of us eating naked was so arousing. I was so ready to fuck.

She smiled happily, accepting the compliment.

Allen patted his belly. "Now you see what I'm up against. It's a constant battle. And she somehow manages to keep herself svelte."

"Well, I work out every day, remember?" She snickered as she licked her fork. Her nipples looked delicious as they hardened, and I couldn't wait to get my mouth on them. "I'm kind of a workout-a-holic."

Allen looked proud. "True, you are babe, and you are one hot mama as a result."

Her face clouded slightly. "Well, I'm more than a mama."

"Oh, that you are, you are my sexy woman." Allen corrected himself quickly with a save.

Maybe he was finally getting it that he needed to treat her like a sexual being more. I made a mental note to talk with him about this once we were back home. It was what Miranda needed. The whole 'love me like flowers and poetry but always fuck me like a whore' sentence rang in my head. I read it in an erotic book once. It was a surefire way to rid a relationship of boring sex, that's for sure.

"Well, I'm horny just sitting here looking at tits and pussies and your beautiful faces. I say we go fuck. Allen?" Kyle stood up and took my empty plate and glass. "Let's clean up while the ladies freshen up and we all meet in the living room. I'd like to fuck while looking out at nature."

In the bathroom, I freshened up my makeup and wiped my parts with after-sex wipes. I was sweetly scented and clean, not that it mattered, but since I had the time, so why not? I fluffed my hair and made my way to the living room.

Allen and Kyle had brought the sex toys from the room and placed them in a pile on one of the recliners.

"Do we want the sex swing in here?" Kyle asked as a suggestion. He clearly liked that thing as much as I did. "Or maybe we don't. We can just go there if we want it."

"Yeah, my hope is we do something as the four of us, so we wouldn't even use it."

I came up behind them as they discussed.

They immediately sandwiched me between them, as they'd done so many times before. I undulated my body between them, enjoying the feel of their hard cocks against my flesh. I worried a bit about Miranda walking in on us like this and her feeling like a fourth wheel. As I started to push back so we'd separated, it was too late. She's already there in the room.

"Miranda, let's be their meat."

She laughed. "I think they are our meat."

"True."

She joined me and we embraced between Allen and Kyle. As they swayed all of us as a unit, Miranda and I kissed.

"Yes, fuck, I love that," Allen said as our kiss grew more passionate.

"Oh, fuck yeah, I absolutely love it. I can't get enough."

As we kissed, their hands cupped, squeezed, caressed, and pinched us all over. My hands meandered Miranda's body as hers roamed mine.

I was so turned on, I moaned as she kissed down my neck. I wished I'd been the one to start that because I really wanted her nipples in my mouth. She took my right nipple in her mouth as both Allen and Kyle groaned out. Listening to their grunts and groans of appreciation, and Miranda's mouth smacking on my nipples, drove my arousal so high I felt a bit crazy, veering to reeling out of control.

I dove in to kiss her neck the second she paused, and quickly trailed my kisses down to her left breast. I licked her nipple and then consumed it. I suckled it hard as she played with my hair, pressing my scalp as she seemed more aroused, her sounds making it clear.

I suckled her hardened fleshy peak to the back of my throat as best as I could. She had such dense breasts that it was tough to accomplish, but I loved trying. Having three sets of hands molesting my body led my limbs to a floppy state. The power exchange shifted as Miranda pulled away from me. Allen scooped her up and Kyle manhandled me like a rag doll.

This was getting juicy and heated quickly.

They carried us to the couch and placed us each to face it. Kyle pushed me forward so my hands hit the couch. He began to caress my clit and he rapidly finger fucked me as I watched Allen doing the same to Miranda. It was intensely sexy to watch her tits swaying when we were side by side. We met each other's gazes and kissed as they manipulated our pussies into a wet lather.

"Let's fuck 'em," Allen said. "She ready?"

"Yes," Kyle stated.

I didn't disagree. I was seriously turned on by them talking this way in front of us.

"Let's do this," Allen said in a gruff voice.

Kyle entered my pussy as Allen entered Miranda's. The sensation was so overwhelming that we fell out of our kiss and groaned out. Our bodies were allowing their control.

A tandem doggy fuck ensued. The act was so sexy I almost came instantly.

Kyle apparently knew because he chastised me. "Don't you come, not yet, baby girl."

"You either, baby," Allen said.

The skin smacks from us being fucked from behind at the same time filled the room, as did all four of our primal sounds of raw fucking.

I danced at the edge, almost unable to stop myself from coming. Allen reached over and gave me a spank as Kyle fucked me, which served to both arouse me and interrupt my orgasm train, which I'd been about to succumb to. This was helpful because I temporarily lost the urge to come. Plus, it helped me feel owned by him. I craved that. The dominance of doggy fucking always made me savor being dominated by them, an emotion I cherished more and more.

I panted as Kyle slammed into my body. The pulsations rode through my pelvis, forcing me to the very tippy edge, then he pulled out of me. I whined in complaint.

Miranda and I had a break, so our eyes met. She appeared so turned on with her eyes all smoky and sensual, falling half closed, then opening again on repeat. We tangled our lips again while we could as the men switched places. I was thrilled as Allen pushed his hard cock into my wet, sloppy pussy. Kyle did the same to Miranda. It was happening. We were swapping in front of each other's eyes. It was intoxicating, a feeling I knew I'd never forget.

The sex sounds gravitated even higher as they aggressively smacked our backsides with their bodies. She and I were getting owned something fierce and it was so overwhelmingly exciting.

"Come for me, Miranda," Kyle commanded.

Allen piped in, "Come for Daddy."

Miranda's body curled and she cried out climaxing, which in turn hurled me off the edge as I obeyed Allen and fell into a luscious ride. My body shuddered as I lulled along the dreamy orgasm wave, panting and making sounds. I was not a quiet orgasmer, and I was thrilled that Miranda wasn't either. Allen ripped his cock out of me with lightning speed and stepped back.

"Whew, fuck, I almost came." His panting was super sexy to listen to as I floated down from a big massive o.

"Same. Fuck, it's even harder to control with the four of us." Kyle was also panting.

I had to admit, hearing them share their struggles was scrumptious.

"Mmm, that was so sexy, Daddies. I loved loved loved that."

"Same," Miranda murmured. She stood up, swiveled, and fell on the couch.

I joined her.

"Can I ask for something?" Her eyes looked worried as she caught my eyes in a lock. "But I don't want to leave you out, though, Alexa."

"Hey, ask away, I bet I can figure out how to fit in," I said as I knew exactly where she was going. I'd been there.

"I'd like to be spit-roasted, but where does that leave you?" The compassion in her eyes was the sweet nectar of a reward for all our interactions to date.

I giggled with glee. "It leaves me to take care of your clit. Are you kidding me? I get the best part!"

"Oh," she said as she realized I was right.

She smiled big, which matched both Allen and Kyle's faces. "Well, that's perfect."

"Be our holes, my sweets," Allen said with his arms spread. "Alexa's right. She'll get your clit ready to serve you as you are serving our cocks."

"Oh, I'm so in." Kyle reached for Miranda. "I'll take her pussy." His declaration was solid.

"Fair enough," Allen said decisively.

They arranged into the appropriate positions, with Miranda on hands and knees between them, her lovely tits hung like ripe melons would if they grew on trees.

The sun was sinking, making the outside take on a romantic dim glow. We had the lights on full blast inside and it was deliciously voyeuristic to consider if someone were outside, they'd totally be able to watch our every move.

Kyle entered Miranda with a deep growl. Allen held his cock in his right hand, ready to guide it into Miranda's open mouth, while he held the back of her head with his other. Once their control of her body was complete, I slid under her.

Kyle held a solid grip on her hips, his fingers pressed into her flesh. I rubbed her clit with my lips. My hands roamed her, taking the tour of his penetrating her as I ran my fingertips from his cock to where it aggressively rode her lower lips.

"Going to fuck you hard until you come, baby girl." Kyle smacked her backside with his pelvis as Miranda moaned her appreciation.

"Take my cock, suck it like you owe me money," Allen dictated.

She grunted her agreement as I suppressed the urge to giggle at Allen's command. He'd said that line to me before.

"Fuck, this is so fucking sexy," I murmured. I pressed her clit hard, then realized I could also heighten this for myself. I crawled over to the recliner with all the toys.

"Fuck, baby girl," Kyle said. "Watching you crawl like that is getting me even more horny." He was panting so came out broken. His declaration really pleased me.

I chose a rabbit dildo with a large head so I couldn't accidentally squeeze it out as I was moving under Miranda. I switched it on and pressed it inside me while I was still on my hands and knees. I moaned as I reacted to the dual pleasuring of the toy.

"I should have crawled over first, then put this in," I chuckled at myself as I reached to pull it out.

"Don't you dare, baby girl. Crawl with it in," Allen commanded in a raspy voice.

I glanced at him, surprised he was even paying attention to me while Miranda was sucking his cock.

I began the crawl obediently, faltering as the waves of pleasure from the toy inside my pussy overcame me. Having my Daddies watch me struggle like that was super-hot, especially as I saw Miranda watching me too. The crawl was difficult and embarrassing because I was failing miserably at moving effectively, but that all turned me on more.

"Come on, baby girl. Get over here and suck her clit," Kyle said in a commanding voice. "Hurry." His tone was urgent and tense.

I could tell he was about to come and he didn't likely want to before Miranda did. I finally made it to Miranda and nestled myself beneath the bridge of her body. The toy was molesting me to almost climaxing myself and I licked at Miranda's clit a bit too weakly as a result.

Her body recoiled in response and both men grunted, reacting to her. Miranda undulated her body against my suck as I fully consumed her clit. I sucked her loose skin in as strongly as I could. She twitched, paused, then her body gyrated as she came. I followed her movements as best I could while still sucking, but I fell off her as I climaxed myself, my body twitching as I lowered to the floor. As I recovered enough, I reached up and spanked her clit. She screamed out and climaxed again, which created a chain reaction. Kyle came next, Allen took his turn, and then I peaked as well.

We sounded like a proper porn film as we all verbalized, rivaling the primal sounds of nature itself.

Miranda fell next to me, and the men flanked us on the floor. All four of us assembled in a pile of bodies and limbs and we slid down the floaty natural high. No one spoke for a few minutes.

"Wow," I said finally. "That was, wow, that was way better than I'd imagined. It was incredible. Positively cosmic."

"It really was. I loved it." Miranda sounded like she might cry, so I pulled her into my arms.

Allen caressed her head as she started to cry softly.

After about thirty seconds, she said softly between gasping sobs, "I don't know why I'm crying, I loved it."

"It's okay to cry. It's likely just an emotional release for you. Go with it, honey." I patted her back gently.

She let out a sob, then her body went completely slack. I kissed her lips and her closed eyelids as both Allen and Kyle caressed her body. She needed touches from all of us.

"Mmmm, wow." Miranda wiped her eyes. "I'm a mess."

"A gorgeous mess. And I'm actually thrilled you cried. It means you opened up and were fully vulnerable with us." I held her gaze as her eyes flickered between unease and comfort.

She nodded as tears wet her face, her lips pressed into a crying fit, but she didn't sob anymore. Instead, she smiled through her tears.

"Yeah, I guess you are right." Her eyes cleared of all the uneasiness, and she looked happy.

We laid together in a group snuggle, soaking up every second of our last evening together, but with excitement for our future.

#

Waking with Kyle again the next morning was beyond wonderful. Again, I let myself wish for more of this in the future. A dangerous indulgence indeed. Having the full length of his body along mine, though, with his morning wood poking my backside was a true gift. I could also savor the present.

He pulled me to face him. We pressed our bodies together tight, with no room for space.

"Good morning, sunshine," he said with a kiss on my forehead. "How did my baby sleep?"

"Really good. Too good. I forgot where I was and when I woke up, it was a wonderful realization to be wrapped up in your body." Yeah, one hundred percent. I could live happy the rest of my life waking this way. Only with Kyle could I be feeling this way so soon after splitting from fuck face. There was no denying we had something special together. It was no accident we'd crossed paths in life.

"Same. I love waking up with you."

He was silent for a minute, and I simply held the feelings in my heart and soul, for all its comfort, sensuality, and purity. For now, I'd want for nothing more than this moment in time. Whatever happened, all this had happened, and it could never be undone.

"Well. I'm going to do it. I've made a decision this weekend. I'm finally leaving her."

My heart stopped cold as I wondered if I had dreamt what he had just said.

There was a sadness in his face that flickered to relief in his eyes as he smiled. "I'm going to do it. Maybe not right away, but we can do that Italian dinner at a restaurant, for real."

A heaviness shifted off my heart as a spark of us as a real couple flared bigger, like a bonfire catching the wind. It almost hurt to hope for it, yet he was saying it. "That would be amazing, Kyle." It often felt weird whenever I called him by his name rather than Daddy. "How do you think she will take it?" My heart pounded with anticipation of this becoming reality. It literally seemed impossible.

He scoffed like a horse snorting. "She will fight me like a starving deranged ape."

I tried not to laugh, now was not the time. Mandy has that undercoat of nastiness that made seeing her as an enraged gorilla very easy. "Yeah, I bet." I stifled my giggle as the urge to laugh at the image of Mandy with her arms hanging to the ground with a grumpy face invaded my brain again. Though it might lighten his mood if I did allow my laughter. But then again, he needed to go through the emotions of this grief to move on.

"It will be very painful." He separated from me with a deep sigh as the thoughts obviously weighed heavy on him. He pulled me close again.

I melted into him, getting more aroused as our bodies settled into each other again. "It will be. Mine was, even with him being such an ass, and I wanted to get away. There's still so much unavoidable baggage with a trauma bond."

"If only she'd realize we could both be happier with another person." He sighed as he pressed his cheek to my breast. "She doesn't want to be ... to admit it ... that she'd be happier with someone else too."

"Some relationships just aren't meant to last." No one planned on believing that, but it was true.

He nodded against my chest while I hugged him to me to comfort him. He let out an exasperated grunt. "She's going to fight me on every little thing. It's going to really suck."

"But why would she want you to stay if you aren't happy?" I was not sure why I asked it, because Mark had been the same way when I told him I was done.

"She's all about image, status, what others see. She doesn't want to be that person who got divorced." He released another big sigh. "She will drag me through the mud."

"Likely she will. People who know you will get it, though, but it is what it is. Can't fight reality. And she might end up happier herself." I stroked his hair as he nuzzled his face into my breasts. I froze my brain from wandering and wondering what this meant for Kyle and me.

He smirked as he mouthed my nipple through my shirt. He popped off and said, "She's going to go nuts when she finds out we are dating."

"Well, she already hates me, so it won't change that much."

He chomped down on my nipple, and I squealed.

"Have I told you how proud I am of you with how you've been dealing with Miranda? Forgiving her and all, and not letting that stand in the way?" He massaged my nipple, chewed it with his lips. "We need to get this off of you."

He helped me remove my tank top and my breasts fell out.

"Mmm," he murmured as he sucked my bare right nipple. He hummed happily to finally have my naked tit.

"I can understand her rather than just condemn her. Though I really loved those flowers. I've learned so much that I can't not forgive her though." I moaned as his mouthing of my nipple continued. "Plus, I really like Miranda as a person."

"Besides, getting her virgin girl pussy last night ... how can you not give a little here?" He snickered as he grabbed my butt cheeks, which were conveniently already bared.

"Oh, that was amazing. I loved it way more than I expected, as clearly did you and Allen." I laughed lightheartedly. "Is this a serious conversation or whacked weird foreplay?" I smiled as I pressed my thighs between his legs so I could cop a feel of his erection.

He chuckled and thrust his hardon against me. "Oh, make no mistake, I'm fucking you to several orgasms before you are getting out of this bed."

"Oh, yes Daddy, please." I let the whininess fill my voice because I wanted nothing more than for him to fuck me into the sweet oblivion of multiple orgasms. The harsh reality of what would play out over the next few months settled in around my brain. We would have to be very careful and not get caught, even more so now. And we all would have to support Kyle, as Mandy would not just step back and fade off into the distance of Kyle's life. She was a viper.

Kyle kept his promise and fucked my pussy into ten orgasms to his two before we reluctantly showered, dressed, and packed up. The leaving of this cabin was going to hurt and I wasn't looking forward to it at all.

Chapter 26

We ate breakfast and planned to pack up the vehicle by the 11:00 a.m. checkout time. The sun beamed as strong as it had the last two days and didn't make our leaving any easier. It was such a gorgeous day. How dare it be a beautiful day on our forced departure!

"I think I need one of these weekends once a month, at least." With a heavy heart, I pulled my suitcase out the front door.

"Agreed," Kyle said in a depressed tone matching my own. He and I would get the worst of it. Allen and Miranda had each other. "Plus, it was so great to not sneak around." Kyle was carrying a cooler with a pack of half-used water bottles on top. It began to slide off and I fixed it.

"Thanks," he said with a frown. "I have extra reasons to not want to go home. Now that I've made this decision, I can't fake it. I'm going to have to tell her." His heart looked heavy in his eyes.

"I'll be right next door when you need me. I'll be at the ready to give you a hug, a massage, or suck your cock to make you feel better."

He smiled at the mention of a blow job. "I might be over really quick. I suspect she will throw things, hit me, or rage out the door in a hysterical fit. It won't be anything calm or accepting. This will threaten her perfect image to the world, and she doesn't take lightly to that."

"Most narcissists don't."

"Let's not tell Miranda and Allen this just yet. I don't think I can handle talking about it much."

I nodded and slipped my arm around his back. "I get it. Don't you want to set that down?"

"No, I'll just put it in now." He carried it to the back of the SUV.

Miranda called me in to help with the making of the beds. Part of the deal was we had to wash the sheets and make the beds, clear out the fridge and freezer, and sweep. The rest of the things the cleaning crew would do.

"Thank you for being so supportive this weekend. I really appreciated it," Miranda said as we fit the sheets on the king bed in the master suite. "You didn't have to be so generous with me. I didn't really deserve it."

"Will you stop beating yourself up over that? You made a mistake. It's not like I've never made any. Plus," I gave her a seductive look, "after last night, consider your debt paid. I really, really, really enjoyed making you come last night. You are so hot when you climax."

She released a single explosive laugh and her face flushed. "No one has seen that face other than Allen for years and years."

"Right, but now you aren't hiding it. I'm so thankful you opened up to both me and Kyle."

"I admit, I felt a little pull when Allen began to fuck you, but Kyle inside made me let that go really quick. He's really a great man and a very generous lover."

"Yeah, he really is," I said dreamily.

"See, there it is. I can see it again." She shook her head. "Shame you two can't be together in real life."

I kept my lips shut to keep Kyle's new secret in. He should be the one to tell Miranda and Allen anyway.

"I know, it really is."

"You two ladies ready to go?" Allen asked as he poked his head into the room.

"Yep, just finishing this bed and we are fully done," Miranda said with a quick nod. Miranda and I pulled the comforter up. "Oh, Allen, don't forget the sex swing! Oh my gosh! We almost forgot it!"

He ran back into the room. "Shit! How did I miss that? That would have been tragic."

"It became a permanent fixture this weekend, so you got too used to seeing it, I bet," she surmised.

He chuckled. "Well, being that we used it again this morning, I should have had it on the brain. Be assured, it's going up in our bedroom the second we are home."

I loved knowing the details of their sex life. "Oh, yummy. I take it that thing is going to be used on a daily basis?"

"I wish. How would we explain that to the boys? They come in our room all the time." Miranda shrugged her shoulders with an exasperated expression.

"I guess I'm going to become an expert at putting it up and taking it down then," he said with a lecherous tone.

"Oh, you'd better. That's like my top favorite thing right now." Miranda added the pillows, and I did the same on my side of the bed.

"And to think, you wanted nothing to do with all this when I brought it up in the past," he said in a teasing voice.

"Yeah, yeah. I get it. I was a fool."

Allen stopped cold and turned towards us. "You are most definitely not a fool, baby. You are the smartest most amazing woman I've ever known, and I'm honored to be your man." He looked so proud, genuine, and adamant.

She beamed and her head tipped to the side.

He pulled her into a hug.

"Agreed. Completely. You are an amazing, sexy, wonderful woman ... and lover, Miranda." I filled my words with as much love as I could muster.

Allen motioned for me to join the hug. We stood there wrapped around each other for a few minutes. We broke the hug.

I gazed into Miranda's eyes and reinforced it. "You are in no way a fool. You got that?"

She smiled and straightened the wrinkle in the comforter.

"Well, you guys are the amazing ones. Waiting for me. Then welcoming me. Despite all I've done."

Allen looked confused, but simply shrugged. She was happy, so he was happy.

I waved my hands and smiled at her.

Miranda returned the grin.

Allen took down the swing, and we all headed out into the living room. After ensuring all the doors and windows were locked and checking the kitchen for any missed items, we exited the front door, leaving the place of the best time of our lives.

On the drive, I reflected on the weekend. It had been more amazing than I'd fantasized it could have been. Packing up and cleaning was a drag, leaving was worse, but we'd still had fun. Nothing could change that. All the flirting had been so luxurious, being sexually suggestive with each other, joking around and. of course, eating an amazing bunch of meals made largely by Miranda had been such a treat. I was a true slacker in cooking this weekend, but that was because Miranda just took over. I had intended to give her a break and do more cooking, but she just took charge and seemed to really get into feeding us all. I took her lead as she gave me little jobs here and there. So, I had gone with the flow. She was clearly very happy directing me, in and out of the bedroom, and it had been so refreshing to see freedom on her lovely face. It had made her even more beautiful.

I could happily live in that cabin forever, the four of us as a quadruple. Unconventional, yeah, but I could see it working for us. But that wasn't in the cards. Some of us had kids under eighteen, way under eighteen in the case of Allen and Miranda, all of us had jobs, but one thing was for sure, our relationships would never be the same again. I was very grateful for that. I despised my old life. I looked to the future with sheer joy.

The drive went way too fast and my moments of talking to and freely touching Kyle threatened to halt to an abrupt stop with each dreadful mile. Another thing that this weekend did was bring Kyle and me closer and define us more solidified as a separate couple from Allen and Miranda. Sure, we were a group, but our triad was also no more. I was delightfully okay with that. I had big fantasies, and even bigger hopes to fill. I'd do it one way or another.

We pulled into the home stretch, the four of us as the latest and biggest of the neighborhood sex secrets. No one knew the sexual blisses we shared, the heights we'd created, nor the boundaries we ecstatically pushed, and they likely never would, but it didn't matter because it was all ours, and ours alone.

Epilogue

It has been three weeks since Kyle spilled his desire for a divorce to Mandy. And neither he nor I could have predicted she'd be so gracious. Kyle was as confused as he had been suspicious, but he didn't look the gift of her nonchalance in the mouth. But it was no wonder, because she admitted to him a week later, once he confronted her, that she had been sleeping with a co-worker for a while. She wouldn't share how long, but it had prompted Kyle to tell her about us. She had pitched a fit, which made no sense, but the world revolved around Mandy, so in her sick universe she declared she was right. Yet I couldn't wrap my head around her views no matter how I tried. Kyle was supposed to be for her only, but she could do what she wanted? Total double standard.

Being Kyle was officially separated, we got braver and showed ourselves more in public. Miranda, Allen, Kyle, and I had gone on play dates with other couples and attended a few clubs together, all of us expanding our sexuality in new ways that were both exciting and titillating. Miranda and I had danced on stage, Miranda had sucked a stranger's cock while Allen supervised, and I had even fucked on stage. It was scary as fuck, but I wouldn't change a thing.

After a long night of partying and fucking, Kyle and I share a pizza at 2 a.m. and lounge on the couch, praying my boys don't come down as they hear the tv on. Finding me with Kyle would be a shock for them, that's certain.

"I just want to be by you. I don't know what that looks like going forward, and we don't need to figure that out now, but I am just so happy when I'm with you. I don't want it to ever stop." The twinkle in his eyes that had appeared after Mandy released him only got stronger by the day. I love seeing it blaze.

I snuggle in close with him and gaze up at his handsome face. "Same, always and forever."

Kyle pulls me onto his lap and holds my face in his hands. "We have freedom with each other that we'd never have with anyone else. It makes you cum harder. It spurs your Daddy on ...makes me more aggressive."

I appreciated focusing on only our sexuality together for a bit instead of the potential of our future life together. I am content to take this new us one day at a time. "Which I love and crave in you," I say with a seductive and happy grin.

His expression turns serious, but full of love. "You and you alone are my girl that I want to dominate ... dominance thru freedom. Because your precious heart is my world ... and I'm the king of your heart."

His words melt me to my core. He's so right. We are living our dream, one that seemed impossible but is now potentially emerging into existence. And I, for one, can't wait to watch it blossom.

THE END

About the Author

Ruan Willow is a spicy romance author, blogger at https://ruanwillowauthor.com/ , sexuality and erotica fiction podcaster at the Oh F*ck Yeah with Ruan Willow Podcast, and an audiobook narrator/ voiceover actress. She is also published on Medium, Frolic Me, and Literotica, and coming soon on Theo Reads. She loves spending time with family and friends, interacting with fans, cooking, sharing/chatting with and educating people about sex, reading, travel, being outdoors, swimming, learning about sex, podcasting, and more sex. Did you catch all the sex? She's giggling right now thinking about you reading all about sex. She values openness and talking about the natural act of sex. And. Yup, she loves to laugh!

Other pen names for Ruan Willow:

RuAnn Willhoe (taboo erotica on Smashwords)

R.U. Ann (Open Door Romantasy)

Ruin Willow (hotwife)

Thank you!

Thank you to all my family and friends who support me. I wouldn't be where I am without you. You are all the magic and the light in my life, the love that grows in my love. I am honestly thrilled and humbled by the supportive people in my life. Love you!

To Fans:

Thank you for purchasing and/or reviewing this book!

I peddle fantasies for the purposes of your enjoyment, entertainment, and expanding your sexuality and openness. Always remember that no fantasies are bad, they take place in your head only, so indulge in your heart's desire to the fullest! You should enjoy your sexuality and your fantasy life as much and as often as you can. Sexual pleasure is your birthright!

Thank you for reading my book! I write for myself and for my fans. My fans are my main focus though, but of course, I want to like what I write too, and I thoroughly enjoyed writing these stories. I love to write about empowered women exploring their sexuality with supportive partners. I love open door because I want the FULL story of the relationship, not a partial view that is chopped off.

In writing erotica/erotic romance, I'm always excited for the erotic journey! I'm on a path of sexual empowerment, enlightenment, and enjoyment. Thank you for reading this and I'm honored to be a part of your journey as well.

I am where I am because fans have responded to me and my content, so I owe everything to you! Thank you! Thank you! Thank you! You are a blessing in my life, and you give me more joy than you will ever know. I love interacting with all of you and I will never give that up.

My stories are erotica, so they have a generous amount of sex in them, as I believe our relationships should have as well. I hope you enjoyed this novel for what it is, literature that is in the erotica genre. It is very different from the sweet romance genre, and there are different levels of heat in the erotica genre as well. Explore them all!

If you'd like more of my work, please see below for my list of published works on the following pages, visit my sexuality and erotica podcast, find my audiobooks, visit my website, my Patreon, visit my profile on Medium, and my linktree with all my links at https://linktr.ee/RuanWillow

Thank you for purchasing this book, I'd love to hear your thoughts in an honest review on the site where you purchased the book from. I'd absolutely love it if you shared my book with others. It warms my heart profusely when I see someone who has taken the time to review/share my book. Love you all very much!

All my best, yours truly, with overflowing love from a full heart,
Ruan Willow
Erotica author, sexuality/erotica podcaster, and erotic book narrator

Oh F*ck Yeah with
Ruan Willow Podcast

It's free on podcast apps! Also airing on the internet radio station Full Swap Radio website and app Tuesdays and 6 pm CST, and Wednesdays 8 am (subject to change, check for the current schedule online) AND the PodNation TV Network/Roku TV station/Fire TV/powered by Podnation Pods anytime VOD on the app, and Sundays and Mondays After Dark Hours around 11 pm Eastern Time Zone (subject to change).

Oh F*ck Yeah with Ruan Willow Podcast on Buzzsprout[1]

Ruan's other books and novellas:

Series:

Ruan's Getaway Series: Heterosexual, MILF Age Gap

Ruan's Cabin Getaway (ebook, paperback, audiobook)

Ruan's Beach Getaway (ebook, paperback, audiobook)

Ruan's Lake Getaway (coming soon!)

The Sex Challenge Series: Heterosexual, Middle Aged 2nd Chance I Dare You

Servicing the Work Men (hotwife with dominant alpha male wife sharing) (8 books)

The Stars Aligned Series: Heterosexual, Twenty-Something's

Skinny Dipping at the Pond on a Hot Summer Day, Book 1 (ebook & audiobook)

The Rush (ebook)

---

1.   https://ohfckyeahwithruanwillow.buzzsprout.com/

Spring Break *(college aged multiple partner fantasy books)*

Spring Break & Stranded with Her Best Friend's Brothers, Books 1, 2, and 3.

GET THE SPICIER VERSION by RuAnn Willhoe Spring Break & Stranded with Her Best Friend's Brothers Plus 6 Men, on Smashwords.

Next Door Temptations *(middle aged couple, second chance at love and sex, friends to lovers)*

Next Door Temptations, Book 1 (in ebook, audiobook)

The Secret's Out book 2 (in ebook)

Seducing Her Ex's Best Friend *(a story of revenge, angst, deception, and romance, HEA)*

Seducing Her Ex's Best Friend, Book 1 (in ebook and audiobook)

Wingless Hunger *(HEA Romantasy, book 1)*

Standalone's:

Decadent Erotica, An Anthology: 10 Tales of Extreme Sensuality, Indulgence, Dominance, and Submission (in ebook, paperback &

audiobook

She Dominated Him Out of a Speeding Ticket (Female Domination story) (ebook and audiobook):

Never Say, Never Swing (a first-time swinging story) (in ebook & paperback coming in audiobook)

Magic In Her Kisses (woman loving woman Domme/sub BDSM) (in ebook, paperback, & audiobook)

The Mardi Gras Unmasking (reverse harem) (in ebook & paperback)

The Licking Sip Coffee Shop (a steamy explicit coffee shop)

Santa Gives the 12 Orgasms of Christmas

Neighborhood Secrets (also Neighborhood Sex Secrets) (ebook and paperback)

The Sugar Daddies (in ebook, paperback, and audiobook)

FRIENDS WITH BENEFITS: A Spicy Four Short Story Adventure (in ebook, paperback, and audiobook)

Spicy & Wicked Tales (in ebook and audiobook)

Hookups & More? (in ebook and audiobook)

Weekend Hotwife Surprise (in ebook, coming in audiobook)

Tantalizing Tales (ebook, audiobook)

Group Fun at Work: Spicy Unions of Three (ebook, paperback, audiobook)

SFW Fantasy audiobook novel narrated by Ruan:

Heroes of the Caroylngian Age written by author Joseph Samaniego:

Audiobooks:

Check out Ruan's books available on online audiobook sellers: Sharing the Itty Bitty Vixen Series, written by Lacey Cross, multiple books written by Amber Collins, books by Luc Lopez, and also Casey Donatello, Benson E Wolf, Joseph S Samaniego, plus her own books as well.

Anthologies and Award Nominations

Ruan has stories in the following anthologies:

He Will Obey (which was AWARDED THE 2020 SILVER PIGTAIL IN BEST ANTHOLOGY CATEGORY

The Femdom Coven (nominee for 2021 Golden Pigtail Smut Awards)

Inside of Ruan Willow (also available in an audiobook)

(this audiobook was a nominee for the 2021 Golden Pigtail Smut Awards)

Decadent Erotica An Anthology **3rd Place Winner in the 2022 Golden Pigtails Smut Awards for Dark/Taboo Category**

Nominations for the 2023 Golden Pigtail Awards include:

Servicing the Trash Man, My Filthy Hotwife Adventure

Dressing Room Domme

Anthology Ruan has a short story in the nominated anthology titled Hearts and Flowers, Whips and Chains

Ruan is in the following Femdom anthologies:

He Will Obey (stories of female domination)

The Femdom Coven (erotic horror and fantasy)

Hearts and Flowers, Whips and Chains (stories of kinks & power exchanges)

Other:

Ruan's website with free erotic stories Ruan Willow Author[2]
Ruan Willow on Goodreads Ruan Willow Goodreads Author page[3]

Ruan Willow on BookBub https://www.bookbub.com/profile/ruan-willow
Sign up for Ruan's newsletter: https://subscribepage.io/ruanwillow

ARC copies are usually on BookSirens and StoryOrigin App. Check those sites for FREE ARC of books and audiobooks.

---

2.   https://ruanwillowauthor.com/

3.   https://www.goodreads.com/author/show/21312130.Ruan_Willow

Featured Book:

Never Say, Never Swing

Two couples have been friends for years. Their families have hung out, but they've spent many evenings alone as just couples, without the kids. They are comfortable together as a group and they've always enjoyed each other's company. So, Miranda and Kyle wonder why not enjoy each other more on a whole deeper level?

One evening when the two couples are enjoying dinner, the topic of sex comes up. They fall into a flirty discussion that launches the foursome into a new topic they've never explored. Much to Karley and Dean's surprise, their friends are secret swingers. As they get entangled more into their flirtations, Miranda and Kyle decide to trek into new territory with their friends Karley and Dean and bring up the often-called taboo topic of swinging. The foursome launches into a negotiation discussion that might just propel them from friends to lovers, couples' style.

With this new exhilarating adventure brewing, each person may just get to saunter down a new path and experience the pleasure of living out a fantasy they've never had the chance to enjoy. Will their new foray into swinging explode Karley's and Dean's sexuality as it did for Kyle and Miranda, or will it leave them devastated they dared to venture into this new alternative lifestyle?